"There's more f[...] whiskey than I've found in this bed for a long time, Amy."

"What did we just do? Wasn't that okay?"

He slipped his arms into his shirt and glared at her in the darkness. "What *did* we do?"

Holding the sheet pressed to her breasts, she wondered why she was having this discussion. It didn't make sense.

He came toward her and leaned forward, one hand on each side of her hips on the mattress, his face inches above hers. "I know what it *used* to be. Lovemaking."

Her chest tightened.

"Do you even love me anymore, Amy?"

Her head roared with confusion and fear. He was her husband. He was Jesse. He'd just known her body intimately for the thousandth time, and yet she couldn't say what he wanted her to say. He needed her.

His need terrified her....

* * *

Prairie Wife
Harlequin Historical #739—February 2005

The Tenderfoot Bride

"Cheryl St.John once again touches the hearts of readers.... Not many readers will be able to hold back their tears as they reach the conclusion."
—*Romance Reviews Today*

Colorado Wife

"A warm and loving story with a strong thread of family. *Colorado Wife* sparkles with fun and romance as it shares the spirit of the holiday season."
—*Romance Reviews Today*

The Doctor's Wife

"Cheryl St.John gives testimony to the blessings of family and to the healing powers of love."
—*Romantic Times*

CHERYL ST. JOHN

Prairie Wife

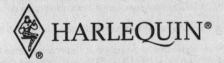

TORONTO • NEW YORK • LONDON
AMSTERDAM • PARIS • SYDNEY • HAMBURG
STOCKHOLM • ATHENS • TOKYO • MILAN • MADRID
PRAGUE • WARSAW • BUDAPEST • AUCKLAND

ISBN 0-373-29339-9

PRAIRIE WIFE

Copyright © 2005 by Cheryl Ludwigs

This edition published by arrangement with Harlequin Books S.A.

® and TM are trademarks of the publisher. Trademarks indicated with ® are registered in the United States Patent and Trademark Office, the Canadian Trade Marks Office and in other countries.

www.eHarlequin.com

Printed in U.S.A.

Please address questions and book requests to:
Harlequin Reader Service
U.S.: 3010 Walden Ave., P.O. Box 1325, Buffalo, NY 14269
Canadian: P.O. Box 609, Fort Erie, Ont. L2A 5X3

This story is dedicated to my faithful readers.
I appreciate you.

Prologue

Shelby Station, Nebraska, 1867

Amy would never know how many shovelfuls of earth it took to fill a grave so heartbreakingly deep and yet so pathetically small. She'd lost count around two hundred or so. The first falls of dirt had been loud, landing on the sanded and varnished wood coffin with a mind-numbing *thud*.

A couple of women had urged her away from the grave, but she'd resisted their efforts and had remained to experience the entire ordeal. It was the least she could do.

Jesse had built the casket. A day and a half it had taken him. A day and a half while she sat beside the small, still body laid out on wooden planks in the dining room, barely acknowledging visitors, gifts of food or expressions of sympathy. The finished project, when he'd carried it into the house, was a work of art. An eloquent expression of love and grief. An outpouring of everything he felt and could express only in this final gesture for his son.

The corners of the heavy oak box had been flawlessly fitted tongue and groove, the entire work stained a dark mahogany, then varnished to a shiny gloss. The interior was padded, upholstered and tucked with a rich blue velvet.

Amy had left the room while Jesse and her father, Sam Burnham, placed the lifeless body of her barely three-year-old child in the casket. When she'd returned half an hour later, Tim looked as though he were merely sleeping upon the luxurious fabric. He looked as though at any moment, his eyelashes would flutter and his blue eyes would open; he'd smile that smile that touched every place in her heart and left her aching with pride and love.

But Tim was as still as he had been since she had pulled him from the creek behind the station and tried to breathe life back into him. He wore his Sunday clothing, dark pants and a white shirt, a miniature string tie. His fair hair was neatly combed, and the obstinate curl that had always fallen over his forehead had been tamed into perfection.

As Amy watched, Jesse ruffled the lock so that it fell upon Tim's forehead in the endearing way it always did. She knew just how soft Tim's hair felt beneath Jesse's loving touch. She had finger-combed it back a thousand times.

Taking a step closer, Amy noticed something in Tim's hand that hadn't been there before. A ray of sunlight streaming through the dining room window glimmered on gold. Her boy held a watch. The pocket watch that Jesse's father had given him, and with which Tim had always loved to play. As a baby, he'd sat on Jesse's lap, enthralled with the timepiece. Jesse had promised the child that one day the watch would be his. It shouldn't have been so soon…and it should never have been like this….

The watch's *tick* was loud in the silent room. The sun caught and reflected droplets on Tim's still tiny hands. Tears. Tears had fallen from Jesse's eyes, tears were still streaking her husband's lean cheeks.

As if in a cocoon of silent unreality, Amy watched without feeling anything. The place where her heart had been was a cavity. Cold. Empty. Jesse had carried on. Jesse had built a coffin. Jesse ate and drank coffee. Jesse *cried.*

Amy was as lifeless as their son.

The least she could do was stand here now and watch it all. Watch as her father and Jesse scooped dirt and moved it into the grave, their shirts growing damp with sweat. It must feel better to do something. But she didn't have to feel at all, did she? Everything would be okay— she could survive without letting out the scream on the inside.

She watched as Jesse paused in his efforts to wipe perspiration from his eyes. Perspiration—or tears? His blue gaze lifted and discovered her standing across from him. If there was a message in his expression, she didn't receive it. He had tried to hold her the night before, but she'd turned away, unable to allow him into her private world of nothingness.

Amy closed her eyes and thought of her precious Tim in his little shirt and pants, lying against the blue velvet. Thought of the watch ticking…ticking…until it wound down…silent forever. Like her son.

Chapter One

Shelby Station, Nebraska, 1868

Jesse entered the kitchen at twilight. After the stage travelers had eaten and gone next door to their assigned lodging, he and Amy always ate a late supper together, and the help thoughtfully left them alone. The room smelled of beef and gravy. Steam rose from a pan of potatoes from which Amy had recently poured boiling water.

"Can I mash those for you?"

He started forward, but his wife grabbed the pan with a pot holder before he reached it. "I'll do it. You sit."

She used to let him help in the kitchen. She used to enjoy his company and having him near. Now she tolerated him.

The change had to do with Tim. And the day their

son had drowned. And the way he had died. And the loss they'd suffered.

That was the day everything had changed.

But Jesse didn't know what to do about it. Nothing he said or did or attempted made a difference. Amy had become a different person. A person who didn't like him much. He doubted she even loved him anymore. As though it had been his fault. As though he hadn't wondered a thousand times if he could have prevented their son from waking from a nap and wandering from Shelby Station unobserved.

So Jesse sat at his place at the table and waited while she mashed the potatoes and set the food in front of him. Sat there like he did every night, waiting for her to talk to him, to look at him.

They ate in silence. Amy was a wonderful cook, and as he did every night, he told her so and ate everything she'd prepared. He didn't bother to pick up his plate or offer to help with the dishes, because that was something else she didn't need him for.

She carried their plates to the sink.

"I have a few chores to finish." Grabbing his hat, he went outside.

In the stable, he drew a bottle half full of whiskey from a nail keg and took a long pull. The fiery liquid immediately warmed his chest and within minutes his tense muscles relaxed. His newfound friend made the emptiness a little easier to bear. A year was a long time to miss a child without someone to share the grief. A long time to miss his wife's touch, her smile, anything remotely resembling comfort or affection.

He worked on repairing harnesses, and by the time the moon was high in the sky, the bottle was empty and his patience was chafed beyond endurance.

His last chores were to check all the horses, make certain the lock on the luggage room was fastened tight, and extinguish lanterns. Two windows in the austere boardinghouse beside the house were illuminated, indicating overnight travelers still awake.

He washed at the pump, the refreshing cold water minimally cooling his frustration, then he entered the house, where an oil lamp cast shadows in the kitchen. Amy stood beside the table, cutting fabric around a paper pattern.

"There's coffee left on the stove," she said.

"No thanks."

She folded her sewing and tucked it into a basket. "I'll get the lamp."

Jesse walked ahead of her up the stairs, careful to keep his movements steady.

Once inside their room, she placed the lamp on the bureau. Jesse shrugged out of his shirt while Amy removed her dress and underclothing and pulled her nightgown over her head. He watched, glimpsing her slender body in the golden light. She'd lost weight in the past year, enough that she appeared too fragile. He'd hired more help for cooking and for cleaning rooms, but Amy worked too hard.

Still watching her, he pulled off his boots and socks. Avoiding his eyes, she moved to her dressing table, where she sat and removed the pins from her hair.

Her aloofness irritating him, Jesse moved behind her, picked up the brush from the table and, starting with the tangled ends, ran the bristles through the silken softness of her honey-colored tresses. Once the tangles were out, he stroked her hair from scalp to ends, the way she'd always loved.

"Your hair smells better than anything," he said, bending to lower his face into the tumble of glossy waves against her neck and inhale. All his resolve to keep his distance melted at her familiar clean feminine scent, and a knot formed in his belly.

"You've been drinking," she said.

It was his turn to avoid her comment. This was his wife, the woman who'd once come to him willingly and eagerly. After placing the brush on her dressing table, he threaded her hair with both hands and then caressed her shoulders through the thin cotton fabric of her nightgown. Her gaze raised to meet his in the glass, then skittered away.

He flattened his palms and slid them down the front of her gown, covering her breasts and cupping them. A groan escaped his throat at the long-missed pleasure of touching her, and he resisted pressing himself against her spine. He'd been in this emotional vacuum too long—way too long, and whiskey could only dull so much.

"Jesse—"

Taking her shoulders, he turned her upper body toward him and bent to cover her mouth with his. She didn't resist, didn't stiffen…didn't respond. He knew she tasted the whiskey on his lips, wondered somewhere in the back of his mind if it had become a familiar—or dreaded taste. Damn her! All she had to do was let his kiss and his touch affect her as it used to do. How had it happened that he'd become unable to reach her—to have any effect upon her? Sometimes he wondered if she'd even miss him if he didn't come to the house for supper. If he never came home again.

A deep aching regret and helplessness surged through him, creating a desperate need to demand the love and acceptance she denied him. He ended the kiss, urging her up from her seat and toward the bed. She turned back the quilt and slipped beneath the covers.

Jesse blew out the lamp, divested himself of his denim trousers and knelt to lean over her. In the moonlight that slanted through the parted curtains, her lovely oval face appeared pale, her eyes dark and luminous. He touched her cheek, skin so soft that every time he experienced its delicacy, he was amazed.

He knew the tender skin at the swell of each breast was just as soft; he raised her gown to pull the garment over her head, and she didn't challenge his right to do so. With his nose and lips, he appreciated the velvety skin of her breasts, pressed gentle kisses in the swells and hollows, inhaled her heady scent and saw stars behind his closed eyelids. He was weak when it came to this woman.

Jesse swallowed back a crashing tide of love and regret and need, greedy feelings that would get the best of him if he didn't go slowly and earn Amy's confidence again. It had been a long, long time.

Cupping her jaw in his palm, he turned her head, touched his nose to hers and kissed the corners of her mouth. *I love you, Amy. Amy, where are you?*

There had been a time when he'd believed his heart spoke to hers, when he'd listened in the darkness and heard her soul-deep replies to his unspoken feelings, when her caresses had answered his every emotional, sensual wish and satisfied so much more than merely his body. *Amy, my love, can you hear me?*

Jesse shifted his length over her, felt the dizzying sensation of skin against skin and shuddered with repressed desire.

He kissed her again, hoping against hope for the responses that would tell him she wanted him, too. She kissed him, but there was no flame, merely submission. He pressed himself against her, urged her thighs apart.

Opening his eyes to gauge her expression in the moonlight, he saw the tears that glistened on her cheeks. Fearful at first that he'd hurt or frightened her, he looked hard into her eyes. There were no tears in the haunted gaze she returned.

It was then he realized the tears were not Amy's, but his own.

Before his grief and loss became a wail he couldn't control, he pushed away from her to sit on the bed's edge and collect himself. He had to get away from here. Away from *her*. Groping, he found his trousers and pulled them on.

"Jesse?" she said softly, the bedclothes tucked against her breasts.

He stopped in the motion of shrugging into his shirt. "What?" It came out more harshly than he'd intended.

She didn't reply immediately, and he almost thought she'd never spoken in the first place. But then she said in a ragged whisper, "I'm sorry."

He tucked in his shirttail and grabbed his socks and boots. "I'm sorry too, Amy," he said. "I'm sorry, too."

And he left.

Jesse hadn't returned the night before. Amy wrapped a towel around the handle of the coffeepot and removed it from the heat. Deftly, she turned bacon, then cracked eggs into a sizzling skillet. There was a bonafide restaurant across the road, but Shelby Station took an ample portion of the stage passengers' business. All the drivers knew the tasty food was reasonably priced and the beds were clean, so they advised travelers thusly.

Jesse could have slept at the stable, or even in an unoccupied room in the building next door. During their five years of marriage, only trips to trade or sell horses had kept him from their bed—those and the night he'd built the coffin.

She didn't blame him for staying away. Nor did she

blame him for the way things between them had deteriorated. She just didn't have the energy to worry about it.

Her father greeted her with a peck on the cheek, poured himself coffee and took a seat.

A well-dressed couple traveling through from Salt Lake City to Washington arrived, introducing themselves as the Buckinghams and taking seats. Amy greeted them. Her kitchen helper, Mrs. Elthea Barnes, poured milk and coffee.

Pearly Higgs, a stage driver with an accomplished reputation, entered the kitchen and doffed his hat. "Mornin', Miz Shelby. Smells mighty fine. I told the Buckinghams here, yours was the best vittles between Atchison and Denver City."

"Why thank you, Pearly. I'll have to take that corn bread out of the oven now, so you can test it."

The slim-as-a-whip driver rubbed his hands together and grinned, overlapped front teeth showing beneath his gray-streaked mustache. "Yes, ma'am!"

Jesse entered the kitchen just as she placed the steaming cast-iron pan of golden corn bread on the table. She nodded, but he hung his hat and the holster that held his Colt on a peg inside the door and took a seat without acknowledgment. His hair was damp and neatly combed, his cuffs spotted from his recent wash at the pump. He wasn't the handsomest man she'd ever laid eyes on—his face was a little too chiseled—but his elemental masculinity gave him an appeal beyond comeliness. He was plainspoken, candid, earthy. She had loved him from the first time she'd seen his smile.

"We need more cooks like your missus on the Overland Trail," Pearly said to Jesse, accepting the generous chunk of corn bread Amy cut for him.

"Mrs. Shelby's a fine cook," Jesse agreed, referring to her the way he always did in front of guests.

"As good a cook as her mama was," her father agreed.

Mrs. Buckingham nibbled at the food on her plate, but mostly pushed it around with her fork. Her husband ate heartily, even asking her if she was finished and then polishing off her share.

"My wife is feeling poorly," he explained. "I have a business in Salt Lake City, but we're going home for a year so she can see her doctor and rest."

The woman blushed, and her husband patted her hand.

Amy immediately knew the woman was expecting a child, a subject too delicate for a gentleman such as Mr. Buckingham to mention in mixed company. Amy turned away from the table and dished eggs onto a serving platter beside the bacon.

"Do you and Mrs. Shelby have children?" Mrs. Buckingham asked sweetly.

Amy gripped the platter. With concerted effort, she relaxed her fingers and placed the food on the table. Jesse had looked up at her, but she kept her gaze on the checkered tablecloth.

"No," he said in reply. "We don't."

Simple. Honest. No hint at the cost of that statement or the pain behind it. No explanation. No words could convey the unfathomable truth.

Pearly ate his meal oblivious to the tense undercurrent in the room, though he had been traveling through this Nebraska station for enough years to have remembered the cherubic infant who had once sat in a wooden chair at this table—the toddler who had followed his father's every step whenever permitted.

Sam gave his daughter a look that conveyed sympathy.

"Pony up with Shelby, here, for your meals and room," Pearly said to Mr. Buckingham, finishing his coffee and pushing back his chair. "We're gonna pull foot so we make Omaha by breakfast tomorrow."

The man took a leather pouch from inside his jacket and paid Jesse in gold coins.

The men grabbed their hats and exited.

"Thank you, Mrs. Shelby," the woman said softly.

"Wait a moment." Amy quickly prepared sandwiches, added apples from the bushel Sam had brought that morning and wrapped the meal in newspaper. "You'll need to eat before Omaha," she said.

The woman accepted the offering gratefully. "You're very kind. Thank you."

Amy followed her through the door, stood on the wooden walkway that led to the stable and lifted a hand to shade her eyes from the sun. Three men who'd eaten breakfast earlier were waiting at the corner of the build-

ing. Shelby Station was the only one along the Overland Trail with sleeping accommodations, and many
travelers had told her that by far, she served the best
food. Most stations were at least half a day's ride apart,
and those stops were usually only forty minutes to
change horses and drivers. Passengers had to sleep sitting up, being jostled about in the coach, so the bunks
her father had built with foresight and a head for business were as good as gold in the bank.

Jesse checked harnesses on the team of matching
grays hitched to a Concord coach. He had trained those
horses well for the task, and they stood attentively. He
was the stock man. He had brought the horses and
know-how into the partnership. Amy's mother, until
she died, had helped Amy cook and feed travelers.

Hermie Jackson, Jesse's right-hand man, had finished loading trunks into the boot and fastened the
straps over the lid. The two stood back as Mr. Buckingham helped his wife into the coach and the men
who'd been waiting boarded and closed the door.

After climbing to his seat and picking up the reins,
Pearly bellowed a "H-yah" and snapped the reins. The
team pulled the coach forward. Hermie strode back to
the stable.

Jesse turned and spotted Amy where she stood in the
sunlight.

They stared at one another for a long moment, a year
of silence cloaking anything they might have wanted to
do or say, a lifetime of regret and guilt closing the door

on what should have been. His partnership with her father had been her introduction to the man she would love and marry. The man who would give her a child.

Jesse adjusted his hat.

Amy flattened her hand against her waist.

He turned and strode toward the corral.

She found her feet and returned to the kitchen.

Though he stood in the shade of the open stable doors, sweat poured from his forehead and upper body as Jesse held the foot of a gelded black between his knees and deftly cleaned the hoof. An intolerable ache throbbed behind his eyes, and he resisted the impulse to go dull it with a hefty swig of liquor. Problem was, he knew he'd feel better if he did, so resisting was a monumental battle.

A soft footfall alerted him to someone's presence and he looked up to see Amy. She appeared fresh and cool in a calico dress sprigged with a tiny green leaf pattern. Her hair was hidden beneath a straw bonnet, green ribbons laced beneath her chin.

He straightened and, still holding the iron pick, wiped his forehead.

"I'm going to place an order at the mercantile. Will you have time to pick it up after Mr. Liscom has filled it?"

He nodded. "Shouldn't be a stage until suppertime. This is the last horse to get ready."

Her gaze flicked over the black gelding. "Anything you need?"

A moment passed and her cheeks turned pink. She waited for a reply without meeting his eyes. Most of their conversations were conducted like this, it seemed.

"You might ask John if the linseed oil has arrived."

"I'll do that." She turned and headed toward the mercantile.

It was a ten-minute walk, but if she'd wanted a horse, she'd have asked, he thought.

Jesse finished with the hoof he was cleaning and spoke to the black, wearily rubbed his forehead and neck. Then he rinsed at the pump and pulled on his shirt before returning to the house.

He entered the kitchen, where Mrs. Barnes glanced up from peeling potatoes. She was a handsome woman, with dark hair turning gray at the temples. Giving her a polite nod, he passed on to the front of the house and stood at the bottom of the stairs, one foot on the first step. This time of day the house was unnaturally quiet. The scent of lemon oil told him someone had been polishing wood.

Silence closed in on him. There should have been a child's voice echoing through these rooms, footsteps on the wooden floors, toys scattered and a small pair of boots standing beside the door. Tim should be here. His precious Tim.

Jesse's chest tightened with a familiar, lonely ache.

A man should be able to share these feelings with his wife, the only other person in the world who knew the same grief.

Jesse glanced up the stairs. There should have been other children, too. Another son. A daughter, perhaps. Not to replace Tim, of course, but to fill this house and their lives.

He couldn't stay here anymore. Couldn't see Amy every night, lie beside her and grieve for the life they'd once had and the things that should have been. He couldn't think clearly when he was here, and he needed to sort things out in his head. Jesse pushed himself into motion.

In their bedroom, he gathered his clothing, comb and brush, and extra boots and placed them in the center of a blanket, which he bundled up and carried quickly down the stairs and across the space between buildings to the plain quarters where travelers slept.

Most rooms held at least six bunks, but he chose one of the two downstairs rooms with only two bunks and deposited his belongings on the bed he had slept on the night before. He could hear someone moving in a room above as he stacked his clothing in a drawer.

Footsteps sounded behind him, and he turned.

Adele McConough, the young woman who changed linens and did laundry, started at finding him. She clutched a stack of sheets to her chest.

"Didn't mean to scare you," he said apologetically.

"That's okay. I didn't expect anyone to be in here during the day." She gave him a bashful smile.

He hadn't wanted to explain, but of course the hired girls would know if he used this room. "I'll be sleeping here. You don't need to change the sheets every day. Once a week will be fine."

"Y-yes, certainly, Mr. Shelby," she said, obviously puzzled.

"And please," he added, "don't mention the fact that I'm bunking here to anyone." Amy didn't need the added embarrassment of gossip.

"I won't," she said, turning to go.

"Appreciate it." He closed the drawer and left.

Back outside, he went to the spring house and raised a bucket containing jugs and jars from the cold water, found a jar of buttermilk and drank it slowly, hoping to calm his stomach and quench his thirst.

Feeling better, he headed back to the stable to finish preparing for the next stage.

The kitchen table was filled with travelers that evening—two businessmen, a young couple, a woman with a son about the age of eight and two elderly sisters. Sam participated in a conversation about the Wells Fargo lines with one of the bankers.

Mrs. Barnes, Adele and the laundress usually ate before the guests, along with Hermie and the other hands. Often Sam joined the other workers, but occasionally, he dined with the guests to stay current with news and happenings on the road.

Catching Amy by surprise, Jesse arrived and seated himself beside one of the older women.

Amy served the meal, and then, while Mrs. Barnes

filled cups, she sliced more roast and cut a thick molasses cake into wedges. Jesse ate breakfast with the guests, but he always waited until they were gone and in their rooms before he came in to share a private supper with her. This change of schedule was an unsettling surprise.

She went about her tasks, and one by one, the diners left, until only Jesse and her father remained. They discussed a mare ready to foal, and as Amy picked up the last dish, Jesse followed Sam out the door without a backward glance.

A sinking shred of disappointment almost made its way into her chest, but she stifled it immediately and, taking her place beside Mrs. Barnes, dug into the stack of dishes.

Eventually, everything was washed and dried and Mrs. Barnes left. She rode in about five miles every day from her son and daughter-in-law's homestead to the west. Her job here was her contribution to their struggle to keep the place going.

Amy picked up the plate on which she'd saved a portion of food for herself and ate a few bites without bothering to sit. She wasn't being fair to Jesse, but she couldn't talk to him. She didn't have anything to say, and she refused to open wounds best left scarred over.

Taking out her patterns and material, she finished cutting two dresses and started pinning the seams together. With little time to devote to herself, this project would take months, but it kept her hands busy this evening. Night had fallen full upon the station and there was no sign of Jesse's return.

She wanted to ignore this problem, too, but maybe she had better go see where he was. After putting away her sewing, she lit a lantern and carried it to the stable.

The lamps were still lit, and that was one of Jesse's last chores, so she searched the building, walking past stalls where horses stood placidly. An occasional nicker prompted her to reach through the gate and rub her knuckles on a bony forehead.

She found Jesse in a large stall toward the back doors, which were closed and barred. He sat on a bushel of hay, a sorrel mare with swollen sides placidly blinking at him.

The swiveling light from Amy's lantern caught his attention and he glanced up. "Hey."

"What are you doing out here?"

"Just keeping her company." Though his words were carefully enunciated, she heard the liquor that laced them.

Spotting the bottle between his boots, swift anger warmed her face and neck. Anger…disappointment… or guilt?

Chapter Two

"And drinking whiskey," she said, her tone flat.

He plucked up the bottle by the neck. "Yeah."

"You've been doing too much of that lately."

He turned his head to look up at her. "What the hell do you care, Amy?"

"It's not an answer for anything—" she began.

"And what needs answering, huh? What's the question? D'you have a question?"

"I mean a solution," she corrected. "It's not a solution."

"Maybe not." He squinted and stared at the nearly empty bottle. "But it's a helluva lot better'n the choices. I'm not hurting anybody out here."

She stood, keeping her silence, hating what she was seeing Jesse become.

"Maybe you ought to try it, Amy." He raised the bottle toward her. "Go ahead. Maybe it'd loosen you up a bit."

"If you're an example of loose, I don't need it."

Pushing unsteadily to his feet, he caught his balance and stepped toward her. "Come on, maybe you'd feel better. Maybe you'd *feel,* period."

She took a step back. "This isn't you talking, Jesse."

"What are you doing out here, anyway?" he asked, anger in his tone. "You can't stand to have me around. I'm giving you what you want, so don't suddenly act… concerned. I know you don't give a damn what I do or where I am. I'm surprised you even—even knew I was out here."

His words found their mark, but she refused to let them wound. If she felt them—like he wanted her to— she wouldn't be able to cope. She turned to leave. "I'm sorry I came."

A crash sounded. Jumping in alarm, she spun to see the broken whiskey bottle lying at the base of the gate frame, amber liquid soaking into the wood and scattered straw. The scent rose and burned her nostrils.

She turned to see Jesse facing away from her, scrubbing a hand down his face. He'd thrown it, but not at her.

"Shit," he said, turning and coming toward her, awkwardly kneeling and reaching for the broken glass.

"No, let me," she said.

He grabbed for the pieces, and Amy watched with dulled senses as a crimson rivulet ran across his thumb and dripped to the hard-packed earth.

"Jesse, what have you done?" She grabbed his wrist.

She turned over his hand and he opened it, revealing a shard of the bottle protruding from a deep gash in his palm.

"I can't even feel it," he commented, staring at the oozing cut.

Amy reacted quickly, gently plucking the glass from his hand and pulling a handkerchief from her pocket. She pressed the clean white fabric against the wound. "Do you have any more of that whiskey?"

He nodded. "Y'want a slug after all?"

"No, you fool, I want to pour some over this cut before I stitch it."

"There's a wooden crate in the tack room. Look under my s-saddle."

"Sit and don't move," she ordered.

He dropped onto the bale and gripped the handkerchief against the cut.

Looking where he'd instructed, she found the case of whiskey, six bottles already missing. She took one out, then ran to the house for her sewing basket and returned with hot water and supplies.

Placing both her lantern and his on either side of where he sat, she knelt before him and guided his hand into the water. While the needle and thread soaked in a saucer of whiskey, she poured more on the cut, then held a clean rag against it.

"Maybe I ought to take a drink of that before you start stitching."

She refused to look up. "You already said you couldn't even feel the cut."

"I can see it."

Finally, she looked at him. His eyes were reddened and his hair mussed. "Don't look."

She turned back and, with a deep breath, steeled herself for the task she had to do. The wound was in the center of his palm, making her chore more difficult, but she had wisely chosen the smallest needle she could find. It took several minutes to neatly sew the cut closed and tie off the thread. She'd performed this unpleasant duty for a few of the stable hands and more than once for her father, but it never got any easier to pierce someone's flesh and draw it closed. By the time she was finished, her stomach felt queasy and her head was light.

"I'll make you some coffee," she said, pouring the water out onto the ground in the corner of the stall.

"I don't want any."

She gathered up the supplies. "You should get some sleep, then." From the corner of her eye, she saw him stand. She took a few steps and paused. "Will you be coming in soon?"

She waited for his reply.

"No."

Her heart stammered, but she collected herself. Well, there it was. Just another situation to ignore. She was good at that.

She crossed the distance to the house and steadied herself with a hand on the porch rail before entering the kitchen. She put away the bandages and ointment, banked the fire in the stove and picked up the lantern and a pail of water.

At this time of night Jesse was usually just behind her, or finishing chores and would be joining her shortly. Not this night, so her footsteps echoed alone on the stairs.

She set the lantern on the washstand and poured the water into the basin.

Slowly, with numb fingers, Amy removed her shirt-waist and skirt and set her shoes aside. In her chemise and drawers, she crossed the room and opened the top drawer of the bureau.

It was empty, except for the velvet box in which Jesse had kept his father's watch. The second drawer held only a packet of letters and the white shirt he'd worn the day they were married.

Amy opened the wardrobe to find only her clothing remaining. She closed it. At the basin she removed her chemise and washed, then pulled on her nightdress and blew out the lantern.

Jesse wasn't coming to bed. He wasn't coming back to this room. From the window, light could be seen shining from the rear of the barn where Hermie slept. A few windows at the boardinghouse were illuminated. Jesse was in one of those rooms.

Amy pulled the curtains closed, turned back the covers and climbed into bed. The mattress dipped and swallowed her into its softness. She lay on her side with her eyes closed against the darkness…against the emptiness.

Tomorrow morning she would rise early to bake bread. There was a social on Sunday after church, so a cake and pies were called for. Mentally going over the list of supplies, she checked that she had everything.

For a brief time after her mother's death, she'd handled all the meals, but then Jesse had hired Mrs. Barnes. Since the woman had been with them, Amy's kitchen chores were less hectic and she had more time to prepare ahead. Adele cleaned rooms and changed linens at the boardinghouse, and Maggie Townsend, whom Jesse had hired last year, did the laundry and helped in the garden.

There had been a time when Amy had done the laundry herself, her son toddling in the yard while she hung sheets to dry. She had spent more time chasing him than she had at her task, but somehow she'd managed to do everything she needed to and look after him, as well.

More than once Jesse had come upon them outdoors and run up to sweep the little boy off his feet and toss him in the air. She could still hear the toddler's infectious giggles and see his fair hair glistening in the sunshine. And the smile on Jesse's face…she hadn't seen that smile since.

Amy clamped down hard on the unwanted thoughts. She willed herself to be strong. *Don't think about it. Don't remember.*

She hadn't realized she'd reached for it, but somehow Jesse's pillow had become clutched to her breast.

She curled herself around it and ignored the unoccupied space in the bed. Everybody made their choices and Jesse had made his. He couldn't move on, and she wouldn't go back. She wouldn't lose sleep over things she couldn't control.

He'd been as good as gone for a long time anyway. For months they'd lain side by side with a mile of hurt separating them. That was just the way things were.

Jesse made a new habit of eating with the hands before the guest meal. Amy adjusted to the change without comment. She saw him at breakfast with her father, half a dozen hands, and the women present. He came in at noon with the others, and then she saw him at supper. The two of them hadn't spent a minute alone since the night he'd cut his hand.

She noticed the bandage had been changed and was clean, so she said nothing.

Finally, when he stepped to the stove for more coffee after Saturday supper, she asked, "Do you need those stitches out?"

"I'll do it myself," he replied. "Thanks."

He carried his cup back to the table.

"Church social tomorrow afternoon," Mrs. Barnes reminded them. "Might be the last one we can hold out of doors before cold weather."

Sam leaned across the table and secured himself another slice of molasses cake. "I'd better practice, in case there's a cake-eating contest."

Hermie laughed. "You're always practicin' for that contest and it's never happened yet."

Sam ate his cake, then stood and glanced at his daughter. He often wore a look that said he wondered what was going on inside of her, but everyone—including her own father—had learned to stay at arm's length and keep their advice to themselves. But she saw it there—the loss. And she looked away.

"I still have more apples for you to dry. When do you want 'em?"

"Monday will be good," she replied.

"See you in the mornin'. Ladies." He plucked his hat from a hook and exited the house.

"Mrs. Barnes, you go on home so you can prepare for tomorrow," Jesse told the older woman. "I'll help Amy clean up after the guests."

"That's right nice of you," she told him. "Hermie, want to see me home?"

The hand got up and escorted Mrs. Barnes out.

There were only three boarders that night. Amy served them supper, and Jesse showed up to help her clean up as he'd promised.

"I can do this," she said uneasily, knowing he'd worked as hard or harder than she had all week, and not wanting to pile additional work on him.

He picked up an empty bowl. "I thought maybe you could stand my presence long enough to get through the dishes."

"It's not that," she said.

He scraped plates into a bucket for the hogs without looking at her. When all the scraps were cleaned up, he carried the pail out the door.

Unexpectedly, Amy's heart chugged. She placed a wet hand over it and collected her thoughts. It wasn't that she couldn't stand his presence. It wasn't. The problem was that when he was around it was more difficult to keep a tight control on her feelings.

She found herself waiting like a fool to see if he would return. The sound of boots hitting the back porch made her jump, and she spun around to appear busy.

She washed dishes.

He carried in firewood and stacked it in the bin beside the stove.

She dried the pans.

He swept the floor and stacked the clean plates on the table for morning.

A well-orchestrated dance of avoidance.

"Has your mare foaled yet?" she asked.

"Two nights ago. A pretty little brown filly with a blaze on her forehead. They're in the barn if you want to see her."

"Okay."

He put away the broom and picked up his hat. "Night, then."

"Jesse?"

He paused, his hand on the open door, and looked back at her.

She wiped her hands self-consciously on her apron.

Didn't he understand this was the only way for her to survive? He believed she had chosen this road. Truth was, it had chosen her, and it took her full-time energy to keep from taking a wrong turn and becoming lost. He wanted too much from her.

She didn't know what she'd planned to say. "Thank you" was all she could think of.

He gave half a nod. "Yeah," he said as he left.

She stared at the closed door.

The first Sunday since Jesse had moved to the boardinghouse dawned as deceptively normal as any other. After preparing and serving breakfast, Amy got ready for church alone in the house. She had selected a dress with sprigs of blue flowers before she realized it took a great deal of effort to button it up the back herself. Her arms ached when she was finished, and she stared at her disheveled state in the mirror.

Quickly, she brushed her hair and pinned it up, found her matching hat and a pair of gloves, and made her way downstairs.

Jesse had polished her Sunday boots and they waited for her beside the kitchen door. She put them on, then gathered all the food she had prepared and placed it on the end of the table, and donned her gloves.

Jesse was waiting at the bottom of the porch stairs. He frowned as he loaded the food into crates in the back of the buggy, and she wondered if he'd had too much to drink the night before. Silently, he helped her up to the seat, and she noted his rifle carefully tucked beneath. They always rode alone to church while her father, Hermie and the other women traveled together in the wagon.

Silence between them used to be comfortable, but now it was loud with unformed thoughts and unspoken questions.

They were greeted at the church door, as usual, and sat together as the service began. Amy took some small comfort from the familiar hymns, the Scripture readings and the drone of Reverend Calhoun's message. It was only here, within these sanctified walls and the safe cocoon of God's house, that she let herself think about Tim. Think his name. But even here her thoughts were carefully controlled and selective. She thought of Tim in heaven, sitting beside the throne of the Father, eternally three, forever happy and free of pain and life's troubles.

Those thoughts gave her the only tiny measure of peace she allowed herself. Once a week for an hour. She never let herself think of her life without him. Or of the loss. Or of Jesse's pain. And if anyone dared to mention her son, which they didn't any more, she pretended not to hear.

It was how she survived.

The service ended and the reverend spoke to his parishioners at the door as they exited.

"Good morning, Mr. and Mrs. Shelby. How are you this fine day?"

"Well, thank you, Reverend," she replied.

Behind her Jesse spoke a few words to the preacher, and then he joined her and they stood outdoors in the sunlight.

Already men had begun assembling tables in the side yard, as the women unpacked their tablecloths and aprons. Jesse carried their crates to a table for Amy, then disappeared while she joined the women in setting out the food.

Leda Bently, a farmer's wife, drew a young woman toward Amy. "This is Rachel Douglas. She and her husband just moved here. Her man is helping with the harvest at our place."

Amy greeted the pale-haired young woman and immediately noticed the faded shawl she held so that the ends covered her swollen belly. It was obvious that her dress was inappropriate for her growing figure, because the front of her hemline was inches above the back, revealing worn boots and black stockings.

"Where are you from?" Amy asked.

"Jack is from England. I met him in New York. We were married there, and he couldn't find work, so we came West."

"You have family in the East?"

She shook her head and glanced at Amy's flower-bedecked hat. "No. I outgrew a foundling home and worked as a maid for two years before I met Jack."

"Rachel is real good at household tasks," Leda told her. "What a blessing for me that Frank hired Jack for the fall. My house has never been so clean."

Rachel blushed. "I'm earning my own keep," she told Amy. "I'm just so glad to have somewhere to settle for a time and not be riding on a wagon, that I'd do anything."

"Amy and her husband and father run the way station," Leda told Rachel. "Even with the transcontinental railroad finished last spring, they still get a lot of travelers."

"Do you need any help?" Rachel asked. "I can clean and cook and do laundry. And Jack is a real hard worker. He'll need work after Mr. Bently's crops are in."

"I have three women who help me now," Amy told her. "Jack would have to talk to Jesse. He does the hiring."

"I'll tell him." Rachel gave her a shy smile.

When she turned to look away, Amy noted her thin frame. The journey west was hard on women, but it must have been especially trying for a young woman expecting her first baby.

"When will your baby be born?" Amy asked.

Rachel glanced back and blushed. "Sometime this winter. Mrs. Bently helped me figure about December."

Amy nodded and, sharing knowledge of the experience the young woman would face, she and Leda exchanged a concerned glance. "Well, I wish you the best," Amy told her. "I hope you and your husband find someplace you like to settle."

"Oh, we like it here," Rachel told her quickly. "I'd

never seen so much wide-open space. The fields are magnificent to behold, all that corn waving as far as the eye can see. Garden vegetables and fresh milk every day. This is a land of plenty, to be sure."

Amy almost felt the young woman's pleasure, almost understood Rachel's sense of wonder at having enough food, and her appreciation of the land. But she held herself in reserve and turned aside to slice pies.

Another half hour passed before the parishioners gathered around the tables and Jesse dutifully sought her out. As Reverend Calhoun said a blessing for the meal, Amy glanced up and unerringly found Rachel. She stood with a tall fresh-faced young man who held her hand to his chest and closed his eyes reverently as the preacher prayed. The two of them were so young, so earnest, so— She stopped herself before she could think *in love*.

Beside her, Jesse held his hat by the brim with both hands. She glanced up to find him gazing out across the landscape.

The prayer ended and the air hummed with voices. Two lines formed and the woman began serving food.

Her father found a group of men and sat with them under the shade of the maple trees growing in the churchyard.

"Sun or shade?" Jesse asked from beside her.

"Sun."

He spread their quilt out on the grass a distance from the crowd, and they sat. The afternoon sun felt good, and she removed her hat to enjoy the warmth on her hair.

Jesse ate his fill of fried chicken, one of his favorites. Afterward, he took an envelope from his pocket. "There was a mail stage this morning."

"Yes, the driver had a quick breakfast."

"I got this letter. It's from my mother."

She glanced from his face to the envelope. He received letters from his mother in Indiana every few months, and Amy often saw him at the secretary in the parlor, writing to her. Because of all his responsibilities here, he hadn't seen her for six years.

"What does she say?"

"She's not well."

"Oh. I'm sorry to hear that. What's the problem?"

"A weakened heart, the doctors have said."

"Would you like to go see her?"

"She's coming here."

Amy blinked. "Oh."

"She's bringing Cay."

Cay was Jesse's sister's son. His sister, Ruby, had run off and left Cay with her mother when he was just a little boy. "How old is he now?"

"Twelve, best I figured. My mother has been having trouble with the boy. He's become more than she can handle, and she asked if we could help."

"What can we do?"

"She wants to bring him here. She needs the rest. And the help. My father died when I was about his age. I know what it's like to grow up like that and I don't want the same for my nephew."

Caught off guard by this announcement, Amy simply nodded. Certainly the woman deserved some rest if she was ill. "She's your mother, Jesse. Of course she's welcome here if she wants to come. We can take care of her."

Jesse's face relaxed somewhat.

The boy was another matter. If he was troublesome, they didn't need that aggravation added to their lives. She felt guilty for resenting the intrusion.

"When will they arrive?"

He glanced at the date on the letter. "Another week, I'm thinking."

"I'll fix the other upstairs room for her. What about Cay? Where do you want him to sleep?"

"He can stay in the boardinghouse. Or he can sleep on a pallet in the parlor."

Parlor was a fancy word for the large room they used for a variety of purposes, among them, extra sleeping space on the floor when necessary.

What would Jesse's mother think of the fact that Jesse didn't sleep in the house? Would he return to their room so he didn't have to explain?

Amy gazed out across the churchyard, took in the various groupings of families sharing meals. Her attention was drawn to Rachel and Jack Douglas. They were seated on a horse blanket, eating leisurely and smiling at one another. Rachel grabbed the plate on her lap suddenly, and looked down. Jack followed her gaze. She spoke, and he reached to place his hand on her belly.

A knife blade of pain cut into Amy's chest, and she jerked her gaze away. She gripped her plate and forced herself to breathe evenly.

"Amy, what's wrong?"

"Nothing."

"You look like you've seen a ghost."

She shook her head. She *had* seen a ghost. The ghost of a young couple in love and anticipating the birth of their child. The ghost of naive bliss.

But ghosts weren't real. So with practiced effort, she exorcised the agonizing glimpse of the past and concentrated on her food.

"Jesse, have you met Jack Douglas?"

"Don't believe so."

"He's working the harvest at the Bentlys'. His wife mentioned he needed work after the crops were in. They're…young."

Jesse studied her curiously. She wasn't in the habit of discussing employees with him, and her mention of the man probably seemed out of the ordinary.

She tried to sound casual when she asked, "Can you use another hand?"

He set down a jar of buttermilk and wiped a white mustache from his upper lip. "You asking me to hire this Jack Douglas?"

"No." She busied herself picking up their plates. "I was just wondering, is all. She asked me, and I told her Jack would have to speak with you."

"If he comes to me, I'll talk to 'im," he said.

That was all she was going to think about that. She had enough to deal with, now that Jesse's mother and nephew were coming. Amy packed their lunch things and watched Jesse lope down the grassy lawn to join a group of men.

Jesse no longer knew his wife. She wasn't the woman he'd married. She wasn't the woman who'd lain beside him in the intimate stillness of a winter night and shared dreams and feelings. She wasn't the woman who'd once loved him so fiercely and well that he'd thought his heart would burst to overflowing.

He lay on the bunk in the stark room he'd taken and stared at the knotholes in the pine ceiling. He could remember so many details of their life together that the memories drove him crazy long into the night.

As cavalry soldiers, he and Sam had met at Fort Kearny during the war. Jesse'd been making a profit selling horses to the Army, and Sam had homesteaded land in Nebraska. Seeing the need for way stations, they put their heads together and came up with the plan to build one in a prime location. They worked out their partnership, and after the war ended, scouted and purchased land with access to water and grazing ranges. It was agreed that the stables came first; horses would be their security and the base of their operation. But until the business prospered, Sam had to provide a roof overhead for his wife and daughter, so once the stables and barns were built, construction began on a sod house.

Jesse remembered the first time he saw Amy. Sam's wife, Vanessa, and his eighteen-year-old daughter had arrived by wagon, bringing supplies and furniture. He'd been surprised that very first day to see Sam's daughter climb down unaided from the wagon she'd driven, using the spokes of the wheel as a step, and turn to help her mother.

From beneath her bonnet, honey-colored hair hung down her back in waves, and she carried herself in a capable and confident manner. She'd spotted her father stacking blocks of sod to form the base of the house and had taken off running. Her bonnet fell back, and the sun glistened from that shiny, thick hair.

Sam Burnham had stopped and straightened, and a smile that would have lit the prairie night split his face. He plucked off his gloves, tossed them down and ran forward to greet her.

She locked her arms around his neck and he swung her in a circle, her laughter floating like a melody on the air.

"Whoo, Daddy, you smell like a goat!" she'd scolded him, backing away and inspecting his stained clothing.

Neither he nor Jesse had bothered to launder their clothes since they'd run out of clean a week or more ago.

"And you smell like a spring flower," Sam replied.

Jesse gazed at the curvy young lady wearing a pale green dress, who looked as fresh as a new day, then glanced at his own clothing. He'd been plowing sod behind a pair of oxen for two days, and his boots were caked with mud and manure, his dungarees stiff with dirt. He smelled like the backside of a buffalo.

He stayed where he was.

Amy Burnham's attention shifted to him, and he was caught off guard by how dark her eyes were—he'd expected blue, but discovered them a rich caramel color. She looked him over, head to toe, an assessing but not critical inspection.

Vanessa joined them then, her greeting less exuberant than her daughter's. Sam kissed his wife on the cheek and she took her fill of gazing at him, as though she was making up for the weeks apart.

"Jesse," Sam said finally, gesturing for him to come closer. "This is my wife, Vanessa, and my daughter, Amy. Ladies, this is Jesse. My partner."

Jesse doffed his hat then, but he stopped a good five feet away from the women. "Ma'am," he said with a polite nod. "Miss Burnham."

"You're younger than I expected," Mrs. Burnham said.

"I'm older than I was yesterday," he replied with a grin.

Vanessa Burnham looked him over. "You're young for a man so financially solvent," she explained.

"I've caught, broke and sold a lot of horses to the Army, ma'am," he explained. "I've outfitted stage lines and buffalo hunters. Then the war scared the nonsense out of me. I met your husband and started thinking about the future, and knew I wanted to settle in one place."

"*This* is the future," Sam told the ladies with an exaggerated sweep of his arm. "A prime spot along the Overland Trail, no other way station in a hundred miles. Once we get the horses ready, we can build sleeping quarters and attract travelers like flies to honey."

"Isn't that like bees to honey, Daddy?" Amy asked with a twinkle in those captivating eyes. "Flies are attracted to…other things." She glanced at Jesse's boots.

He'd recognized the teasing glimmer in her eyes, and though he'd blushed, he hadn't taken offense. She wasn't prissy, not then and never since. Over the years he'd seen her work hard and find satisfaction in the growth of the operation and in their success. She was the woman he loved beyond reason, the woman who made every day of his life and all the effort he'd put into Shelby Station worthwhile.

She was the woman who'd cut him from her life as though he were a loose thread. And day by day something inside Jesse was dying.

Chapter Three

Bless Mrs. Barnes, she never minded extra work or additional mouths to feed. Earlier in the week a wagon train had camped to the west, and the female travelers had been eager to pay for hot baths and fresh vegetables. Truth be told, Mrs. Barnes seemed to welcome the chance to talk with other women, and often made herself a profitable exchange for the scented soap she made and kept wrapped for such occasions.

Jesse had dealings with the Army that same week, and a cavalry troupe sent to obtain horses had camped overnight at the station while Jesse trained the soldiers in special commands and care of his stock.

Mid-morning of the second day Amy browned rabbit parts in two enormous skillets, then dropped the meat into a pot of bubbling water, which would be stew by dinner. She'd waved down Pitch Gittleman that morning and asked if he could spare a few hours to hunt rabbits. The stocky bowlegged ex-cooper was always ready to hunt game when the need arose. He had a knack for finding sizable rabbits, and didn't mind skinning them before he brought her the meat.

She'd rewarded him with a napkin full of doughnuts she'd just fried. He'd grinned a broad smile that showed a gold front tooth.

"I'm gonna hide these and make meself a pot o' coffee."

She had wondered if he'd enjoy his coffee and doughnuts before any of the other hands sniffed him out.

At supper the soldiers raved over her stew and dumplings, told Jesse that they regretted having to leave that afternoon, and thanked her profusely as they filed out of her kitchen, picking up their guns from a pile outside the door.

Amy dropped to a trestle bench and caught her breath.

Mrs. Barnes was already scraping dishes and shaving soap into the dish pan. Adele, too, had stayed to help clean up.

From the yard came a familiar call. *"Stage a comin'."*

"Oh Lord," Mrs. Barnes muttered.

Wearily, Amy stood. "There's still stew in the pot and I can add potatoes in a hurry to make it stretch."

"I'll whip up a pan of corn bread, Miz Shelby," Adele offered.

Amy nodded her appreciation and Mrs. Barnes bustled to clear the table and reset it.

After she'd added the potatoes to the pot, Amy dipped water from the bucket beside the house and filled the two washbasins kept on crates along the porch wall for travelers.

She glanced across the distance to the stable yard, where the coach was stopped and Hermie and Pitch were changing teams. Where was Jesse? He always helped with that task and his absence was unsettling. She frowned when she saw him standing at the opening in the fence that separated the yard from the stable area. A boy who barely came to Jesse's shoulder stood beside him.

Something was wrong. She knew it from the way her husband held his shoulders.

Amy gathered her skirts and descended the porch stairs, making her way to where Jesse stood. Before she reached him, he moved and took the boy into his arms in an awkward embrace.

"Jesse?" she called.

He released the boy slowly and turned to watch her approaching. "Amy."

The boy quickly swiped his face and raised his chin to look at her. He had hair a little darker than Jesse's and eyes the same color of blue. Cay? So Jesse's mother had arrived? Amy glanced toward the coach.

"Amy, this is Cay."

She stepped forward. "How do you do?"

The boy didn't respond, and her gaze raised to Jesse. His eyes held a peculiar sheen.

She experienced a twinge of fright in her chest. "Where's your mother?"

Jesse looked out across the north pasture and grimaced before composing his expression. He rubbed the bridge of his nose. "She died on the skirts of Manhattan and they left her in town. I have to go get her."

Amy couldn't think for a moment. Her hand rose to her breast on its own. "Oh my—oh, Jesse."

"It's a day's ride," he said. "I'll leave first thing in the morning."

"I wanna go with you," Cay said immediately.

It was the first she'd heard him speak, and his voice was childlike, with a hint of the change soon to come.

"You can go with me," Jesse replied easily.

Should she offer to accompany him? She wasn't good at knowing what to do or at offering solace.

Four dusty passengers were heading toward the house. "Do you want to eat, Cay?" she asked.

He shook his head.

He'd lost his grandmother and Jesse'd just learned he'd lost his mother—and all she could do was offer food. Should she ask how it had happened or should she leave them alone?

"She knew she didn't have long," Jesse said. "I thought she'd make it here, though. I figured we'd have time to take care of her."

Amy tamped down whatever it was that had started

to rise in her chest. She filled her lungs with the sage-scented breeze and pressed her fingernails into her palms.

Cay shifted his feet and didn't raise his gaze. "She din't look good ever since we left Fort Wayne."

Amy needed to see to the guests who had reached the house. She hadn't put out extra towels yet. "I'm sorry about your grandmother." She couldn't look at Jesse again, couldn't bear to see his face and his pain and feel inadequate over her inability to share it. "I'm sorry, Jesse." She caught up her hem. "I'll go see to the guests. Have Cay bring his things to the house. He can stay in the room I got ready."

She buried her feelings by showing the travelers where to wash, slicing bread and filling cups. She and Mrs. Barnes worked compatibly, their relationship comfortable and familiar. Amy collected payment for the meals, and the pocket of her apron grew heavy with coins from the day.

Afterward she used her key to let herself into the small locked room behind the kitchen, where she recorded the amount in a ledger and placed the money in a metal box. At the end of each week Jesse paid the employees, set aside enough for groceries and supplies and took the rest to the bank.

A while back he had mentioned his desire to make a trip to Indiana to see his mother, but there never had seemed to be a good time. He was probably regretting not acting on that wish.

By supper the stage was on its way, and only two passengers had stayed over for a night's lodging. Jesse brought Cay in to eat with the hands, but the boy barely touched his food. Cay watched Amy with a mixture of resentment and blame in his expression, and she wasn't sure why he would feel either toward her.

When night fell, Jesse accompanied him back to the house. Cay's hair was wet and his clothing wrinkled, but clean. He'd apparently been to the bathhouse at Jesse's prompting.

Amy should have thought of it.

"You didn't eat much at supper," she said. "Would you like something now?"

Cay didn't look at her, but replied, "I could eat."

"Sit down and I'll fix you something."

He took a seat at the kitchen table, while Jesse removed himself to the locked room, probably to look over the day's earnings.

After slicing bread and ham, Amy placed a sandwich and a cup of milk before the boy.

He reached for the food.

"'Thank you' is called for," Jesse said from behind Amy, surprising her, because she hadn't heard him return.

He too had bathed, and she inhaled the fresh clean scent of his skin and hair, smells that triggered responses over which she had no control and caught her off guard.

"Thanks," the boy said sullenly and bit into the meal.

Amy poured Jesse a cup of coffee and cut him a narrow slice of apple pie. She knew he liked something sweet with his coffee at night, but lately he hadn't been coming in during the evening.

He thanked her and took his place at the end of the table. Amy sat across from Cay, while the two ate.

"We'll leave at first light," Jesse told her when he'd finished.

"I'll pack food for you. How long do you think the trip will take?"

"With the wagon, probably a day to Kansas and a day and a half taking it easier comin' back."

They'd be returning with his mother's body. What a difficult trip that would be.

Earlier in the day Jesse had deposited both his mother's and Cay's bags in the parlor. Amy thought of their belongings now. "Will you carry Cay's bags upstairs, please?"

Cay stood. "I can do it."

"Okay." She removed her apron, folded it and placed it on top of three others to be laundered. "Jesse can help you put things away and get settled in your room."

"I don't need any help. Just show me where."

After Cay found his bags, she picked up a lantern and climbed the stairs ahead of him. Jesse followed with the other lamp. He hadn't been upstairs for over a week. She had wondered what he would do when his mother arrived. Now it was Cay staying in the other bedroom, and she was still anxious. Would Jesse leave and have the boy speculate as to why he didn't sleep in the house?

She entered the room she had readied for Jesse's mother and placed the oil lamp on the bureau. "You can put your things away in these drawers. When you need your clothing laundered there's a basket by the door— just set it out in the hall. If you should need anything tonight…" She paused, confused over saying *I* or *we* would be close by.

"…we'll be right across the hall," Jesse supplied softly.

Amy's stomach knotted at his words. "Good night, Cay."

He didn't respond.

Jesse handed her the other lamp, and she carried it to their room. She had removed her shirtwaist and washed before Jesse opened the door and entered.

He walked to the window and stared out at the darkness through a slit in the curtain.

Something wild fluttered in Amy's stomach at her husband's nearness.

"I remember when your mama died." His voice was rough with emotion.

She removed her underclothing and quickly donned her nightdress. Without sitting at the dressing table, she loosened her hair, picked up her brush and made quick work of brushing and braiding. Her mother's death had been the first loss she'd experienced. She'd been brokenhearted and Jesse had been there for her. He'd offered silent compassion, as well as companionship to her father.

"There'll be one more marker on that little hill."

She hadn't been back to the pair of graves on their land to the east since last year, and she didn't want to think about them now.

"Both of Tim's grandmas will be there with him."

Amy dropped the jar of glycerin she'd been rubbing into her hands, and it hit the wood floor with a resounding *crack*.

Jesse turned from the window.

She looked from the jar on the floor to his weary face and bent to pick up the glycerin. A knot of anger formed in her chest and she took a deep breath to dispel it.

She was angry with herself—furious over her inability to dredge a scrap of feeling from her dead soul. She didn't know how anymore. She'd nailed everything up and lost the tools to let anything out. Some of her anger seeped over toward Jesse, as if he were to blame for making her feel so empty inside.

Anyone with a heart and blood in their veins would go over and touch him, offer him some small measure of comfort. She could see herself doing just that, imagined crossing the room and placing her hand on his firm chest, drawing him close to her body and sharing her warmth. She imagined his heartbeat against her breast, steady, strong, pictured her head on his shoulder and smelled his familiar scent.

Pain knifed across her chest and sucked the breath

from her lungs. She set the jar on the dressing table and practically staggered to the bed, where she turned back the covers and slipped between the sheets, drawing the top one to her breast.

Jesse removed his clothing and she didn't look away. The sharply defined muscles of his chest and shoulders flexed with each movement, and his body tapered to slim hips and strong hair-dusted thighs. Memories of touching him, lying with limbs entwined and pulses racing kept her attention fixed. He was a good man, not greedy, not selfish. He was kind and gentle, yet strong in all the ways she'd ever needed him to be strong.

She had failed him so many times, had let him down, shut him out, hurt him. Yes, hurt him. And that was the worst. The shame she couldn't bear was that of her own wrongdoing.

She watched as he folded his pants over the back of a chair and moved to blow out the lamp. The bed dipped, and Amy squeezed her eyes shut against the sudden panic that threatened to find a crack in the armor around her heart.

She smelled him. Soap. Man. Jesse.

She heard his breath. Ragged.

She sensed him turn to look at her. Felt the length of his body stretched out beside her, though he wasn't touching her anywhere.

Jesse needed her.

Without further thought, but with a purpose born of her self-loathing, she turned toward him and placed her hand on his chest. His skin felt warm and supple, as she'd known it would.

His hand came up and wrapped around her wrist, bringing her fingers to his lips and kissing them. His lips were hot and moist, and though she didn't want to, she remembered the feel of them on other places on her body.

He rolled toward her then, cupped her face, and she imagined he could see her in the shadowy darkness.

"Amy?"

There was no scent of liquor on his breath this night, only coffee.

He needed her.

He moved close to gently touch his lips to hers. The kiss was too sweet, too tender, leaving too much room for thought and choices, so she pressed harder. His lips parted and his tongue sought hers. Along with his desperation, she tasted the coffee and her pie.

After several earthshaking moments, he paused to bury his face against her neck and wrap his body around her. "God, I miss you, Amy," he said, his voice a low rasp.

It had been so long that it felt awkward, but she raised her hands to his hair and found it thick and silken beneath her fingers. He groaned at the simple caress, and her shame grew to a beast that filled every shadowy corner of the darkened room.

He touched her through the cotton nightdress, stroking her hips, her belly, her breasts and against her thigh she felt his desire. She didn't resist when he raised her gown and touched her skin in all those same places. With a minimum of urging, her nightdress ended up in a puddle beside the bed.

She had spent the past year erecting barriers and shields, and to her bewilderment they served her well now. The furious trembling that had begun inside her subsided. A small sound came from her, like a sigh, but she didn't connect it with herself.

The faint sliver of moonlight that came through the curtains cast a sheen on his hair and a glow across her skin when he pulled back the sheet to look at her.

Jesse rose over her then, his weight achingly familiar and yet disturbingly foreign at the same time. Deliberately initiating a long deep kiss, he entered her body the same way...with purposeful, yet slow movements...too tender...too intentional.

He needed her.

Amy had a lock on her emotions. Her body was another matter. Jesse knew her body. And he used his knowledge to woo a physical response. He knew she liked a long, slow buildup, so when she tried to hasten his movements, he held her still and played her nerve endings with patient fingers and coaxing lips.

He knew kisses across her shoulders and her collarbone made her shudder with heightened sensation, so when she tried to duck her chin, he held her jaw aside with his thumb and touched his mouth to her skin in enticing nips and plucks.

She closed her eyes and tried to escape the onslaught of sensation, but he was unwavering, and ardent and good…oh so good. He cupped her head to kiss her and his fingers snagged in her hair. A ripple cascaded across her scalp while another pulsed from the recesses of her body and engulfed her, his sought-after goal coaxed and fed and *grasped.*

And he *knew* he'd brought her release, so he pressed his lips against her cheek, grasped her hips and spent himself inside her.

His heart beat like a war drum against her breast, and their damp skin cooled in the air. Jesse moved his cheek against hers, and she felt wetness. Had she cried? She didn't think so. A person had to feel to cry.

She sensed an awareness that slowly bled into Jesse's body, in the nearly imperceptible tightening of his limbs and the turn of his head. He raised himself, found the sheet to cover her nakedness, and moved to lie on his back at her side, one arm flung over his head.

She wanted to say something. He expected it. But it was his expectations she couldn't deal with.

"I'm sorry about your mom, Jesse."

When his voice came, it was hard. "Is that what this was, then? Pity?"

She shrank inside herself at his accusation. At her shallowness. She couldn't give him more, she couldn't. "I would say comfort."

He sat up, stretching the sheet taut. "Well, shit,

Amy. How about love, huh? That word drop out of your vocabulary?"

She hated it when he placed demands on her this way. She didn't know what to say.

He bolted out of bed and was yanking on his pants before she could think of anything.

"Where are you going?"

"Away from here."

She sat up. "Where?"

"To the boardinghouse."

"So you can drink?"

"Maybe. There's more fire in a bottle of whiskey than I've found in this bed for a long time, Amy."

"What did we just do?"

He slipped his arms into his shirt and left it hanging open to glare at her in the darkness. "What *did* we do?"

As she held the sheet pressed to her breasts, he came toward her and leaned forward, one hand on each side of her hips on the mattress, his face inches from hers.

"I know what it *used* to be—lovemaking."

Her chest tightened.

"Do you even love me anymore, Amy?"

Her head roared with confusion and fear. He was her husband. He was Jesse. He'd just known her body intimately for the thousandth time, and yet she couldn't say what he wanted her to say. He needed her.

His need terrified her.

Slowly, he straightened. While he put on his boots,

she consciously admitted her faults to herself, knew he deserved more and curled into a ball on her side.

The door opened and closed, and he was gone.

God help her, he was gone.

And it was what she deserved.

Amy slept only a couple of hours that night, and woke early to dress and tiptoe past the room where Cay was staying and down the stairs. She prepared a chicken and several sandwiches, wrapped slices of pie and jars of water and lemonade and packed two crates full of food.

When Jesse entered the kitchen dressed in his buck-skins, the ever-present Colt revolver on his hip, she had a breakfast of ham, eggs and biscuits ready. He looked tired, but not hungover. After he'd gone up to wake Cay and returned without him, they avoided eye contact.

She indicated the crates on the end of the table nearest the door. "That's your food for the trip."

"We'll only be gone three days at the most."

"It'll probably only last two. And you should find Cay some milk along the way."

Cay showed up in overalls, carrying a hat. He sat at the corner opposite Jesse, and Amy served his breakfast.

He raised his blue gaze to Amy, then to Jesse, and said reluctantly, "Thanks."

After he'd finished his meal, he helped Jesse carry the crates out to the wagon in the door yard. Jesse had harnessed a handsome team of blacks, and they stood in the pink light of dawn, swishing their tails.

Sam approached on horseback, just arriving from his place a mile away. He dismounted and walked his horse to where Jesse and Amy stood several feet apart.

"Don't worry about anything," Sam told him. "We'll handle the place until you get back."

Jesse shook his hand. They'd been partners to start with, but were now family. The words weren't necessary.

And no one needed to mention that Amy would be looked after. Sam was her father, after all.

Jesse climbed up to the driver's seat and Cay scrambled to sit beside him. The back of the wagon held the crates, their bedrolls and a small tool chest.

If Sam thought it odd that Jesse hadn't said goodbye to Amy, he kept it to himself. He'd been around them every day for the past year, and he already knew things were strained, so this probably didn't seem any more out of the ordinary than any other day.

Cay, on the other hand, looked back at Amy with an expression she couldn't decipher. She assumed he didn't like her. And that was fine by her. Another month, six weeks and he'd probably run off anyway. Even if he stayed for the time being, another three or four years and he'd be out on his own.

Sam approached her, would have given her a hug if she hadn't taken a step back. He studied her for a moment, the look in his eyes telling her he saw it all, saw through her and wouldn't hold his silence much longer. He led his horse toward the stables.

Mrs. Barnes arrived and waved a greeting before she entered the house.

Amy stood alone watching the wagon disappear. Then she watched the horizon until the sun was up and sounds of life and work came from the barns. Occasionally Jesse made a trip for horses or other business, so having him gone for a few days wasn't unknown. He'd even made a couple of trips over the past year while they hadn't been on the best of terms.

But this was different. It felt different. Because of the occasion. Because of what had happened last night. Because she was having trouble keeping a lid on her carefully guarded thoughts.

Work was good for keeping her mind occupied, and there was always plenty of that. The men would be coming for breakfast, so she turned and hurried toward the house.

Travelers from a wagon train that had camped nearby the night before rode into the door yard in mid-morning. Their horses were thin and dull-coated, and the travelers themselves looked as though a stiff wind would send them back to Kansas.

While the men were apparently working out a trade with Sam for fresh horses, Amy invited the three ladies in for tea.

Penelope Cross was a motherly looking woman, with

deeply tanned hands and cracked red spots on her nose where she'd burned in the sun. These women spent much of their days on a wagon seat, reins in their hands, and every other moment cooking, washing clothing and collecting firewood. Penelope blushed with pleasure at being invited in.

"You can't know what a delight it is to sit in your kitchen."

Amy knew very well the difficult months these women were experiencing. Hers was quite likely the only roof they'd seen over their heads since leaving their homes.

Amy poured tea and Mrs. Barnes set a plate of sliced applesauce cake and sugar cookies on the table.

Penelope chewed a cookie slowly and closed her eyes. "Heaven."

Rebecca McDonald was Penelope's sister-in-law and Katy Montgomery was Rebecca's daughter. They planned to settle in Colorado before winter.

"Mrs. Shelby, does the mercantile nearby trade?" Penelope asked.

"Not often," Amy replied. "The problem out here is having someone to sell the traded items to. The people coming through need food and practical supplies, not the belongings that were dispensable to the previous owners. I'm sure you understand."

"I do," she said, but her expression showed her disappointment.

"What is it you need, Mrs. Cross?"

"I was hoping for eggs, and perhaps cheese and butter."

"And what do you have to trade?"

Penelope got up and crossed to the door. She disappeared for a few minutes and returned with an object wrapped in a blanket.

Amy watched as the woman carefully unwrapped the bundle and revealed a lovely cherry-wood mantel clock with a round glass face and gilt-edged legs. She took a brass key from a tiny drawer in the back and wound the timepiece, then opened the glass door and started the pendulum swinging.

"Mrs. Cross, that's worth far more than a few eggs and some cheese, don't you think?"

"My father brought it over from England. But it's doing me no good right now. I get up when daylight dawns and don't go to bed until work is finished. Not a lot of call for knowing what time it is."

"But someday…"

"Someday doesn't count much when my family needs to keep up their strength and their spirits."

Amy studied the ticking clock. She had a solid home and her daily needs were met without worry. Comparing her situation to that of these women, she felt fortunate. "Tell you what. I'll do you better than the eggs. I'll trade you two of my black laying hens, a rooster, a brick of cheese and two pounds of butter."

Penelope's face brightened, and she and her companions shared excited smiles.

"My father can fix up a cage," Amy added.

It had seemed a simple enough solution, but the three women acted as though they'd traded for a king's ransom. When it came time for them to leave, regret plainly showed on their faces. Amy accompanied them to the stage yard.

Penelope thanked Amy again and gave her an impulsive hug. Amy felt herself stiffen, but she didn't pull away. Everyone who knew Amy had learned to keep their distance, but this woman had no reason to realize her spontaneous act was unwelcome.

If Penelope noticed, she gave no indication. Her smile was as bright as before when she joined her party and rode away.

Amy watched them go, thinking of the hardships they were enduring on their way to their new land.

Back at the house, she polished the clock and gave it a place of honor in the parlor. She'd met countless families making their way to what they hoped were better futures, and she recognized the sacrifices they made during their travels. Several pieces of furniture in this very room had been abandoned along the trail, discovered by Jesse or her father and brought home. Sometimes she wondered about the owners, hoped they'd reached their destinations.

She had so much to be thankful for. And that fact only added to her guilt and inadequacy. What weakness in her kept her from being the person she wanted to be?

That evening Amy worked on the dress she'd been

making. Though Jesse hadn't been sleeping in the house, the rooms were all the more silent with him gone.

From her seat in the rocking chair in the parlor, the *tick* of the clock on the mantel was her only company.

And something about the sound, about the elusive familiarity of it, disturbed her. Before she went up to bed, she opened the clock face and stopped the pendulum.

Chapter Four

"What are we gonna do with her?" Cay asked, giving Jesse a sidelong look from his spot beside him on the wagon seat.

They were descending the last hill that led them along the Platte Valley on their return to Shelby Station. Since they'd left Kansas, the boy hadn't spoken much, hadn't eaten much, and didn't seem inclined to share more than the seat and a campfire with his uncle.

"With your grandma?"

Cay nodded.

"Well, normally, we'd lay her out in the parlor and have visitation. Then bury her with a service and all. But the sorry truth is, it's been too many days, and we can't do more than put her in the ground."

The boy beside him showed no reaction.

Jesse had spent most of the miles of travel regretting having not taken time to visit his mother or send for her before it was too late. Now he was the only family Cay had left, and his mother had known Jesse would accept responsibility for him. Jesse didn't have a problem with that. Family was family.

"We're lucky to have her so we can bury her on our land, Cay. This whole valley is a graveyard for folks who died on their way west. We're on the Overland Trail here. Oregon Trail's the same."

Cay checked the surrounding vista with a concerned gaze.

"The graves aren't marked," Jesse said. "So you won't be seein' 'em. After the person's buried, their family or friends roll their wagons over the place so Indians or animals won't find it."

At that the boy looked a little pale. "Oh."

"So having her buried on our land with a marker is good. Even if we don't have a long drawn-out mourning time like back home."

Cay nodded his understanding.

The boy seemed withdrawn, and Jesse hadn't managed to find a subject that interested him. Cay was grieving and Jesse felt powerless to offer him comfort. He'd already learned that you couldn't force consolation on a person who didn't want it.

From the direction of the river came a sharp yelping sound. Both of them turned their attention toward the noise.

A small butterscotch-colored dog with darker fur on its ears and chin bounded across the dry prairie grass, sending grasshoppers whirring into the air. Keeping its distance, the dog ran alongside barking furiously.

"Where'd he come from?" Cay asked.

"Probably got left behind or lost from a wagon train," Jesse replied.

"How will he live?"

"Catching mice and prairie dogs, I suppose."

"What about winter? Don't it get cold here?"

"Mighty cold." Jesse glanced at the dog, then at Cay's face. It was the first interest he'd shown in anything. If a dog could be a comfort to the boy, Jesse was all for taking the mutt home. "You thinkin' you'd like to keep 'im?"

Cay shrugged. "He'd probably die out here when it got real cold."

"Probably. Whoa, there, whoa." Jesse stopped the team, and Cay jumped to the ground.

The feisty critter barked and ran in circles.

Cay took a few steps toward it, and the dog ran about ten feet, then stopped and darted back to bark again. Cay squinted up at the wagon. "We got any o' them biscuits left?"

Jesse twisted back to reach the crate they'd been munching from since morning and tossed Cay a biscuit.

Kneeling down, Cay held out the offering. "Come get this, boy. You need a place to bunk? Ain't nobody gonna hurt ya."

Jesse listened to the childish coaxing, instinctively knowing Cay was saying the things he needed to hear and know. His mother had cast him off like an old shoe and never come back. Now his grandmother was gone.

After a few minutes of coaxing, the dog finally wagged its tail and moved cautiously forward, eating the biscuit from Cay's hand, then licking the boy's fingers.

Cay picked him up and rubbed his ears.

"What're you gonna call 'im?" Jesse asked when they were back on their way, the dog settled in Cay's lap.

Cay petted the animal, who'd already shown a fondness for having his ears scratched. "Biscuit?"

Jesse grinned.

"That okay?"

"Fine by me. He's your dog."

An hour later, Shelby Station came into sight, and the view moved Jesse as it always did. Cottonwoods formed a windbreak across the south. The buildings were spread out in a nook between two hills of pastureland, a hay field to the west and the river to the east. A windmill turned lazily in the breeze, and a clothesline full of white towels and linens flapped beneath the sun.

"This is your home now," he told Cay. "You're family, and I'm glad you're here."

Cay said nothing, but studied the station a little more intently.

A dozen fine horses grazed in one of the pastures, and twenty others stood in paddocks. The repetitive ring of an anvil was proof that work never stopped. Once this had been everything Jesse had ever wanted.

Here were the horses he'd planned to train and sell. The operation he planned with Sam Burnham was a success. The woman he'd met and taken for his wife was here.

A sense of hopelessness washed over him at the thought of Amy.

He couldn't see the spot from here, but his gaze unerringly traveled in the direction of the rise of land that already held two markers. He'd *almost* had everything he'd ever wanted. He didn't know what he wanted or needed anymore, except the ability to survive nights and days he'd just as soon forget.

The horses knew their feed and stalls were just ahead, and he had to keep a tight rein, finally halting them in the door yard.

Pitch hurried out with his peculiar bowlegged stride. His gaze moved across the tarp-covered coffin in the back of the wagon.

"Unhitch this pair and bring a fresh team," Jesse said. "These fine girls deserve a rest."

"Sure thing." Pitch hurried to do the chore.

Amy came down the porch steps then, as pretty and fresh as the first time he'd seen her.

"How was your trip?"

"Mostly uneventful."

Cay climbed down and set the little dog on its feet. The critter scurried to sniff the corner of the porch and the last dying blooms of Amy's flower garden.

"That your dog?" Amy asked Cay, shading her eyes with her hand.

Cay looked at Jesse, then replied, "Yeah."

"Yes, ma'am," Jesse corrected.

"Yes, ma'am," he amended.

"Teach him not to water my flower bed, will you?"

Cay made a dash to stop Biscuit from peeing on Amy's petunias, but he was too late. He chased the dog across the yard.

Jesse took off his hat to run a hand through his hair, then settled it back on his head.

"What will you do now?" Amy asked.

"Get a shovel, I reckon."

"Already saw to that." Sam approached. "Me'n Hermie took turns the last couple o' days. Thought it would make it easier for you."

"Thanks, Sam."

"No thanks needed."

"Cay and I need a bath. After that, I'll pull the wagon up to the site. Will you ask some of the men to give us a hand with the…." He gestured with his thumb over his shoulder. "With this?"

Sam nodded.

"We could send for the preacher and wait, I reckon," Jesse said. "Or we could lay her to rest our own way." He glanced at Amy. "What do you think?"

"I think she'd like it just fine if you said a few words yourself. We can sing a hymn."

Jesse's chest felt so tight he couldn't speak, so he nodded.

"I'll send Adele to get your water, and I'll bring you clothes," she said.

With a jerking movement, he got himself headed toward the bathhouse.

Half an hour later, clean-shaven and dressed in his dark trousers and white shirt, Jesse watched as his men carried his mother's plain wooden coffin from the wagon bed to the side of the grave, then laid it on ropes and lowered it into the hole. He had always thought there was time left. Time to visit his mother, time to bring her here to meet Amy... But his mother's time had run out.

He couldn't even be sure Amy was breathing beside him. Her face was pale, and she looked steadfastly at Jesse, not at the box that held his mother or at the small grave beside it.

As far as Jesse knew, Amy had not been to their son's grave site since the day of his burial. If the rosebush Jesse'd planted was a surprise, she didn't let on.

Something was expected of him now, so Jesse opened the Bible he'd found among his mother's belongings and located the page she had marked. "'The Lord is my shepherd,'" he read. "'I shall not want. He maketh me to lie down in green pastures.'"

It wasn't a long Psalm, and when he was finished, he looked at Cay to find the boy's face pinched, tears glistening in his eyes. Jesse's mother was the only mother Cay had known; she had raised him from the time he was small.

With Jesse's permission, Cay had brought the dog, and Biscuit lay at his feet, its keen brown gaze watching the proceedings of the humans with curiosity.

Jesse looked at Amy then, and gave her an encouraging nod.

Her sweet girlish voice led them in all the verses of "Amazing Grace." His mother would have loved this place, this land. She would have loved Amy. Wrestling with regret was a waste of time and energy, but Jesse tussled with his feelings anyway. He'd lost his last opportunity for seeing his mother again and had missed introducing her to his wife.

Somehow he kept up his end of the song, and when it was over, Jesse took a shovel and scooped dirt into the hole.

Cay knelt and buried his face in the dog's fur.

Hermie and another hand stepped forward to take over the task, but Jesse refused their help. This was his job. "You can all head back now," he told the gathering. "I'll finish here."

One by one, the hands went back to their chores, the women to their tasks, and Sam settled his hat on his head and took Amy's arm to lead her away.

Only Cay stayed until the grave was filled. Then he released the dog and stared at the fresh mound of dirt, his throat working.

Jesse wiped perspiration from his forehead and watched as Cay got down and used his hands to smooth the dirt. He sat back on his haunches, his gaze moving to the two wooden markers bearing Shelby names. Jesse anticipated the question.

"Who're Vanessa and Tim?"

Jesse tucked his handkerchief away. "Vanessa's Amy's mama. Tim's our boy."

That answer seemed to be enough, but there was more on his mind because he frowned and asked, "What about a marker for Gran?"

"You can help me make one." Jesse worked the other two crosses from the hard-packed ground. "These need a new coat of paint while we're at it."

It didn't take long to make a simple wood cross, paint Jesse's mother's name on it and freshen the paint on the other two markers. He and Cay had all three finished and set into the ground by supper. They stood side by side on the hill, each lost in his own thoughts.

Jesse took moderate comfort in the fact that his mother and Amy's mother lay on either side of his son. They weren't really there, he reminded himself, and glanced up at the sky where the sun headed for the horizon. *Take care of each other.*

"Well, I'm hungry, how about you?" he asked Cay.

The boy shrugged and followed him to the basins beside the porch to wash.

During the meal, Sam brought Jesse up to date on the travelers who'd been through while he was gone. Amy took special care in placing the best pieces of meat on Jesse's plate and freshening his coffee. If she stopped long enough to lay a hand on his shoulder or lean against him, the last shred of his brittle soul would shatter.

As it was, the ache inside grew like a hunger he couldn't seem to appease. When he'd finished eating, he pushed back his chair and waited as the others filed out.

Only Mrs. Barnes remained, and she was busy washing pans in a tub of suds.

"Come here, Amy," he said, and motioned for her to follow him toward the back room, which he unlocked.

She hung back until he gestured again, and then she entered hesitantly. He closed the door, confining them in the small space.

Amy clasped her hands before her and waited, her expression impassive.

Jesse knelt to the bags he'd stored there for lack of a better place. Among his mother's clothing had been her jewelry and personal things. He took out a silver case engraved with roses and stood to hand it to Amy. "This is for you."

It took several seconds for her to accept the box. She ran her fingers over the top. "It was your mother's."

"There are a few pieces inside. Go ahead and look."

She opened the hinged lid, revealing a few brooches, a locket and two pairs of earrings.

"You don't have to wear them if you don't like them."

She raised her gaze. "I do like them, Jesse."

"Well. I want you to have them."

Amy owned jewelry that had belonged to her mother, as well. If they had a daughter, she would inherit the pieces someday. None of the items was particularly valuable, except for the sentiment they held. Jesse didn't say what he was thinking. They didn't talk about things like that anymore, and chances for more children were slim. Their plans for the future and a family were all buried in that little plot on the hillside.

He wanted to tell her how bad he felt that she hadn't met his mother, how many regrets he'd experienced these past days. But he didn't.

Amy closed the lid. "Thank you. I'll keep this on my bureau."

If she touched him, all the pieces of his soul would come together and he'd feel whole again. If she touched him, he'd know she was doing it out of duty or pity and not because of any great love she felt for him. If she touched him and he showed his weakness for her, he'd hate himself later.

But he didn't have to concern himself, because she kept her distance. He felt so cold, he didn't know how it could be only late September and not the dead of winter.

"A trunk came yesterday," she told him. "Probably more of her things. It's in the parlor."

"I'll look through it in a day or so. You can open it if you like."

She shook her head and reached for the doorknob.

"Good night, Amy."

She left, and what little warmth had remained in his bones seeped out. Jesse locked up, crossed the kitchen and made his way to the barn.

In the tack room, beneath his saddle, he found the remainder of his case of whiskey and popped the cork on a fresh bottle.

The burn started at his throat and a path of fire spread to his belly. After several swigs, his limbs were warm and the cavity in his chest glowed like a coal furnace. He was damn tired of denying himself. Tired of disapproval and guilt and helplessness, and if this eased the loss of everything he'd once held dear and no longer had, well, who the hell could blame him?

Jesse wrapped the crate in a horse blanket and carried it to his room at the boardinghouse.

The following morning Amy encountered Cay in the hallway on her way downstairs.

"Morning," she said.

He merely nodded.

"Is your room okay? Do you need anything?"

"Room's fine." He made a point of looking directly at her and saying, "Thank you" before sliding past her and hurrying down the stairs.

She watched him go with conflicting emotions. He was young and would be alone if not for them. But she wasn't going to get her hopes up that he'd blend right in to their family and way of life. Hope had a way of turning sour and it was best to be practical.

She'd been in the kitchen only a half hour when a stage driven by Pearly Higgs pulled into the station. The gray-bearded ribbon-sawer made his way to the house, hung his hat and holster on a peg and rubbed his hands together in glee. "I been a-waitin' for a stack o' your flapjacks, Miz Shelby."

With fanfare he pulled a gold coin from the pocket of his buckskin shirt and plunked it on the table.

Amy poured him a cup of coffee and set a plate before him. "It'll be just a few minutes while I get the griddle hot again."

"Watchin' you work only makes the waitin' more pleasurable," he said with a grin.

Sam entered through the back door, poured himself a cup of coffee and took a seat across from Pearly. "What's this I hear about a train derailing?"

"A party of Cheyenne tore down telegraph wire and lashed a stack of rails to the tracks. Train came along last night." Pearly cracked a fist into the other palm to demonstrate the collision.

Amy winced.

"Cheyenne are just tryin' to protect their land," Pearly said with a shrug.

Sam took a sip from his mug. "Yeah, but the Army will see this as an act of war and reinforce their efforts to round the Indians up."

"Were many people hurt?" Amy asked.

"Don't rightly know," Pearly replied. "I heard it from a rider comin' from the south."

Thinking of all those people stranded on the prairie, Amy looked at her father. "Do you think there's something we can do? Should we go see if they need doctors and stages?"

Sam scratched his chin. "I s'pose we could take a few wagons and see if anyone wants to come back to the station with us. They can catch rides from here."

Amy looked to Mrs. Barnes. "Can you handle things if I go with my father?"

"You go ahead—we'll do fine," the woman assured her.

"You're fixin' to go?" Sam asked his daughter.

She removed her apron, then placed the twenty eggs she'd boiled that morning in a clean coffee tin and covered it. "No reason that I shouldn't."

Knowing better than to argue, Sam raised a brow and turned to Pearly. "Exactly where did this happen?"

While her father got directions, Amy packed food and stacked blankets and crates on the porch.

Jesse pulled a team and wagon into the yard and stalked toward her. Apparently her father had told him Amy's plans.

"Amy, you can't go off like this, it's not safe."

She gestured to the gun lying with her belongings. "I have my rifle. And I'll be with my father."

"Maybe so, but we don't know about the Cheyenne that attacked that train. They could still be out there."

"We've always been on good terms with the Cheyenne," she replied. "They see the trains as the threat, not us. Their actions have been more like deterrents than attacks."

"You can't be sure. I'll go, and you stay here."

"You need to run the station," she told him logically.

"Then I'll send one of the hands in your stead."

"That will only leave you more shorthanded. I'm going, Jesse. There are women and children out there who need help. It's the right thing to do."

His gaze took in her determined expression. He looked away for a moment as though gathering his thoughts, then met her eyes. "I'm against this, but I know I'm not going to stop you. Keep that rifle with you at all times."

Jesse had taught her to shoot the rifle during their courting days, and she was a fair shot. He'd been adamant about her being able to protect herself. "I will."

He caught her arm and she glanced up into his intense blue gaze. Obviously he wanted to say something more, but the moment grew awkward and he released her.

"Not knowing how many passengers you'll find, I had three teams harnessed to wagons. Hermie is going with you."

Sam and the hand approached as if on cue.

"If you're not back by tomorrow night, I'll come after you," Jesse told her father.

Sam shook his head as he replied, "Wait 'til light the next morning."

He and Jesse shook hands, and Jesse slapped Hermie

on the shoulder. Jesse helped Amy up onto the wagon seat and stood on the side of the wagon for a moment. Without giving her time to think or object, he leaned forward and kissed her, then jumped to the ground.

She raised a hand in silent farewell and lifted the reins.

Amy had plenty of time to think over Jesse's objections and his reaction to her determined plan. She'd never had cause to question his feelings for her. He'd never been anything but straightforward, attentive, protective. Everything that was wrong between them had started out as her fault.

Everything. And that was the single insurmountable fact she couldn't live with.

They stopped for a quick meal at noon and, with the sun high in the sky, filled water jugs from a stream. Shortly after, they found the railroad tracks and followed them east. The air cooled toward evening, and lightning streaked the distant sky and thunder rolled across the prairie. Sam had grown frustrated at not having located the train. They'd been following the rails for several hours.

"I think we're going to have to camp here and try to find the train come light," he called back to Amy.

She nodded her understanding, but as she did, she noticed a plume of smoke in the sky. "Look!"

"Could be them. Or could be Cheyenne," her father called back. "I think we'd best wait 'til daylight."

She trusted his judgment, but knew this delay would make them late getting home and that Jesse would worry.

Jagged lightning split the sky close by, thunder rumbled and Hermie's mumbled cussing could be heard as they hurriedly ate a meal and stored their gear, fat raindrops splatting on their heads and shoulders.

Amy and her father ducked under her wagon to sleep on the pallets they'd prepared. Hermie had taken refuge under another.

"Are you doin' all right?" Sam asked.

She settled her hips, trying in vain to find a comfortable spot on the hard ground, and made sure her rifle was dry and within reach. "I'm fine."

"You have gumption, Amy. Aren't many women who'd come out here in the off chance that they could help somebody they don't know."

"I have a good life, Daddy," she told him, softly calling him the name she reserved for when they were alone. "I know the hardships out here. Nearly every week I see women torn from everything safe and familiar, living out of wagons, risking danger just to find what they hope is a better life for their families. Sometimes I don't know how they do it."

"They do it just like you and your mama did when we first got here. You've had some hard times, too."

She didn't reply.

Rain struck the tarpaulins covering the wagon beds and poured off in sheets to the hard-packed ground, the sound loud and steady. Amy tried not to think of her comfortable home and soft, dry bed back at the station.

After several minutes Sam said, "Either you or Jesse

is gonna have to make some changes soon. The two of you can't go on with things the way they've been."

Her heart constricted painfully. Of course her father knew. But now her private troubles were out in the open, plain as day.

"A bottle of whiskey is a poor substitute for a lovin' wife and a warm bed," he added.

Her father had seen Jesse's drinking. Her shame grew. "Has he said anything to you?"

"Not about you. He respects you too much."

"Don't worry yourself about it."

"Well, I do worry. The man is your husband. We're a family. At least, we used to be. Don't feel like it much anymore."

Amy turned on her side away from her father, away from his probing words. She didn't need her glaring imperfections pointed out to her. Talking only made her feel more and more like a failure and less like the woman everyone expected her to be.

"Good night, Daddy."

Sometime later, a soft snore told her he slept. And when she was sure he couldn't hear her, she let her ragged breathing escape and struck the ground several times with a fist.

Later, much later, she slept.

Rain continued to pour through the night and into the early-morning hours as they harnessed the teams and headed east. The sky cleared temporarily as they came upon the derailed train a half hour later. The area was littered with flimsy tents constructed of soggy blankets, tarpaulins and piled trunks. Seats and bunks had been removed from the railcars to provide beds for the injured.

Fortunately for the passengers traveling the Union Pacific, a doctor had been among them, and those hurt had been cared for. There were at least fifty who needed transport. Riders had gone ahead and behind to alert the railroad officials and delay any scheduled trains.

While Sam was thinking through the options, another caravan of wagons found the site, so the drivers met to discuss which travelers each would take.

Amy helped Hermie take care of their horses while the gathering divided and collected belongings. Amy couldn't remember ever being so wet or physically miserable. Trunks and valises were loaded as thunder again echoed across the heavens.

Ready to join them for the trip back to Shelby Station were twelve adults and six children. Two of the adults had been injured—William Hunter, an elderly gentleman with his arm in a sling, and Eden Sullivan, a pretty brunette with her foot in splints.

Sam carried Eden to the back of his wagon and settled her as comfortably as possible. By the time everyone was situated among the trunks, they barely had time to get moving before another rain shower drenched them.

Amy again pulled her slicker over her head and

shoulders. Instead of stopping for meals that day, they ate hard tack and jerky, but with the added weight and on increasingly muddy ground, travel was slow. When night fell, they were forced to camp. Amy helped her father rig tents out of tarpaulins and poles, then she strung ropes as close as possible to the fire to dry their clothing.

"Will those Indians come after us?" a wide-eyed Eden asked Sam as he fed the smoldering fire.

"Nah, they caused what trouble they set out to do and are probably long gone."

"I think we're fortunate to be alive," a man by the name of Barnett said. He picked up a stick and lit a cigar. "I've heard stories about the Indians out here in the territories."

"Some of those stories are probably true," Amy told them. "But what you don't hear are the counts of Army regiments wiping out entire villages of Sioux and Cheyenne, women and children included. The bands are protecting themselves and their hunting grounds the only way they know how."

"Did a party attack the train or the passengers?" Sam asked.

"I call derailing tons of steel an attack," Barnett replied.

William Hunter spoke up. "We saw them from a distance only. They sat on horseback and observed our predicament. I suppose they think they're discouraging travel by rails."

"I suppose they do," Amy said. "But the Army seems determined to drive them away. This incident will no doubt cause more regiments to be assigned to the area."

"Is your station safe from attacks?" Eden asked.

"We've never had trouble with the Sioux or the Cheyenne who live nearby," Amy answered. "In fact we've often traded with them. More so right after the war, before the Army refocused its attention on getting rid of all Indians."

Amy didn't care if she sounded defensive. People coming west had a right to know the truth. The subject was dropped, but she didn't know if their minds were set at ease. She guessed the new pot of coffee had been boiling long enough and used a flour sack to remove it from the fire.

Eden was sitting hunched beside the fire with the rest of the bedraggled travelers, her injured foot propped on a valise. She had long dark eyelashes, and a way of speaking with a charming little pout. "Is Nebraska always this miserable?"

"You never know about the weather in these parts, Miss Sullivan," Sam replied. "The ground can sure use the rain, though."

"Are you a farmer?" she asked.

"No, but I have a small orchard to fulfil my homestead agreement," he told her.

"What kind of trees?"

"Mostly apple. My Amy here makes the best apple pie this side of the Divide."

"Where were you traveling, Miss Sullivan?" Amy asked.

"I'm on my way to look after my sister's children. She's been sick."

"I'm sorry to hear that. Where does she live?"

"Denver City."

Amy handed her a cup of coffee. "You won't have that much farther to travel after your foot's had a chance to heal."

"What's your town like?" Eden asked.

"Well, it's not much of a town, really. There's a restaurant down the road a way. We run the stage station, trade horses and do any smithing that's called for."

"Smithing?"

"Blacksmith. One of our men works steel for horseshoes and wheels, tools and such."

"Oh, so there are others at your station?"

"Yes, we're the only station with beds for the night, so we get a prime share of business."

"So you have a hotel?"

"Not a hotel." Amy glanced at her father, and they shared a grin. "More like a boardinghouse. There's a mercantile not far away. Our mail and shipments are delivered right to our door, so we don't want for much."

Eden wrinkled her nose in a delicate grimace. "What *is* that smell?"

"Buffalo chips, Miss Sullivan," Sam replied. "They're ideal for fire when they're dry, but this rain tends to soften 'em up."

Eden brought her blanket up over her nose. "I believe I'd like to lie down now. Do you mind, Mr. Burnham?"

"Not at all." Sam picked up the young woman and carried her to one of the wagons, under which he and Amy had laid out a pallet of blankets.

William Hunter accepted a cup of coffee from Amy and sat cradling his injured arm. "It's kind of you to come for us, Miss Burnham."

"It's Mrs. Shelby," she corrected him.

"Sorry, I was thinking since you were Mr. Burnham's daughter that your name was the same."

"That's all right. My husband and father are partners. Shelby Station belongs to all of us."

"And your husband allows you to place yourself in danger out here?" Barnett asked.

Amy cast him a glance. "My father taught me to ride when my family came to Nebraska. When I met my husband, he taught me to shoot and protect myself, Mr. Barnett. I'm not helpless and my husband doesn't treat me as if I was."

William Hunter hid a smile at Amy's response and continued as though Barnett hadn't interrupted. "My son started a newspaper in a small town west of Denver City," he told Amy. "He wrote a while back, asking me to come join him now that he has the shop operating and has built a house. So I sold my little cobbler shop in Pennsylvania, and took a train. I thought I'd be at my destination tonight."

"It should take only another day or so to get you there," she assured him.

Hermie joined them, and a few minutes later Sam returned. His knees cracked as he knelt beside the fire. "Cussed rain gets to my joints every time," he said.

"Your knees seemed fine whilst you were totin' Miss Sullivan about," Hermie observed.

Sam pointedly ignored that comment.

Hermie and Amy shared a sly glance. Come to think of it, her father had been showing Eden considerably more attention than he had the other travelers.

"Do you have children, Mrs. Shelby?"

William Hunter's innocent question jerked Amy's thoughts in another direction and caught her by surprise, twisting the knife that was always at the ready in her heart. Quickly picking up her rifle, she stood. "I'll make sure the rest of the women get bedded down, and then I'm turning in."

"Did I say something wrong?" William asked Sam.

Sam shook his head. "She's a little tetchy on the subject."

"Fine daughter you have there."

"Finest daughter a man could ask for," Sam agreed. But his expression showed more than pride as he watched Amy assisting the women. Compassion was her nature. She'd always been ready to offer help or sympathy or just an ear. He'd seen a change come over her after his grandson's death. It was as though she'd put her life up to that point behind her, and her new life had started the day after they'd buried Tim.

The briefest mention brought censure. Sam, Jesse,

even the help had been abiding by her wishes for the past year. No one, not even Jesse, forced her to talk about Tim.

And things had grown worse than that.

Though Sam went home to his own place every night, talk got back to him that Jesse had been staying nights at the boardinghouse. He couldn't shake his growing feelings of concern, but he didn't know what to do to help her.

Chapter Five

By morning, the rain had turned low sections of the prairie into knee-deep mud. Two of the wagons were mired nearly to the axles, and the tired teams couldn't budge the conveyances forward. The smells of wet animals and soggy wool clothing permeated every breath. Amy and her father considered their slim choices.

"We could try harnessing all the horses to one wagon to pull it loose," Sam suggested.

Amy nodded, mulling over his idea. "But we'd have to do that to both wagons, and the animals are already tired. I wouldn't want to risk injuring them. Besides, how could we even be sure they could continue pulling the loads once we got the wagons out of these holes? We could easily just roll into others."

Sam peered at her through the battering rain. "Jesse would have my hide if his horses came to harm."

"He'd want us safe first," Amy was quick to say. "But that plan won't guarantee to keep us moving."

Frustrated and wet, Sam and Amy reinforced the shelters. They'd run out of dry chips and kindling, so they didn't even have warmth or coffee. The poor travelers they had taken under their wings huddled chilled and wet to the bone beneath the makeshift tents, forlorn and miserable.

It had been Amy's suggestion to come out here and get them, and now they were worse off than before. Back at the train, they could have used coal and wood for fire, and eventually someone would have found them. Amy berated herself for her shortsighted plan and her stubborn insistence on coming. Silently, she also cursed the rain. If Jesse had come in her stead, perhaps he would have done a better job.

One of the women opened a box of chocolates she'd been taking to her intended husband and shared the confections. Amy ate her ration without enjoyment, wondering how long they could keep up their strength without real food.

She pulled a brimming pail under the tent. At least water wasn't a problem.

After more thought, she took her father aside at the corner of their shelter. "I think I should take one of the horses and head for the station."

"No, Amy, it's not safe with the Cheyenne up to no good. You could run into trouble."

"I don't think we have much choice."

He seemed to consider their options. "I'll go."

She knew he was the wiser choice for the job. Without argument, she nodded.

Jesse had intuitively placed two saddles under the canvas in the rear of a wagon, so Sam got a horse ready. Amy touched his arm, refusing to let herself think of the dangers he might run into alone.

"I'll be fine," he told her.

She nodded and released him. In the past he would have hugged her, but he merely placed his foot in the stirrup and mounted with a creak of leather.

Amy ducked back under the tent as he rode out. Hard as she tried to bridle her thoughts, she imagined him riding through the storm—and sent up a prayer for his safety.

Less than an hour later, a whinny and the sounds of harnesses alerted her to someone's approach. It sounded like too many horses to be her father returning, and Amy stood, peering apprehensively. The Cheyenne didn't shoe their horses, but on the soggy ground she couldn't tell by the sound whether the animals were shod.

Through the downpour, she made out two figures on horseback leading a dozen more horses. Her father and…Jesse. She'd never been so glad to see anyone in her life.

Amy ran out into the rain to meet them.

Both men dismounted. A grin split her father's face. "Look who I ran into."

Rain streamed from the brim of Jesse's hat. "I'd been following the rails hoping I was heading in the right direction when I saw Sam riding toward me."

Amy noted the horses he'd brought. "You knew we ran into trouble."

"Figured as much, with all this rain. You all right?"

She nodded. "Just wet. Who's looking after Cay?"

"Mrs. Barnes. Let's get you home."

She followed him and her father to help harness the additional teams. Jesse approached one of the mired wagons with a spade and used the tool to shovel mud away from the axles.

Within minutes the muscle of the additional horses had all three wagons moving.

Amy and Hermie gathered their belongings and took down the tarps. "I need some help," Amy called to Jesse.

Jesse responded by hurrying to where Amy stood beside a woman seated on a crate. She looked to be a little older than him, with dark hair. She held a shawl tucked around her shoulders.

"This is Eden," Amy told him.

"How do, ma'am."

"Her foot's broken."

Jesse picked up the woman and carried her to a wagon.

"It's 'miss,'" she said from beneath a dripping bonnet. Her admiring gaze took in his features appreciatively.

"Pleasure," he replied.

"You're a sight for sore eyes."

He nodded politely and hurried to get the teams moving forward, then climbed onto the seat beside Amy. She handed over the reins and he took the lead.

"I knew you'd worry," she said.

"Last night when I saw the rain wasn't letting up, I headed out." He wanted to wrap his arm around her and pull her up against his side to reassure himself that she was all right.

"I never thought we'd get stuck like that."

"You had no way of knowin' how much rain there would be."

"Maybe if I'd let you come instead... I just pray no one gets sick from exposure."

"It wouldn't have been any different if I'd been along," he assured her. "In fact, it would have been worse, because you couldn't have readied more teams and brought them alone."

"Do you really think so?"

"Yes, ma'am."

Somehow his wife had felt responsible for the safety of these people from the very first. She'd made it a way of life, caring for others; it was her nature to take on the additional effort. But it didn't set well with him that she blamed herself for something out of her control. "We'll get them to the station and have them dry and warm in no time."

Six horses hauling each wagon made for quick travel, and by late afternoon, they pulled into Shelby

Station. Biscuit darted from the barn, barking excitedly and sniffing the passengers who climbed down.

Cay hurried out and shushed him, sending him back inside the barn with a gentle command. When their eyes met, Amy thought he wanted to say something, but he turned quickly and lent his hand to helping with the animals.

Amy had never been so glad to let the hands take over the care of the horses and wagons. She assigned her guests to rooms at the boardinghouse, placed a few of the men in the barn and had Adele help arrange pallets in the parlor.

Mrs. Barnes greeted her with a pat on the shoulder. "Go get yourself a hot bath and some dry clothes."

"You don't have to tell me twice."

Adele and Maggie had hot water and towels at the ready, and it was so good to be in out of the rain that Amy didn't mind standing in line for her turn in the bathhouse.

Rarely were all three tubs in use, but this evening they never stood empty. Adele and Maggie continuously carried water and hung towels around the stove to dry.

After Amy's bath, she helped the dark-haired woman bathe and dress and get settled in a room on the main floor of the boardinghouse. Sam had fashioned Eden a crutch, and Amy gave it to her now. "My father made this so you could get around in your room."

"How thoughtful of him. He's a dear man."

"I'll bring your supper," Amy told her. "You stay put and rest that foot. Call out if you need something. There's usually someone nearby who will hear you."

"You've been so kind already," Eden said, "but I would surely enjoy a cup of tea."

"I'll see that you get some."

Back at the house, Pitch was helping Mrs. Barnes fry ham and potatoes.

"Have the hands eaten?" Amy asked.

"They have," Pitch replied. "Mrs. Barnes figured we'd do a first shift for the guests who've finished with baths and then feed the rest on the next."

"Good plan," Amy told them with appreciation. She looked around the roomy well-appointed kitchen. "I wasn't gone that long, but it's sure good to be home."

Mrs. Barnes swept past her with a plate of sliced bread. "Some days seem like weeks, don't they? You sit now. I won't take no for an answer."

Amy sank gratefully onto a bench.

Just then, Jesse opened the door and stepped inside. He'd dressed in dry clothing and had left his boots out on the porch. He hung his holster on a peg. "Can I get a meal? Thought I could wait until after the boarders, but my belly's eatin' a hole in my backside."

"No, you won't wait," Amy told him, and waved him onto a seat beside her. "Where's Cay?"

"Sticking close to Sam. Helping him with the

horses." She took slices of bread and slathered them with butter and jelly for the two of them.

Mrs. Barnes placed thick portions of ham on their plates. Pitch scooped crispy potatoes wedges into a serving bowl. "There's slaw here, too," he said.

Amy and Jesse ate together, then sat back to enjoy a hot cup of coffee before the guests from the parlor came in to seat themselves. When they did, the Shelbys gave up their seats and moved to drink their coffee in the other room while it was temporarily vacated.

Amy carried in their cups while Jesse stoked the fire in the fireplace. She sat in her favorite side chair; Jesse took the rocker, crossing one ankle over the other knee.

"When was the last time you saw so much rain?" Amy asked.

"Spring. Have you forgotten?"

"I guess I'm never right out in it for that long at a stretch. I thought it would never stop."

Jesse glanced out the window and rocked the chair with the stockinged foot on the floor. "It hasn't yet."

"I even felt sorry for the horses."

Jesse turned his blue gaze on her.

The house settled with a creak and a gust of wind whirred down the chimney.

Jesse's gaze flickered across the clock on the mantel. The time hadn't been right since she'd stopped the pendulum.

"We sure can get a lot of miles out of talkin' about the weather, can't we, Amy?"

Cringing inside for fear of what he'd bring up or expect of her, she sipped her coffee and said nothing.

"Was going the right thing to do?" His question wasn't what she'd been expecting, but she didn't mind answering it.

"Yes."

"Then I guess you did the right thing."

Amy shrugged. "I'd like to think someone would do the same for me."

"I'd like to think they would, too."

"Cay did all right while we were away?"

"He did fine. During the day, he helps with the stock and the chores. Of an evenin' he's hearing stories from the hands, learning to tie knots and such. It couldn't hurt him to have another influence as well." Jesse paused, leaving her to wonder what kind of an influence he meant. "I've been thinking he needs to finish his schooling. I can order books. Between the two of us, we should be able to teach him."

She wasn't sure what she thought of spending evenings with Cay, and she hated how selfish that made her feel. "I don't know. How will we know what he needs to learn?"

Jesse shrugged. "I reckon we could ask Leda Bently what a boy his age should be studyin'. She teaches her children during the winter." He jerked a thumb toward the kitchen. "Maybe one of the women in there'd have an idea."

"Maybe."

He stopped rocking. "If you don't want to help, I'll do it."

"I just worry about you becoming too attached to the boy, Jesse."

"For heaven's sake, why?"

"Your mother told you he was already making trouble. I'm afraid he'll only cause us problems and then run off at the first opportunity."

"Well, he hasn't made any trouble yet. His mother ran off and left him when he was little more than a baby. He's had a sickly woman motherin' him and no father. You'd see the need for us—for a family if you'd let yourself."

She raised a palm to stop Jesse's ire. "I'll help teach him."

He stood. "I don't know what you have against the boy. You're hangin' back when it comes to helping 'im, but you risked your neck to save a bunch of strangers."

He was right, and the fact that he'd pointed it out shamed her. "I said I'll help."

"Nobody wants to feel like they're not wanted." His voice was low and filled with emotion. "Don't make that boy feel like he's not welcome here."

"Of course he's welcome. I'm just not sure how well I can teach him."

"You'd have been teaching Tim if we hadn't lost him. You'd be teaching more children—if you wanted to have them."

Not this. Not this again. What was it he wanted from

her? Couldn't he just leave the subject alone? Talking about the past wouldn't change anything. She got up and headed for the kitchen, where she could lose herself by keeping busy in the crowd of strangers.

From the corner of her eye, she saw when Jesse followed and set his mug beside the basin. The door squeaked opened and closed.

Pitch gave her a curious glance from across the room.

She knew their conversation had been too quiet to overhear, so he must have seen something on Jesse's face or in the way he carried himself from the room that made him question Jesse's abrupt leave-taking.

Or maybe a telltale look was on her face.

Before the second shift of diners arrived, Mrs. Barnes gently eased Amy away from the stove and pushed her toward the other room. "Go on upstairs. You've been out in the weather and gone without decent rest, and you're ready to fall over where you stand." She waved the hem of her apron as though Amy were a pesky fly. "Shoo."

Amy wearily climbed the stairs and entered the bedroom. In the darkness, she stood in front of the window and gazed down on the outbuildings where light poured from windows and doors. Shelby Station was always filled with comings and goings. People from all walks of life passed through for various reasons and headed to their destinations. Strangers who eased Amy's discomfort in having to live with herself.

Conversation drifted up from downstairs, chair legs

squeaked on floorboards and iron kettles clanged. Living as she did amid a constant stream of activity and purpose, how was it she always felt isolated and adrift?

Amy survived with her heels dug into the here and now to keep from sliding off into the past or the future where nothing was safe and where she risked the chance of caring too much. Sometimes she thought that so much of her spirit had bled from her that she was nothing but a walking, breathing shell.

And then Jesse had gone and said something that proved there was more on the inside of her after all—more to board up with walls of denial and secure with self-preserving nails. But she was good at construction. She didn't even have to think about building barriers anymore—it was survival instinct.

With the muted sounds of life beneath her, Amy undressed and crawled into bed. She went through the routine she had devised, thinking about the chores she had to do the following day and not about what had already transpired.

But the image of Jesse riding through the rain, sliding from his horse and looking her over, wedged its way past her guard. She saw his face, blue eyes squinted against the rain that drizzled from the brim of his hat, the set of his jaw and his unspoken relief. She had a man who loved her beyond her failings and her barren heart. Few people in this sorry world were loved that completely—that unselfishly. Any other woman—a whole woman—would glory in that.

Rain poured from the heavens and soaked into the earth. Heat blazed from the stoves and the fireplace; light gleamed from the outbuildings and every window of the house except hers. But within this room, within this heart, it was dry and cold and dark.

And for the first time Amy recognized dimly, as though looking through a gauzy veil, that hers was a heart condition that hurt as much as anything physical. And maybe more.

A rainbow was a beautiful thing. Jesse squinted at the ethereal colors from the corner of the corral. Birds sang morning greetings and the countryside smelled clean and alive.

His head throbbed and his tongue felt like he'd chewed sawdust half the night. Even dunking his head in the rain barrel hadn't cleared the morning-after cobwebs.

Half an hour ago a Concord coach had arrived from the West, dispatched by telegraph for the sole purpose of picking up a particular passenger, but seven others would benefit from the ride, as well.

A man Jesse recognized as one they'd brought from the train and served in the kitchen last night appeared from the barn, a leather satchel in hand. He wore a tailored black suit coat and trousers, a white shirt and shiny tie, fancier garb than was the norm in these parts.

"I owe you, your wife and father-in-law a debt of gratitude, Mr. Shelby." He placed his bag on the ground and extended a hand. "Castlewhite's the name."

Jesse shook his hand. "Call me Jesse. Pleased everything turned out all right."

"I own a few investments in Denver City," the man said, leaning back on his heels. "A hotel among them. The White Castle Hotel."

"I believe I've heard of it."

"Consider it your home whenever you chance to be in my city, Jesse. There will always be a room and meals for the Shelbys."

"Thank you, Mr. Castlewhite. I'll keep that in mind."

"Clive," he said with a grin.

Jesse nodded.

Hermie and the driver had loaded baggage, and Hermie came to get Clive's satchel. The other passengers who had been chosen to travel with the hotel owner called their thanks to Jesse and boarded the coach.

By the third day all but three of the displaced passengers had ridden out on departing stages. Only William Hunter, Eden Sullivan and Mr. Barnett remained.

On the fourth day the two men were gone, as well, and the boardinghouse held the usual sprinkling of guests, plus the still-hobbling Eden.

She'd made no mention of moving on, and continued to pay her dollar a day for room and board. It was a steep rate; the Shelbys could charge it because of their locale and appeal, but it was a mystery why Eden didn't mind paying it—and how she could afford to.

"Hello?" she chirped from her room as Jesse passed through on his way out early Friday morning.

Hesitantly, he stood outside her partially open door. "Yes, miss?"

"I'm dreadfully bored and couldn't possibly rest another moment. Will you be so kind as to assist me to the house for the day? I'd like to take meals with the others and converse a bit."

Hat in hand, Jesse opened the door and peered around it to find the woman perched on the side of the narrow bed, dressed in a spring-green dress, her dark hair artfully arranged in an upsweep of curls.

She motioned for him to come closer.

He glanced out toward the hall.

"Come on in. I'll need your strong back and arms."

He approached her uncomfortably.

"Come on, I won't bite."

When he drew beside her, she stood and reached one arm around his neck. He placed his hat on his head quickly and lifted her up against his chest, one arm around her back, the other behind her knees.

"I'm positively *aching* for company," she told him as he carried her out of the room.

She smelled like powdery roses. "I'm sure my wife and Mrs. Barnes will be good company."

"I asked the maid if Mrs. Shelby was your wife."

"She is."

"I wasn't sure, because you stay here nights."

Heat burned up Jesse's neck, but he passed off her comment as though it didn't disturb him. They were out of doors and he made quick work of traveling the board walkway that stretched to the house. Four steps up to the porch, and he paused so she could reach for the handle on the door.

Amy stood at the stove, stirring something in a pot, her back to them as they entered. Mrs. Barnes looked up from kneading dough.

"Amy, bring a chair, will you, please?"

She turned to discover her husband standing just inside the kitchen doorway, a sweetly smiling Eden in his arms. Wiping her hands on her apron, Amy walked quickly from the room, returning with the rocker.

Jesse deposited Eden on the seat, backed away as though she were a stick of dynamite and he held the match, then nodded to Amy before slipping back outside.

Eden watched the door close, then swept dark-lashed eyes around the kitchen. "I couldn't bear another moment in that room staring at the walls. Your Jesse was kind enough to avail me of his strong back."

Amy picked up a bowl of potatoes and a knife and placed them on a bench within Eden's reach. "I'm glad you're here. We can always use another hand in the kitchen."

Mrs. Barnes hid a smile by turning away and wetting a towel to drape over the shaped loaves.

As the men filtered in for their morning meal, each pair of eyes made a brief and appreciative inspection of the fetching woman seated in their midst. Eden smiled and greeted each hand politely, but reserved the magnitude of her charm for Sam and Jesse.

Sam scooted her rocker closer to the table and reached for cream and molasses for her oatmeal. An injured foot hadn't affected Eden's appetite up 'til now; Amy had observed that she'd eaten all the meals carried to her room. But this morning, she ate only a few spoonfuls of oatmeal and a couple of bites of toast.

"I can't hold any more," she told Sam. "But I'm delighted to have company for my meal. I've been dreadfully lonely."

"Well, you just sit tight here and you'll have company for all your meals," he told her. "Amy and Mrs. Barnes are in and out most of the day, so you won't be alone."

"You've all been so kind to me." She drew a lace-edged hankie from the pocket of her dress to dab the corner of one eye. "I can't thank you enough."

Amy glanced at the males around the table. Deezer, the youngest of their help, swallowed, and his Adam's apple bobbed as he stared at her wide-eyed. Hermie and Pitch paused with spoons halfway to their mouths. Jesse glanced from Eden to the door and downed his coffee. Even Cay stared as though a heavenly apparition had been placed in their midst.

Sam patted Eden's hand awkwardly, then moved her chair back to its original position. "No need to get carried away thankin' folks," he said. "We're all real glad you and the others are safe and sound."

"Well, I wouldn't be if it weren't for your bravery. Yours and Jesse's."

Jesse stood then, grabbed his hat and settled it on his head. "Going out to look for you was my wife's idea. Be thankin' her." He glanced to his nephew as he buckled his holster. "Cay, oil the harnesses this morning."

He left, the door swinging shut behind him.

Cay scraped his bowl clean and trotted out with a perfunctory "Thank you, ma'am."

Their departure prodded the others to finish their meals and head out. Sam wished the women a good day and joined them.

By the time Amy had finished clearing the table, she noted that Eden had managed to finish her oatmeal. Must be the men who made her lose her appetite, she thought. She set the empty bowl beside the tub where Mrs. Barnes was scrubbing dishes and they shared a knowing look.

Amy thought of the comical expressions on the men's faces and realized that her father's was the one that disturbed her the most. She scoffed at herself with her second breath. Sam was twice Eden's age—too old and far too wise to be taken in by such obvious feminine wiles.

Wasn't he?

Sam was too damn old to be moonin' like a tongue-tied schoolboy and finding excuses to stop by the house during the day. Or was he? He hadn't even neared fifty yet, and he was still fit enough to wrangle a horse or carry a featherweight woman to the boardinghouse each night and back again of a morning. That part had come to be a pleasure. Eden was softer and curvier than anything he could think of, and she smelled like rose petals. His wife had been gone a fair number of years, but until now he hadn't realized how much he missed havin' a woman in his arms.

Her skin was dewy and fair, and her hair held the midnight sheen of a newborn colt. She was a delicate distraction from his otherwise male-oriented and harsh days. It wasn't as though the woman's stay was permanent. She would be movin' on—had family expectin' her—had a life of polish and refinement far from here. No, life on the frontier was hard on women.

Sam had impressed that fact upon Jesse from the first time Jesse had shown an interest in his daughter, and again when Jesse and Amy married. A few years back, news had traveled that a homesteader's wife over by Wolf Creek gave birth to her seventh child, got up and baked a blueberry pie, then went out to the barn and hung herself from the rafters. Sam and Jesse put their heads together on the spot and hired more help. Sam's wife had died too young, though.

"I don't want a hard life for Amy," he'd told his son-in-law.

Both of them had done their best to give Amy the skills she needed to survive while shielding her from the harshest elements. But Eden was definitely not cut out for life on the Overland Trail.

There was no reason Sam shouldn't enjoy the fresh

picture Eden painted on his otherwise monotonous days, though. Last time he checked, he wasn't dead.

On Saturday night he asked Eden if she would like to attend church with them on Sunday, and she accepted. The next morning Sam carried her to a buggy he'd rigged for the occasion. He pointedly ignored his curious family and the gawking hands as he and his female companion left together.

Jesse stood beside his own buggy, watching them go, then sensed company at his side. Looking fine in her blue dress with the lace neck and sleeves, a hat shading her eyes, Amy had joined him. She was so pretty he felt all soft inside. He turned his attention to Sam's buggy in the distance.

"What do you make of that?" he asked.

She smoothed her white gloves over her fingers. "I guess he has a right to his folly if he chooses it. Or, could be she's looking for a man and a home."

Jesse wasn't so sure about the home part. He assisted his wife up to the seat and climbed to take the reins and utter a command to the horses.

"Do you think Cay would want to ride with us?" Amy asked.

Her question surprised him, but pleasure overrode any hesitation about her intentions. "Whoa there. Whoa." He tied the reins to the brake handle. "I'll see. Is he in the house?"

"No, he left a little while ago."

Jesse got down and loped to the barn, returning moments later with Cay. Dressed in his good shirt and trousers, the boy scrambled into the small seat at the rear. Jesse resumed his place beside Amy.

As they participated in the service that morning, Jesse rolled Amy's words from earlier in the week around in his mind. She sat on his right, as always, Cay to his left. She had said she was afraid he would get too attached to his nephew and then Cay would leave. Was she thinking of Jesse being hurt? Or was she protecting herself—because she'd been hurt by loss and couldn't bear it again?

A Sunday morning never passed that Jesse didn't think of the squirming fair-haired toddler who used to sit between them, sometimes falling asleep on Jesse's lap with his thumb in his mouth. Did Amy think of Tim on these mornings, too? Or had she completely erased every memory because of the pain they caused? He knew Amy, the real Amy, knew her caring nature and her tender heart. She wasn't locking out Cay because she didn't trust him or because she resented the intrusion. Intentionally or unintentionally, she was trying to protect them both.

But today she'd suggested that Cay ride with them. Jesse wanted to reach over and take her hand, thank her without words. *Is the Amy I remember still there? Is the girl I fell in love with and gave my heart to a ghost? Come back to me, my love. My heart. Don't leave me here all alone.*

Jesse prayed for strength. And for forgiveness.

And for strength to forgive.

Chapter Six

Sam had forgotten what it was like to be around a female other than his daughter or Mrs. Barnes. Another week around Eden proved she was a woman to catch a man's fancy and tickle it good.

The following Sunday they'd attended church again. Afterward she sat beside him on the buggy seat as he headed the horses toward home. Wearing a bright pink dress with a square-necked bodice that showed a man enough cleavage to thoroughly addle his thoughts, she was a new spring flower on a late-fall day.

She tucked her arm through his. "I don't even know where you live, Sam."

"It's on past the station just a mile. Not far."

"A house?"

"A small one. Serves me well."

"I'd like to see it."

Sam glanced down at her uptilted face. Her beguiling smile was irresistible. "Now?"

"Unless you prefer not. But I surely would enjoy the scenery in that direction."

"The scenery looks just the same either way, but I don't mind takin' you there."

She gave his arm a delighted little squeeze that unwittingly pressed her breast against his arm. A tremor shot through his body.

A short while later his homestead came into view—the orchards to the east and south of the house, a well in the yard and a red barn. "This is it." He pulled the buggy up in front of the house. "I could fix us some lunch if you want. I don't have much, but I can put together somethin'."

"That would be most kind of you. I am quite hungry after a whole morning of singing and praying."

She leaned on her crutch as Sam unhitched the horse and tethered it where it could find dry grass.

He ushered Eden inside. The house was only two rooms—a wide kitchen open to a sitting area, and a bedroom. The last years of their life together. He and Vanessa had shared this little house, taking most of their meals at the station but spending evenings and nights here.

Since Vanessa's death, Adele came over and cleaned for him and Amy made sure he had supplies laid by. It wasn't much of a home anymore. He looked at the rooms through a city woman's eyes and they came up sorely lacking.

"It's not much," he said with an apology in his tone. "I don't spend much time here."

"It's rather quaintly charming, actually," she said, touching the edge of the table and the rungs of a ladder-back chair. She had a way of touching people and things, as though she experienced them through her fingertips. "It has possibilities."

Sam couldn't imagine what possibilities, but he took her wrap and hat and hung them beside the door. He blinked at the unaccustomed sight of the feminine garments, a knot in his chest. Catching himself, he turned to his task, raised the stove lid and stirred the fire to life with the poker. Sparks floated toward the ceiling. From the stack beside the stove, he took a chunk of wood and added it, then set about slicing ham and opening a can of beans. A whoosh flew up the stovepipe as the fire caught, and he heated their meal.

Eden found plates and silverware and set the table. "I don't suppose you have any tea?"

"'Fraid not."

"I'll drink water. I haven't developed a taste for your western coffee."

He forked slices of ham onto the plates and set the hot beans on the table in the pan. "Quite a bit about the West takes some gettin' used to. I should have put those in a bowl."

He reached for the handle of the pan, but she caught his wrist. "It's all right, Sam. You don't have to do anything fancy on my behalf."

He looked at her hand, small and pale and soft. Not the hand of someone who scrubbed laundry on a washboard or made soap or milked cows. She was like a traveler from another time and place set down in his kitchen, and he couldn't quite grasp the marvel of her presence. That she even wanted to be with him was a wonder.

"Are you exceedingly hungry?" Her dewy lips formed that delicate pout.

Sam shook his head in a lie. He was always hungry at dinnertime.

"Neither am I." She released his hand and touched his lips with her finger. Taking another step closer, she breathed, "But I do have a craving for something sweet."

Heat rushed through Sam's veins and his body reacted immediately and potently. No, he wasn't dead by a long shot. Unless he was missing the mark, Eden was as eager for something to develop between them as he was. He might miss the signal, but he wasn't going to miss the opportunity to see if he was right.

Wrapping one arm around her waist, he drew her solidly up against him. Her eyes darkened with sultry excitement as she held his gaze. There was no mistaking his desire pressed between them. Her nostrils flared with anticipation.

Lowering his head, Sam kissed her. She responded with a growl in the back of her throat. He didn't know if he'd ever kissed a woman who threw herself into the act like Eden. She used her teeth and her lips and her tongue until both of them were breathing hard.

With pauses for breath, she leaned back and made quick work of Sam's tie and shirt buttons, freeing the tail and pushing the garment off his shoulders and down his arms.

She ran her hands over his chest and arms appreciatively. "You're so bumpy in all the right places. Here—" She tested his biceps. "Here—" That said with her tongue lapping his shoulder.

Sam gritted his teeth.

In a wash of rose perfume, she turned and presented her back. "My buttons, Sam."

The tiny things taunted him, but he was persistent and laboriously peeled each one away from its mooring. Her ivory skin was exposed an inch at a time, until the dress fell away and she stepped out of it, turning back. She stood before him in a lace-trimmed corset, her breasts spilling over the top and stealing his breath.

"You're the prettiest thing I've ever seen," he told her.

She gave him a provocative smile. "Is that the truth?"

"I wouldn't say so if it wasn't."

She leaned in to brush her softness against his chest. Large dusky nipples peeked over the top of her corset.

With catlike grace, she moved around him, touching him where he stood, stroking herself against his back, coming to face him again. With the back of her hand she reached down and brushed against his erection.

Sam tensed his body and felt blood rush to the place

she had touched. He'd never dreamed such feverish goings-on in the middle of the day. He'd been married twenty years and never done this in the kitchen in broad daylight.

He definitely received the message that she was willing. No pussyfooting around between them. He liked that.

Sam swept her up and carried her into the bedroom, where he tossed her into the middle of the bed and followed. She laughed and scrambled to her knees, then watched him with hooded eyes while he removed her corset and plumped her breasts in his palms.

Her gaze constantly moved across his arms and chest, down to the front of his trousers, as though she was eager to see more. What kind of heaven on earth had he gone and found himself without even trying?

She shucked off her pantaloons and stood on her knees before him in the middle of the bed, pale skin creased by her corset, her breasts full and round with rosy nipples. Her eyes devoured him and her full pouty lips begged for his kisses. He leaned toward her, but she stopped him with a hand on his chest.

"Your turn, cowboy."

Sam stood beside the bed to remove his trousers.

Unembarrassed, she watched. Sam didn't know if his wife had ever looked at him naked. If she had, she'd never let him see her looking.

"Touch me here, cowboy." She took his hand and guided it where she wanted him to explore.

Uninhibited. He'd never known the full implication of the word before. He learned it now.

Two hours of pleasure with Eden had him more physically spent than a week of mucking stalls and handling horses. She liked it fast, she liked it slow; she liked it fierce, she liked it easy. Eden just plain liked it.

All that and her hair was barely even mussed. Later she sat across from him at the table, dressed in his shirt with the sleeves rolled back over her slender white arms, and she still looked as fresh and pretty as she had that morning. Hellfire, but she was young.

"I don't know how I got so fortunate," he said, finishing a bite of cold ham. "But I'm gonna take gifts to those Cheyenne if ever I learn who they were."

Eden giggled.

"I kept thinkin' all along I was too old for you."

"You're not old, Sam." She pushed the beans around on her plate and ate a bite of bread. "You're *seasoned.* Just right."

He chuckled. Minutes later, pouring himself coffee, he sobered. He had no idea what was going to come of this. And he was too proud to ask. Would Eden think about staying now? They'd done things backward, but he would jump for a chance to court her. She hadn't mentioned her plans.

"I don't suppose we should let on. About this."

"It would be prudent to keep our silence," she agreed.

When they returned that afternoon, he told the others they'd gone for a ride. No one seemed to think strangely of it. And the afternoon wasn't mentioned again.

He and Eden shared secret smiles…and Sam considered his options.

Another two weeks went by, bringing colder temperatures and frost. Coats and caps and gloves came out of storage, and a supply of firewood was laid by.

Amy was adding salt pork to a pot of beans one afternoon when there was a tap on the kitchen door. No one ever bothered to knock; their home was accessible all hours of the day and most of the evening. Puzzled, she walked to the door and opened it.

Rachel Douglas stood on the back porch, a frayed coat pulled around her girth, her nose red from the wind.

"Come in," Amy urged, taking her sleeve and drawing her inside.

Rachel pulled a scarf from her head and stuffed it in the pocket of her coat along with her wool mittens.

"It's so good to see you," Amy said.

"I'm here to work." A hesitant smile brightened her features.

"Work?" Amy asked, puzzled.

"Your husband hired on Jack. But I'll earn my own keep."

Jesse had hired Jack Douglas. Amy had seen the Douglases in church, but she and Jesse hadn't discussed them since the day of the picnic when they'd first met them. She had had no inkling that Jesse needed another hand.

The door opened again and Jesse ushered Jack inside. "Amy, you know the Douglases," he said. "Jack's hired on."

"I can earn my own keep, too," Rachel insisted.

"Any duties Amy has for you will be of her choosing." Jesse addressed Amy again. "I set the boys to cleaning up the soddy a week or so ago, laying up wood and such. If you and Adele could rustle up blankets and a few homey things, it'll make a nice place for Jack and his missus to stay."

Amy nodded her agreement.

"Amy and her folks lived in the sod house before this house was built," Jesse told Rachel. "And Amy and I lived there for a time when we were first married. It's not fancy, but it's dry and warm."

Rachel had tears in her eyes after she exchanged a look with her husband. She turned to Amy. "Thank you."

"Your husband's a fine man, Mrs. Shelby," Jack said in his crisp English accent.

She looked at Jesse. "Yes, I know."

Jesse seemed embarrassed by the praise and led Jack back outside.

Mrs. Barnes came upon the women then and Amy introduced Rachel.

"Hang your coat," Amy said. "After dinner, we'll get the soddy all set up for you. You'll get by just fine out there."

Leda Bentley had been right about Rachel's skills in the house. She dove right in to help with meal preparation, and what she didn't know how to do, she asked about and learned.

"We have crates of cabbage in the root cellar that I want to get made into sauerkraut," Mrs. Barnes told her. "You can help me with that tomorrow."

Rachel smiled with satisfaction. Amy planned to limit the girl's activities due to her condition, but she sensed how important it was that Rachel feel she was pulling her own weight. She wouldn't take that away from her. There were plenty of light duties that would keep her busy and be a big help at the same time.

At dinner, Jack proudly joined the men at the table. He'd already been dubbed "the Duke" because of his accent, and he took the ribbing good-naturedly.

That night, with the Douglases tucked away in the cozy little soddy, Amy sat by the fire in the parlor, sewing. Her hands fell idle. Jesse's words that afternoon had dislodged a memory she'd been unable to stuff away again. She couldn't shake what he'd said about their first months and years of marriage.

This house had just been built; she and her parents had spent only a few weeks living in it. Jesse had moved from the barn to the soddy. After their wedding, they had retreated to the privacy of the sod house. They'd spent their wedding night there, and all the nights that followed…until her parents had decided to give them the big house and live at the homestead.

Amy pictured the young couple staying in the sod house now, preparing for bed, relishing the seclusion. She saw Rachel in her nightgown, her belly swollen with their child—and her rock of a heart betrayed her again.

Her throat felt thick and she could barely swallow.

Amy looked down to see she'd gripped the fabric so hard that the needle had pierced her thumb. The drop of blood that glistened there reminded her of Jesse cutting his hand and saying he couldn't feel it.

Standing, she grabbed a shawl and stepped out on the back porch. Light spilled from the barns and the boardinghouse as usual. Across the expanse she saw Pitch carrying a bucket of water.

"Pitch?" she called.

He stopped in his tracks. "Ma'am?"

"Ask Jesse to come up to the house, will you, please?"

"Yes, ma'am."

Amy went back inside and fed a log to the fire. She rubbed her hands together and was lost in the flicker of the flames when she heard a floorboard creak behind her.

She turned to find Jesse in his sheepskin-lined coat. "You needed somethin', Amy?"

"Sit down. I'll get you coffee and a slice of peach pie."

He removed his coat and sat in the side chair. The rocker, Eden's personal throne, was still in the kitchen.

After Amy brought his dessert, she perched on the ottoman before the fire. The room seemed unseasonably chilly this evening.

Jesse ate slowly. "I like your peach pie the best."

"I know."

He finished and set the plate on the floor. His gaze traveled the room and stopped on her clock. "Your clock ran down."

"I didn't really need it," she said. "It's a bother to keep it wound."

"I s'pose those families are enjoyin' their eggs, though."

"I suppose they are."

"You asked me to come in so you could feed me?" he asked finally.

"No." She arranged her skirts and finally looked at him. "I wanted to thank you. For hiring Jack."

"Why should you thank me?"

"We see less stages through the winter, Jesse, I know you didn't need the help."

"It'll work out. Deezer and one of the others are heading East for the winter."

"Okay. So you didn't do it for me."

He pursed his lips momentarily, then said, "I thought you were worried about Jack not having work over the winter and Rachel bein'...the way Rachel is and all."

"I don't think I was—worried I mean. But I'm pleased that she's here safe and sound."

"You're a caretaker, Amy, no way around it."

She didn't respond, but turned to gaze at the fire once again.

"Haven't seen lights in the windows of the soddy for a long time," he said reflectively. "Reminds me of when I used to come home to you at night."

Amy's pulse belied a hardened heart.

"You used to have a slice of pie ready for me then, too."

The hammering of her heart drowned out coherent thought.

"Sometimes we skipped the pie and went right to the lovin'."

She didn't feel the chill any longer. The fire seemed to be prickling her skin, setting her blood ablaze.

"Sometimes we didn't even sleep—"

His voice was right behind her ear, but she hadn't heard him move. He had knelt beside her.

"We had that quilt your aunt gave us for our weddin', and we'd lay it on the floor in front of the fire and let our skin touch everywhere and our hearts be filled to overflowin'."

"Jesse, don't—"

"Wasn't anything could have kept me away from you for a night then."

His breath tickled the hair on her neck and sent shivers skittering across her flesh. Her overheated body turned to liquid.

His teeth nipped her ear gently, and she made a sound like a newborn kitten mewling.

Jesse turned her on the ottoman so that she faced him instead of the fire. It didn't take much urging to insinuate his body between her knees and bring himself up against her. He cupped her head in both hands and kissed her breathless. He tasted like peaches and promised pleasure, and it was a seductive drug in her veins. His words were picture memories, vivid and searing. They showed her what they'd had…what they'd lost.

As if he was afraid to give her time to breathe or think, he plied her mouth with urgency and her senses with his inordinate brand of heady seduction.

Jesse separated their lips, and she opened her heavy lids to look into his eyes.

"Do you remember, Amy? Do you remember it wasn't pity or guilt or grief back then?"

She hadn't forgotten. She had buried. Built. Abandoned and moved on.

"If I went upstairs with you now, I'd know you were thanking me. Just like the last time when you were pityin' me. It wouldn't be you wanting me. Not the way I want you."

He released her and stood, letting air flow around her and chill her once again. She sat with her skirt draped between her wide-spread knees, her body thrumming and the taste of peaches on her tingling lips.

"Jesse," she whispered.

He turned. "'Night, Amy."

His broad form filled the doorway and disappeared.

"Jesse," she whispered again. The back door opened

and closed. She squeezed her eyes shut and felt him. Heard his voice. Tasted his kisses. What had she done to him?

What had she done to *them?*

Nearly two hours later Jesse pulled the cork on the next bottle. He'd replenished his stash that week and a fresh crate had become his bedside table. He'd picked up the last bottle to find it half gone already, and had polished it off before he'd finished checking the horses.

This bottle was going down a lot smoother. He liked it when the whiskey slid down his throat so easily. He tried to hold out, tried to make it through a night without givin' in to the craving that now seemed to be in his head and on his skin, but he was so dry, and his belly ached with the need for just a little to soothe him to sleep.

Still, he wasn't hurtin' anybody. He didn't let his work suffer or his morning head stop him from taking care of business. Nobody cared. Amy didn't even really care, because when he was out here he wasn't bothering her, and she wasn't obligated to act like a wife.

He thought he heard a pounding in his head, but he hadn't even fallen asleep yet, so it couldn't be morning.

There it was again.

"Jesse?"

"Amy?" What was she doin' out here? He hid the bottle under his bunk and went to let her in.

He blinked. Dark hair. A green dress. Not Amy.

"I hate to disturb you so late, but I'd be much obliged if you'd give me a hand."

Eden. Even her name was linked to dangerous temptation.

"What's wrong?"

"I had Adele help me into this dress this morning. It's not a practical garment for a woman who must dress without assistance, and I'm afraid I can't reach the buttons by myself."

"I'll— I can find Adele."

"No, no, I don't want to wake her, it's much too late. If you could just lend your assistance ever so briefly." She turned her back and lifted her hair with one hand.

Jesse squinted to focus on the row of tiny buttons. His fingers were too big and blunt. Unfastening them took forever, and he just wanted to be rid of her.

"This is so sweet of you," she purred.

The row of buttons seemed to trail into infinity. "Why don't females…make their dresses suh-*sensible,* so they can button 'em up the front?"

"Fashion simply defies logic, does it not?"

He had reached the end of the row of buttons, and Eden turned to face him.

"I especially like those buckskins I've seen you wear," she said. "A simple little lace by your throat to loosen and you can pull it off over your head."

She raised a hand and ran one finger teasingly across his shoulder and upper arm. "I wondered what you looked like without your shirt."

Dimly, he realized he'd removed his shirt some time ago.

"I've watched you with the horses, seen you load the coaches. You're very strong."

A belated warning went off in his head, deadened by alcohol, but there just the same. This woman was trouble.

"It's not right, you sleeping out here all by yourself," she said. "Not a deserving man like yourself."

"I don't think…I'm not…" Wrong, *wrong*. This was all wrong.

Eden used his confusion to inch herself forward and latch her forearm around his neck to bring his head down to her. "A woman like me knows how to appreciate a man."

Before her behavior registered on his sluggish brain, she kissed him full on the mouth. Not primly, not hesitantly, but hungrily, her lips widening over his.

A tap sounded on the door. "Jesse?"

Eden hung on.

The door smacked against the wall.

Jesse raised his head and realized his hands were on Eden's waist, whether to push her away or not, he didn't remember.

In the open doorway, gripping her shawl with white-knuckled fingers and wearing a stricken expression, stood Amy.

Chapter Seven

Amy opened her mouth but no words came out. Her chest felt as though someone had struck her with a two-by-four. She stared at the scene before her, her befuddled mind grappling with what her eyes conveyed. Chest bare, eyes hooded, Jesse stood with his hands on Eden's waist. That sight captured her breath and drew out the painful moment like living a nightmare.

One strand of Eden's hair draped against her ivory-skinned neck. The bodice of her unbuttoned dress hung forward, exposing the tops of her breasts where they were pushed upward by a lacy corset. She lazily drew her hand across Jesse's shoulder and stepped back to adjust her dress. Wearing an expression like that of a cat who'd just lapped up a bowl of cream, she tucked away the strand of hair.

"Well, hello, Amy. We weren't expecting you."

Amy found her voice. "I can see that."

Jesse reached a hand toward her. "Amy, it's not—"

Following her first instinct, she turned and fled. She ran out of the boardinghouse and across the yard.

"Amy!"

At the sound of his voice and his steps behind her, anger roiled up inside. Balling her fists, she changed her direction and, instead of heading into the house, she spun around, heading straight back for him.

Jesse saw her coming and planted his feet.

Amy came to a stop a foot away. Without forethought, she slapped him as hard as she could, jolting his head to the side. He stood that way for an endless moment, the night wind ruffling his hair. Slowly, he turned to look at her. He swayed on his feet as though the breeze might knock him over.

With her hands fisted in the fabric of her skirt, she used every ounce of control she possessed not to hit him again. Her breath came out in tight-chested pants. "Do not follow me into the house. I'm going to lock the door. And I'm going to lock the bedroom door."

She whirled and marched toward the porch.

"Amy."

"Don't say my name!" She ran again. Inside, she did as promised, turning the locks back and front, making her way upstairs and slamming down the wooden bar that barricaded her in her room. Diving onto the bed, she covered her head with the pillow as if hiding beneath it could shut out this last prevailing horror.

Images flashed in her mind's eye, each more unbearable than the next. Jesse's hands on Eden's waist. His eyes staring at her across Eden's bare, rounded shoulder. Him standing steadfast with his face to the side after she'd struck him.

Throwing off the pillow, she stood and took deliberate, calming breaths. She was stronger than this. She wasn't going to bury her head and wallow. She always picked herself up and went on, no matter what. In three steps she reached her dressing table. The mirror reflected her wild hair, her face pale with disgust and confusion. With trembling hands, she performed her nightly ritual, changing her clothing, braiding her hair, all done while feeling nothing.

A thousand torturous images had already been buried in the recesses of her mind and the untouched places of her heart. What were a few more? Visions of Jesse with Eden in his arms would have to be added to those. Closed up. Locked away. But she had to capture them first…

It was as much her fault as his. *No guilt!* Tuck that out of mind too.

What the hell did she care? *Jealousy?* Not allowed.

She knew he still loved her, she knew it! *Doesn't matter, no regrets.*

So many times she had lamented and questioned what she had done to their relationship, agonized over her responsibility for the breakdown of their marriage. But her world had slipped tonight. Everything familiar, no matter how wrong, had been lost and a new doubt had been born.

What had *Jesse* done to them?

* * *

A rooster crowed and Jesse rolled over on his bunk with an agonized groan. His mind was a woolly gray mass and his head ached so bad he thought it would split in two when he lifted it off the mattress.

He was already wearing his trousers, so he stumbled outside and around the corner. Knocking aside the lid of the rain barrel, he plunged his head deep. He stayed that way, holding his breath, feeling his pulse pounding in his ears and the cold seeping into his numb brain, bringing cells to life.

With a gasp, he straightened and flung his head back, cold water running down his chest and back, air hitting the rivulets and sending painful messages to his body.

This was the worst. He'd never felt this bad, never come this close to staying in bed and saying to hell with a day. Never before had he felt the need to go right back in and open a new bottle to work off some of the pain behind his eyes.

He gritted his teeth.

And then he remembered. Dread gripped his heart.

Eden. Coming to his room. Kissing him.

Amy. Walking in. Hating him.

He fell to his knees and grasped dry weeds and grass as self-loathing washed over him. Staggering to his feet, he stumbled to the rear of the building where he retched, muscles spasming, until his belly ached.

Don't follow me. Don't say my name.

Anger and hurt and betrayal had weighted every

word she'd spoken. Shaken her voice. Darkened her eyes. He could have continued sleeping in their room and endured the nights. He could have resisted the lure to drown everything out with whiskey. He could have been the man she needed him to be until she found a better way to cope with their son's death.

Jesse's hands shook, and he stared at them as if they belonged to someone else.

They did. He'd become a stranger.

Sam rode his horse into the barn and slid off. He removed the saddle and let the mare into the corral. Smoke spiraled from multiple chimneys this morning, from the house, the soddy, the bathhouse—a homey, welcoming scene. His steps were light, and he whistled softly as he crossed the yard.

The boardinghouse was silent when he stuck his head inside. He sighed in disappointment. Over the last few weeks his Sunday afternoon "rides" with Eden had become a much-anticipated event. The rest of the days, she cast him furtive looks and those soul-burnin' smiles. Sometimes if he caught her alone of a mornin', she would invite him into her room and tease him senseless. Around the others, however, they hadn't let on that something was happening between them—and that had started to feel wrong.

Last night he'd decided. He was going to just come out and ask her to stay so he could court her proper. He'd been thinkin' it was disrespectful the way he'd been taking his pleasure with her without a commitment. Maybe she wasn't sure of him, either. Maybe one of them just needed to say something out loud.

Sam moseyed up the back stairs to find the kitchen door open. Voices slowed his pace and he paused, unease creeping into his bones.

"Fine man like that needs looking after, and it's plain you don't intend to do it," a feminine voice mewled. "I'm more than happy to take your place if you don't want your husband in your bed."

Eden? Those confusing words made blood roar in Sam's head.

"You've worn out your welcome at Shelby Station," Amy replied in a hostile tone Sam had never heard. He stepped right up to the door and listened. "Pack up your things and be on the next stage—I don't care which way it's headed. If you don't, I'll put you on it. I don't care if I have to strap you to the boot with the other baggage!"

"You are a coarse, drab, unfeminine bore," Eden replied haughtily. "This place is uncivilized and backward. It's obvious you belong here and, as you so rudely pointed out, I do not. It no longer amuses me to stay, and I choose to leave on my own."

The screen door flew open and Eden practically ran into Sam. He steadied her by taking hold of her elbows. "What's goin' on?"

Her face was flushed and she wore an expression of disdain. After glancing up at him, she jerked away, held her skirts aside and hurried down the stairs.

"Don't forget to pay for your breakfast," Amy called from the doorway.

Sam stared after Eden, a sick feeling raising bile in his belly. He wanted to chase after her, but Amy would never understand. He turned on his daughter. "What the hell is going on?"

Amy pursed her lips and stood with her hands on her hips. He'd never seen her so angry, and half expected her to fly after the retreating woman and snatch her hair out.

He couldn't have heard right. "Did she say something about takin' your place in Jesse's bed?"

For the first time in over a year, Sam saw tears come to Amy's eyes. She blinked them back and controlled her quivering chin by raising it a notch to look him in the eye. "Last night I found her in Jesse's room at the boardinghouse."

"What?" Jesse and Eden together? His mind wouldn't wrap around it. "Doin' what?"

Her cheeks flushed and her eyes glistened with unshed tears.

"In—in bed together?" he asked.

She pressed a hand to her cheek. "No. But getting there, I'd imagine. He had his shirt gone and her dress was nearly off. He was—" She stopped and bit her lip, fought for composure. "He was kissing her."

Stunned, Sam absorbed the facts. Amy had seen this with her own eyes. She was relating the truth. His ego was takin' a monumental beating, but Amy—good

Lord, Amy. All his well-hidden doubts bubbled to the surface.

"Oh, honey," he said, stepping forward to lend her comfort.

She backed inside and he followed, but she kept him at arm's length with a shake of her head and an out-stretched arm. "Don't" was all she said.

She was too proud, too hurt, too afraid of letting herself feel. Anger rose in Sam's chest and riled his blood. For a minute nothing but Eden's soft curvy body and succulent kisses were in his head. He drove them out and thought of his daughter's pain instead. Sam was a damn old fool, but Jesse was a married man!

"I'll kill the son of a bitch." He turned and stormed out.

"No! Daddy, no!" Amy cried, following him. "Let us handle this."

"That's the problem. You don't handle anything!"

"Stop!"

Adele popped her head out of an upstairs window at the boardinghouse.

"Jesse up there?" Sam growled.

She shook her head and watched them pass.

"Jesse!" Sam shouted, heading for the barn. Inside, he crossed the hard-packed dirt in determined strides. "Jesse!"

Pitch darted out of Sam's path, slopping water from the bucket he carried.

Jesse stepped from the tack room in the rear. His skin

was paler than normal except under his eyes, where dark semicircles gave him a weary appearance.

"What the hell do you think you're doing?" Sam demanded.

Jesse swiped a hand down his face and his gaze traveled to Amy, where she hung behind, then back to her father. "I need a chance to explain. I know it looks bad and I was in the wrong but—"

"It'd take a heap of explainin' to fix this. I don't think you have that much wind in ya."

A few of the hands had heard the commotion and gathered nearby.

Sam waved his arms. "Get the hell outta here and earn your pay!"

They scattered out of the building.

Sam stomped toward Jesse until they stood face to face. "I know my daughter hasn't been a proper wife to you this past year. But that's no excuse for *stupidity.*"

What was he saying? He was equally as stupid. Just not married. Who was he mad at? Himself? Eden? At the thought of her and the way she'd let him think she wanted *him,* Sam saw red.

"You're right." Jesse looked from Sam to Amy. "I'm sorry. I'm so sorry. I was *stupid* drunk and I wasn't thinkin' straight. I shouldn't have been out here." He drew a shaky hand over his face. "I should have stayed in our room no matter what. It shames me just to face you now, Amy. It's killing me for you to see what I've become. If I could change things, I would. If I could take us back to before all this, I'd do it. But I can't. And I don't know how to fix so much wrong."

Amy heard the regret in Jesse's voice, saw the misery in his eyes. He was sorry, truly sorry. This was an opportunity for forgiveness and healing. More than anything she wanted to let down her emotional barriers and believe him. But her defenses had been constructed well and reinforced daily, and her fear of being the tiniest bit vulnerable held her rooted to the spot and kept her lips sealed.

She remembered striking out at him the night before, and the way he'd stood there as if the punishment was his due. He'd come right out at her father's call as though prepared for his anger. She knew as well as she knew night would fall that if her father hit Jesse, he would not fight back.

Moving beside her father, she said, "I think we've all said what needed to be said this day. Jesse, I hear your regret for what happened. I have regrets, too. We all need some time now."

Sam's anger seemed to have seeped away, and he took a step back. He looked like he might throw up.

"Are you okay?"

"I'm fine." He jerked his gaze to Jesse's. "Amy's right. I'm going to get some work done." With hunched shoulders, he turned and walked to the open double doors and disappeared outside.

Jesse pushed his damp hair back and stood with a hand on his hip. "Amy, I have to explain somethin' to you."

"If it makes you feel better."

"What you saw last night was all that happened. She asked me to help her with her dress. I did and she kissed me. It all happened so fast and my head was so sluggish. I don't have an excuse. I'm not makin' an excuse. But you have to know that I wouldn't have made love with her."

"I guess I don't know that. I don't know what I believe anymore." She looked into his eyes and felt familiar confusion knot her stomach, remembered him kissing her in front of the fire. The heat of humiliation burned in her chest. "You could have stayed with me last night," she said, willing her voice not to break. "It's never been that you *can't* take your ease with me, Jesse. It's that you put conditions on it that I can't fulfil."

A muscle ticked in his jaw.

He was a man with many layers—pride, ambition and honor among them—but he'd never been insincere.

"Sam thought she was interested in him," he said, as if it had just occurred to him.

"I know." She thought for a moment. "Maybe you'd do him a favor by putting her on the next stage and leaving him to his work. I made it clear she wouldn't be spending another night at Shelby Station."

"You want it to be *me* that sends her packing?" Jesse asked.

She studied him. "I think you want her gone as much as I do. Am I wrong?"

"Maybe more."

"Then the pleasure is all yours." She turned to leave.

Jesse caught her arm and she stopped, but she didn't look at him.

"Amy, please." His voice was gruff with emotion. "Look at me."

She did. He looked awful, with dark circles under his eyes.

"I'm sorry, Amy. There's no other way to say it. Don't leave me feeling like this. Don't."

She was as responsible for what had happened as he. She'd shut him out. He needed his conscience purged, and she held one of the keys. Regardless of the fact that she held her affection in reserve, he was the man she loved. Part of the reason she'd locked herself away was how much it hurt to see him suffer.

"I accept your apology. I do."

"Something has to change," he told her. "We can't go on like this anymore."

He was right. He was always right. She nodded, but she had to look away from his probing blue eyes.

Jesse released her arm. "We'll talk after supper tonight."

Change was in the wind. Part of her fought the fact with every self-protective instinct. But another part was like a captured butterfly anticipating freedom. Heart thudding, she nodded again.

"Yes."

Sam was coming from the stables when the morning stage stopped for water. The guests enjoyed a breakfast while he and Jesse changed horses and Jesse checked the wheels and axles.

As the passengers filed back to the coach, Jesse strode into the boardinghouse and returned with two black bags, which Sam helped him strap to the boot atop the trunks.

Eden appeared in the doorway, wearing a deep blue cape around her shoulders and a matching hat that hid her hair and shaded her eyes. She paused on her way to the coach and approached Sam with sashaying steps and no crutch in sight. He wasn't about to reveal his wounded pride for her devious pleasure, so he simply looked at her, willing himself not to react to her beauty.

"It's been a pleasure, Sam," she purred, throatily emphasizing the word *pleasure* and letting her gaze caress his lips.

Her sweet-as-honey voice and ladylike appearance had soured for him now that he knew her true character. "Goodbye, Miss Sullivan."

Disappointment flickered across her expression and she continued on to the coach. When she looked about for a hand up, both men stepped back. Sam stuffed his hands in his pockets and Jesse found particular interest in a spec on his sleeve.

One of the male travelers reached out to assist her.

Sam turned and strode into the barn, the sound of the coach pulling away behind him.

Thoughts of Eden's deceit nagged him all afternoon. When the hands washed and trudged to the house for dinner, Sam called to Hermie that he was heading home.

He saddled his horse and rode out. The sky was a blustery gray and the temperature had dropped by the time he had his horse put up and entered the house.

His attention grazed the cloth he'd draped over the table last Sunday. He'd never done that the whole time he'd lived here alone, until Eden started coming to the cabin with him. He took the checked fabric off and tossed it over the back of a chair before starting a fire in the stove.

After making coffee, he heated a skillet and fried potatoes and a pile of eggs. Taking a seat at the table, he ate half of the food he'd prepared, then pushed it away.

In the bedroom, he opened the top bureau drawer and took out a lacy handkerchief and a small oval tintype, the likeness of his late wife. Amy looked so much like her, he thought, rubbing his thumb over the image in a caress.

Would you be ashamed of me, Vanessa? Or would you understand a man needed someone from time to time? If Eden had stayed and wanted to make a life with him, what they'd done would have seemed right. But the fact that she'd been dallying with him for her amusement while fancying Jesse sullied everything.

He was a damn old fool.

At least he hadn't hurt anybody.

His thoughts turned to Jesse and Amy. They'd been through so much already. Seemed it never rained but it poured woe on those two. He couldn't forget Amy's face when she'd told him what she'd seen. Nor could he stop thinking about Jesse looking so dad-blamed guilty.

Humiliation chapped his hide. He should've known better. He should've used some common sense. He should've kept his pecker on the shelf.

Damn old fool.

"Where's my father?" Amy asked the men seated around the table at noon.

"Said he was goin' home," Hermie replied.

"Was he sick?"

"Looked fine."

Amy set the last plate on. She glanced at Jesse and he gave her a shrug that said he didn't know anything about Sam's leaving. "If he's not back for supper, somebody needs to go check on him."

"I'll go," Hermie said.

Cay lifted his fork to gesture and said, "I'll come with ya."

As it was, they didn't need to go. Sam showed up to work that afternoon and later came to the kitchen for supper.

He didn't seem his usual self to Amy. He didn't join in the bantering, and more than once one of the hands cast him a quizzical glance. But how did she know what was normal anymore?

After making four apple pies disappear, the men made their way out, and Sam and Jesse accompanied them.

Amy had cleared the remains of the meal and Mrs. Barnes was washing dishes when Jesse returned with a package wrapped in brown paper. He untied the string. "These came the other day."

He revealed several books, two slates and chalk.

Amy dried her hands and picked up the top book, a reading primer, and glanced through the pages and lessons.

"Days are gettin' shorter," Jesse said. "I think we should start now."

She met his eyes and nodded.

Jesse glanced at Mrs. Barnes's back, then motioned for Amy to follow him into the other room. Hunkering before the hearth, he used the poker to stir the fire and added another log.

Slowly, as though thinking over his next words, he stood to face her. "There are chores, of course, but… it's probably best if I spend more time here of an evenin'."

She mulled over his statement. He wanted to spend more time with Cay? Or with her?

"I won't be stayin' at the boardinghouse anymore. I'll be sleepin' in our bed."

She wanted him to know she was in agreement with anything he planned. "I never sent you away."

"No, but I made a bad decision. I'm fixin' it now. I need to be *here*." He pointed to the floor where he stood.

"Okay, Jesse." There was something she wasn't picking up on. Something in his voice and the way he stressed the importance of being in the house. Eden was gone. That temptation was removed.

The point he stressed was just beyond her grasp. If he wanted to talk about things better left alone, she didn't know how she'd deal with it. But she would find a way. She would.

He moved forward and pulled her to him then, held her against his chest and kissed the top of her head. His entire body felt tense, as though he was prepared for a bullet to come at him. Was she the bullet?

It had been a long, long time since Amy had felt safe. Since there'd been any peace or contentment in her soul. She wanted those things, she did. If Jesse could just move on like she had, maybe they could find a new beginning.

Like a barely detectable hairline crack on an egg shell, an infinitesimal fissure marred the protective armor of her heart, and Amy felt exposed and vulnerable. If any feeling could penetrate her defensive shield, it was love for this man.

He had no reason to or intention of hurting her. She was safe with him. She knew that as well as she knew she stood here right this minute. What terrified her was letting that crack open enough to make her susceptible to other things—feelings she couldn't allow. Her heart took control at that moment, and she wrapped her arms around Jesse's waist and clung to him, pressing her cheek against the front of his soft chambray shirt and squeezing her eyes closed.

"I'm not proud of what I've become." His voice was low, the tone full of regret.

"Because of Eden?"

"She's just a fly on the shit pile I made out of things."

Amy withdrew and leaned back to see his face. "I know you didn't have any feelings for her."

"Hell, no."

"It still…well, it was a shock seeing the two of you. My head jumped to conclusions."

"And you know I love you, Amy. I always have."

A knot formed in her throat. She nodded. "I do know."

From the kitchen Mrs. Barnes called, "I'm leaving. See you in the morning!"

"Good night!" Jesse and Amy called together.

He took a step back. "I'll go round up Cay."

She nodded, removed her apron and stole a few minutes to go upstairs to wash her face and straighten her hair. When she returned, uncle and nephew sat on the rug before the fireplace.

"We made you tea." Jesse pointed to the cup and saucer sitting by her chair.

"How thoughtful! Thank you." She looked at Cay. "Are you ready?"

He shrugged.

"Did you like school in Indiana?"

"Not much."

"Do you like working with your uncle Jesse?"

His blue gaze skittered to Jesse and then down at the floor. "It's fine."

"He's a natural with the horses," Jesse told her. "You can see their attention when he talks to 'em and grooms 'em. He has a real way about him."

Cay might like the horses, but he still hadn't warmed to Amy. She made up her mind that she was going to do her best to make him feel a welcome part of their family. "This is going to be good for me and Jesse, too," she told him. "Brushing up on our reading and numbers can't hurt. Maybe we can pick a book and take turns reading out loud each night. Would you like that?"

Again Cay glanced at Jesse.

Jesse raised a brow, showing the boy he was waiting for his answer.

"Whatever you want," Cay answered.

Amy and Jesse exchanged a glance. Cay wasn't giving them any hint of encouragement, but she guessed she shouldn't expect any. Ever since he'd been here, she'd kept busy with her chores and the guests, preoccupied as always. Why would he think she'd suddenly take an interest in him?

She vowed then to change things. Jesse's nephew had been through enough and shouldn't have to suffer because of their problems. "I want us to spend time together."

Jesse smiled, that crooked half smile that told her she'd said just the right thing.

Cay raised his gaze to hers, and in eyes much like her husband's she read mistrust and doubt.

Many things had to be learned. Numbers. Spelling. History. Trust.

Amy prayed she was up to the challenge.

Chapter Eight

The room was warm and cozy, a fire flickered in the grate. Cay was a bright young man and already read well, but he needed help with numbers. Amy was pleased with the effort he made and with how well he remembered their teaching.

As the evening stretched out, Amy made hot cocoa. Jesse had taken to pacing the room like a trapped cougar. He used the poker to stab at the fire when it didn't need tending, then stood over Amy where she sat on the floor beside Cay. She looked up and tried to interpret his mood.

He had run his hands through his hair so many times, it stood up in wild disarray. He hadn't shaved that day, and the shadow of his beard lent him a dispirited appearance.

After another half hour of him pacing and torturing the burning logs, she closed the book she and Cay had been looking at. "Cay's been yawning. Jesse, why don't you light the lamp in his room while I put these things away?"

She picked up the books and slates and carried their mugs to the kitchen.

Minutes later, Jesse's boots sounded on the stairs. She turned to find him standing on the other side of the kitchen.

"Would you like coffee or anything?"

He shook his head.

She set a kettle on the table. "Would you mind bringing me water? I'm going to soak beans for tomorrow."

Without bothering to grab his jacket, he picked up the pan and headed out the back door. When he returned he set the full pan on the back of the stove, then took a seat at the table.

Amy went to the pantry for beans and just as she returned, the back door banged shut. "Jesse?"

After pouring the beans into the kettle and adding salt, she placed the lid on top, then took a wrap from a hook. His erratic behavior this evening had been disturbing, and she hadn't figured out what was bothering him. Grabbing the lantern from the table, she followed.

Moonlight illuminated the front of the boardinghouse. Stepping off the back porch onto the board walkway, she glimpsed Jesse carrying something to the barn, Biscuit running at his heels. The door opened, then closed man and dog inside. If Jesse'd gone to do last-minute chores, she would feel silly for following him, but something unexplainable drew her.

She reached the barn and let herself inside. The scents of animals and hay were familiar, but the sound she heard wasn't. Jesse cursing.

Amy hurried her steps.

He was in the tack room, just rising after having bent to pick up a crate. She'd seen a similar crate before, the night he'd cut his hand and sent her to fetch whiskey.

"What are you doing?"

He carried his burden past her. "I have something to take care of."

Biscuit tagged along, tail wagging.

Again she followed Jesse, this time out the back and across the dark yard to a stand of young maple trees on the slope that led down to the creek.

There was already one crate on the ground, and he placed the second one beside it.

He plucked out a bottle, and she thought he was reading the label, but in the darkness he couldn't possibly see the lettering. With a burst of energy, he flung the bottle toward the base of a tree. Amy jumped at the sound of shattering glass. Whining, Biscuit ran behind her skirts.

Another bottle followed the first, and another.

After half a dozen, the pungent smell of strong whiskey assaulted her nostrils. There were eight in the top crate and twelve in the bottom. With deliberate, angry motions Jesse continued until each bottle lay in shards, its contents seeping into the black earth.

He didn't look at her, but stood with his feet planted wide and dropped his head back.

Biscuit came out from behind her skirts, trotted to the spot beneath the tree and sniffed. Immediately, the animal backed away and shook its head, giving a canine snort.

"I had to do that."

Jesse seemed out of breath, but relieved, as though he'd run a race and won.

"I couldn't have it out there."

Amy drew her shawl more tightly around her. Suddenly Jesse's behavior became clear, and she chided herself for her oblivious lack of understanding. She hadn't understood the magnitude of his penchant for whiskey until that moment. All along she'd seen it as a choice he made to avoid her. Now the problem was bigger than that. Maybe it had started out as a choice, but with practice his drinking had gone past simple avoidance to something he needed to get through the nights.

He'd said so many things that morning when her mind had been focused elsewhere. He'd spoken of the shame he felt when he faced her. *It's killing me for you to see what I've become.*

She understood now.

Without hesitation she walked forward and wrapped her arms around him. His body was tense, and when he placed his hands on her waist, they were trembling.

"It's going to be all right, Jesse," she promised him. "Whatever it takes, it's going to be all right."

"I don't know if I'm strong enough," he said against her hair.

"You are. I know you are." And with that, she took his arm and led him back to the house. She made him coffee and he drank half a cup before they went upstairs.

In their room he stood at the foot of the bed, not looking at anything, not making an attempt to change out of his clothing. His body had begun to shake.

With confident movements, Amy unbuttoned his shirt and pulled it off, revealing his union suit. "Sit on the edge of the bed."

He did so and she worked off his boots. Then she had him stand so she could unbutton and tug off his underclothes and trousers. When he was naked, she urged him into the bed and drew the covers around him. Still fully dressed, she climbed on top of the quilt beside him to hold him close.

He drifted to sleep, but woke after half an hour. Perspiration dotted his forehead. She got up, wrung out a cloth in the basin and bathed his face and chest.

"That feels so good."

She wiped his lips tenderly.

"I'm gonna be sick."

Amy dashed around the end of the bed, grabbed the chamber pot and made it back just as Jesse lost the contents of his stomach.

"Damn, I'm sorry," he told her.

"It's all right." She wiped his face again. "Remember the time I was so sick and you sat beside me all night long?"

"That was different."

"I don't see how."

He rolled to his back and stared at the ceiling. His lips were frighteningly pale. "I'm afraid this is only going to get worse."

She set the chamber pot away and rinsed the cloth before returning. "Maybe so. But we'll handle it."

While he dozed, she stayed awake, washed the chamber pot and brought more water.

As she passed Cay's room he peered out. "What's wrong?"

"Jesse isn't feeling well. It's okay, you go back to sleep."

A stricken look flattened the boy's features. He stepped out into the hall, wearing a baggy union suit. "Is he gonna die?"

"No," she assured him. "He's not going to die."

"How can you be sure?"

Amy studied his fearful expression. "You can come see for yourself."

Carrying the pail of water, she led the way into their bedroom. Jesse was curled on his side, holding his belly. A groan escaped him.

"What's wrong with him?" Cay asked. "Should we get a doctor?"

She rinsed a fresh rag and perched on the side of the

bed to wipe Jesse's forehead. "I don't know that a doctor would help. Jesse's not—not sick exactly."

Cay didn't believe her. He stared at his uncle with fear on his young face. He'd lost so many people already. Amy recognized his distress and sympathized with his feelings.

"Cay," she began. Jesse was beyond listening to her or caring what she was saying at this point, so she plunged ahead. "Jesse's been drinking for months and months."

Recognition flashed across the boy's face. He'd seen it.

"Whiskey," he said.

She nodded. "He doesn't want to get drunk anymore. But it's not an easy thing to stop. His body is crying out for the liquor."

Beside her, Jesse retched. Cay was the first to grab the pan and hold it for his uncle. Amy marveled over his genuine concern which erased any distaste he may have felt. Cay waited patiently until Jesse rolled back with a groan and closed his eyes.

The night stretched endlessly. Cay and Amy took turns napping on the other side of the bed while the other one watched over Jesse. They continuously bathed his face and chest with cool water.

As dawn broke, Jesse sat on the side of the bed and gripped his head in both hands. For Cay's sake, Amy got up out of the rocker, padded to the bureau and found Jesse a pair of drawers.

"Do you think you could eat anything?"

She assumed the palm he held up was a no.

"Maybe later we could try some tea and toast."

"Hopefully by then I'll be dead," he replied.

Her gaze shot directly to Cay, who was sitting up on the other side of the bed. Apparently Jesse's words hadn't upset him, because he said, "You're gonna be fine, Uncle Jesse."

Jesse turned to blearily peer at Cay sitting beside him. Jesse had two or three days' growth of beard, and his eyes were red. "This isn't fittin' for the boy to see."

"Cay has been here all night," Amy told him. "He's concerned about you, and I appreciate his help."

"I'm gonna use the outhouse. And maybe I'll try the tea. But that's all."

Amy only had to look at Cay, and he got up to follow his uncle.

By mid-morning Jesse was back in bed. Cay assured Amy he could watch over him and that he'd call her if he needed help. She put on breakfast with the other women, did the cleanup and prepared for dinner before making her way outside to find her father.

Sam was measuring molasses into buckets of grain when she found him at the stables. He looked up.

"You look tired. Jesse okay?"

"He's feeling poorly," she admitted. "Last night he broke all his bottles of whiskey so he wouldn't be tempted."

"Takes a strong man to get over a cravin' like his." Sam straightened and studied her. "He's a strong man."

She nodded. "I know he is. He most likely won't be up to his work for the time being. I don't know…" Amy shrugged. "How long will he feel this bad?"

Sam shook his head. "Could be quick, could be slow. I'd guess at least a couple of days of bein' sick. After that, every day will be tough until he has that thirst whipped."

They were both absorbed in their own thoughts for a few moments. Then Sam surprised her with his tone of voice when he said, "There's somethin' I need to tell you."

"What is it?"

He glanced behind her as though making sure no one would overhear. "I made a fool of myself."

She jumped to a conclusion. "Yelling at Jesse?"

He shook his head. "No. He had that comin'."

"What then?"

"There's more behind it." He scratched his jaw with his thumb. "I'm an old fool. I, uh, got myself tangled up with Eden."

"I suspected you had feelings for her. I'm sorry you were disappointed."

"I was sorely disappointed. But, Amy, I'm tryin' to tell you that I know Jesse wasn't sniffin' around her. She had an appetite for a man, and she wasn't picky about where she satisfied it."

Amy gave her father a curious look. "What exactly are you saying?"

"I'm just tellin' you that Eden went after what she wanted. I was duped into thinkin' I was the only one she wanted. I'm convinced she tried to take advantage of Jesse when he'd been drinkin'."

"I believe that, too," she replied.

"Just don't turn that occurrence into something it wasn't."

"He blames himself enough." She glanced away. "He said if he hadn't been out there and if he hadn't been drinking, it wouldn't have happened."

"Well, those are the facts, but you both had a hand in him bein' out there."

"I know, Daddy."

He stepped forward and reached to tip up her chin so he could look into her eyes. "So you two won't be lettin' Eden be another thing that comes between you?"

"No."

He kissed her forehead and released her. "I could sit with him a while so you can sleep."

She shook her head. "I'll sleep whenever he does tonight. Cay is with him now. Thanks for the talk."

"Thanks for listenin'."

On the way back to the house her steps were slow. She could easily fall asleep if she stayed in one place for longer than a minute, but she climbed the stairs determinedly.

Cay sat in the rocker beside Jesse's bed, his chin resting on his chest. She stood beside him for a moment, her hand involuntarily reaching to touch his hair, but she stopped herself and brought it back to her side. She couldn't help thinking about his situation. He'd lost the only person who'd ever cared for him and come to live with strangers. If she'd been uncomfortable with his arrival, she couldn't imagine how awkward he felt.

And here he was, taking care of Jesse and being an incredible help to her. Strange how things turned out.

Amy checked on Jesse, kneeling beside the bed to silently pray for him, then left them both to sleep.

The remainder of the day passed much the same. The hands were subdued at supper. She couldn't imagine what they were thinking. They'd overheard part of the quarrel between her father and Jesse, and Jesse's bottle-smashing rant had probably attracted attention the night before.

Amy had saved broth from the beef Mrs. Barnes had prepared. After adding barley and a few tiny pieces of vegetables, she carried up a bowl.

Jesse refused her help and ate the runny soup with his hand shaking. Afterward Amy waited anxiously, but the meal stayed down and he slept.

The following day he ate more, and his balance was steadier. His hands didn't tremble and he didn't spill his tea. Cay watched him finish his meal that night and smiled broadly.

"You're gettin' better, Uncle Jesse."

"I think I am. Maybe you won't have to dig a hole for my sorry bones after all."

Cay's smile dimmed.

Jesse reached out and hooked the boy around the neck, drew him closer and ruffled his hair. Cay grinned. When he sat back, he and Jesse studied each other.

"Thanks," Jesse said.

Cay shrugged as if the long, exhausting days hadn't been of significance.

"I think we can both use a bath," Jesse added. "Go grab clean clothes. You can help me heat water in the bathhouse."

Cay hurried to obey.

Amy sat in the rocker and watched Jesse gather clothing. His body was more sinewy than it should have been, and whiskers darkened his jaw. She would have to see that he ate well in the following weeks.

"Shall I come with you?" she asked.

"And embarrass the boy? I'll do fine."

She said nothing.

"There's no whiskey in the barn, if you're worried I'll slip out there."

"I wasn't."

He stood with his clothing in his bare arms, his hair tousled and his expression weary. "I wish I wasn't."

"Remember what I told you. You are strong enough to lick this, and whatever it takes, we'll get through it. Nothing worth doing ever comes easy, Jesse. Shelby Station is proof of that. But you did it."

He studied her. "*We* did it." He nodded then and left the room.

Amy made her way to the kitchen, where Rachel was helping Mrs. Barnes with the last of the supper dishes.

"You've been a blessing ever since you came," she told Rachel.

The young woman hung towels on a line near the fireplace, then turned and smiled. "We saw Mr. Shelby passin' through. Is he feeling better?"

"I believe he is."

Mrs. Barnes smiled, and Rachel came to give Amy a hug. She was one of the few people who didn't know Amy's history and hadn't been conditioned to keep her distance.

Amy allowed the brief embrace, then busied herself with preparations for the next morning. "You head on home, Mrs. Barnes. You've stayed past your usual time nearly every night this week. I'll handle the rest."

"You get yourself some sleep," the woman replied. "You're lookin' mighty peaked yourself."

"I will."

By the time Jesse and Cay returned, the women were gone and Amy had finished her chores. Jesse and his nephew smelled like soap and fresh air. Jesse had shaved and his skin was pink.

"We filled a tub for you. We'll get a start on lessons while you have a turn. Take your time. There's a hot kettle on the stove if your water needs heating again."

The idea of a peaceful bath sounded marvelous, and Amy hurried to gather clothes and make her way to the bathhouse.

The interior of the building was warm and humid, and the isinglass window on the stove washed the room with a golden glow. She emptied the kettle into the already full tub, undressed and slid into the hot water. It felt so good, her skin broke out in gooseflesh. She inched down and rested her head against the iron tub, relishing the treat of taking time to soak and relax. More than just the hot water, the fact that Jesse and Cay had thought to prepare her a bath eased tension from her mind and body.

It wasn't that she didn't have opportunities to take more time for herself, she thought dimly. Her father and Jesse had always worked to make things easier for her. The fact was, she never allowed herself the risk of having too much time without her mind occupied. Reflection would be more than she could handle.

Tonight, though, exhaustion had settled into her bones; she felt as though she'd run a race and won. It had been Jesse's victory, however. He was the one who had suffered and endured. She had no illusion that this would be the end of the problem. The possibility of his going back to his old ways would always hang over them. She roused herself to wash and rinse her hair, then lathered with the sweet-smelling soap Mrs. Barnes supplied.

Too weary to concern herself with emptying the tub, she left the water for the girls to dump the following day and returned to the house.

Minutes later, sitting on the ottoman before the fire, she untangled her hair with her comb and fluffed it out to dry.

"Cay and I chose a book," Jesse told her. "Tonight I'll read."

While turned away, she hadn't noticed Cay leaving the room, but now he returned with mugs of tea. Amy accepted hers with a surprised smile.

"Jesse tole me a good man takes care of the women in his life." His voice was unusually deep, as though he was trying to sound more mature.

She'd assumed that Cay resented her, but perhaps he just needed a little advice and a good example.

She glanced at Jesse where he sat in the rocker. "Listen to him and you'll learn to be a fine man."

Their eyes met. He *was* a fine man. Nothing harmful in saying so. Or in telling Cay his admiration was well placed.

She sipped her tea. Cay sat on the rug and crossed his legs.

"Did you like school back in Indiana, Cay?" she asked.

"Not much."

"Why not?"

He shrugged. "The schoolmaster made us stand in the corner if we couldn't answer right. I thought that was dumb."

"Well, it wasn't very nice," she agreed. "Did you enjoy reading?"

"I like stories all right."

She smiled and Jesse opened the book and began to read.

Cay listened attentively, smiling from time to time. Once, he and Amy shared a smile.

Half an hour later, Jesse closed the book. "Time for you to get a good night's sleep in your own bed."

The boy got to his feet. "Night, then."

"Good night, Cay," Amy said. "Thank you for all your help."

Jesse stood. "I'm going to check the stables and the barn, make sure the luggage room is locked and that the lamps are all out."

That had always been his end-of-the-day routine. Events over the past months had disrupted their habits, but Jesse was returning to the house again. He would learn to get by without the whiskey.

She carried their mugs to the kitchen and went upstairs. Just removing her shoes and clothing seemed a chore that night. She was barely in her nightgown and under the covers before she'd drifted into slumber.

She was vaguely aware when Jesse climbed into bed behind her, smelling like shaving soap and the night air. It didn't seem out of the ordinary to her tired brain when he molded his long, warm body along the back of hers. His breath heated her neck.

"I love you, Amy." Barely a whisper.

I love you, Jesse. A fact of life.

Amy dreamed she had a baby. It wasn't a new dream; in fact, it was one she had often. Sometimes the baby was a girl, but usually it was an infant son she was responsible for. In this dream, she'd carried him with her while she hung clothes on the line, and placed him in a basket where she could see him. The piles of laundry seemed never ending. When she turned from hanging hundreds of changing cloths, the baby wasn't where she'd left him.

Panicked, Amy ran inside and frantically checked each room. No one was in the house, no one to ask for help in finding her baby. Outside she ran from building to building, searching, until finally she heard a thin cry. The sound came from the old soddy.

The door wouldn't open when she tried it. She beat on the wood, then ran to each dirty window, where caked-on soot prevented her from seeing in. Finally she found a cracked pane and broke it inward. Cobwebs brushed across her face as she climbed on a stack of aged lumber and entered the house through the tiny square window. She barely fit through, but the baby's insistent cry drew her.

It was so dark she couldn't see. She followed the sound to the old rope bed where a pile of covers hid the source.

Amy pulled away the quilt.

The cry echoed into nothingness, as though it had never been.

Wrapped in the quilt was a doll, a jagged crack across its porcelain face.

Amy jerked awake and sat up.

Chapter Nine

Beside her, Jesse rose on one elbow.

Her heart was beating so hard her chest hurt.

Jesse placed a hand on her shoulder and turned her to face him. "Amy?"

She lay down and he smoothed her hair back. She hadn't braided it, and his fingers caught in the tangled length. "I was dreaming."

He drew her against him and gently cradled her. "Want to tell me?"

She shook her head against his shoulder. His skin smelled so good. "Are you feeling okay, Jesse?"

"I was havin' a spec of trouble sleeping, but I'm fine."

With her eyes closed and his warmth surrounding her, the disturbing dream faded away, and she dozed.

She didn't think much time had passed when she grew conscious of Jesse's lips on her cheek. He held her close, and her hand rested on his bare hip.

Adjusting their bodies, Jesse shifted so he could open the front of her gown and trail kisses across her skin. When he couldn't reach past the opening, he nuzzled her breast through the fabric, dampened it with his tongue and teased her that way until she found the hem and pulled it up so she could feel his mouth on her skin.

Shivers skittered across her flesh, and she squirmed against him. She'd missed the feel of his skin against hers and the tingling in her breasts when he teased and caressed them. She almost felt as though this was another dream, a better one—a much, much better one—and she floated on a sea of sensation.

She reached to stroke his sides and his belly. His body was a familiar comfort, but her growing impatience for closeness was fresh and new. Together they eased her nightgown over her head and he tossed it away.

His kiss, when he covered her lips with his, was full of need, and she shared the same craving. It had been so long since there'd been no heartache between them, since all that mattered was the moment and the feelings they had for each other.

Jesse, all warmth and eagerness in her bed, was in fact better than a dream. She surprised herself by having no other thoughts in her head than these pleasurable sensations.

He nipped her ear and breathed the question, "Do you want me?"

She bracketed his face with her hands and kissed him eagerly. "Yes."

"Say you want me, that you're not feelin' sorry for me or taking care of me out of obligation."

"I want you, Jesse. I do."

He moved over her, and she trembled, feeling him pressing hot and hard. Grasping his shoulders, Amy moved her body to take him inside her, and he thrust deep. She forgot to breathe. The world closed in and around them until all she knew was the two of them at this moment...sighs of pleasure...sounds of urgency, the beating of their hearts and the intensifying slide and pull at the center of her being.

Jesse knew how to make a good thing last.

She appreciated the coiled strength of his muscles, his gentle domination and the way he simultaneously teased and fulfilled. He urged her with whispered encouragement and purposeful strokes. She stifled a cry against his neck and shuddered. Jesse's release followed immediately.

She wrapped her arms around him and didn't let him move. She needed to experience his splendid weight, revel in their closeness and hold the world at bay forever.

But she couldn't, of course, and eventually, he moved to her side. The urge to cry swept over her so suddenly she had to turn her face away and bite her knuckle.

Jesse urged her gently onto her side, facing away from him, and cradled her from behind. He stroked her hip until eventually his hand fell still. His rhythmic breath caressed her shoulder. Amy's world hadn't felt this right for a long time. With only this solitary night in her thoughts, she fell into blissful slumber.

Jesse ate at the table with the hands the next morning. No one questioned his absence during the previous days, and everyone seemed glad to have him in their midst.

He overheard Mrs. Barnes asking Amy, "Did you sleep well last night?"

Pink crept into Amy's cheeks and she kept her face averted while she turned flapjacks. "Oh, yes."

He studied her over his coffee, but she deliberately avoided looking at him. He wasn't under any delusion that everything had been fixed by one night's love-makin'. He still had a long way to go fightin' the demon that called to him at night. And most of the wall that had been constructed after Tim's death was still between them.

But he was hopeful now. And hope was more than he'd had for a long time.

The following weeks passed uneventfully until one afternoon a stage stopped and a tall man wearing a black suit and hat dusted himself off and sought out Jesse. "You the Mr. Shelby who runs this station?"

"I am."

"I'm looking for a woman who was on a train that derailed over a month ago. I tracked her to this place. Dark hair, not very tall. Is she still here?"

"Eden?" Jesse asked.

Sam sauntered up to stand beside him. "She's not here."

"She was going by the name of Eden?" the man asked.

Sam squinted. "Who're you?"

He extended a hand. "Name's Milton Price. I work for a detective agency in Philadelphia."

"A detective?" Jesse's brows rose. "What do you want with Eden?"

"Her real name's Lark Doyle. She was working with a con man by the name of George Gray. Sometimes he uses the name Frank Benjamin." He glanced from Jesse to Sam as if gauging their reactions to those names.

Both men shook their heads.

"The two of them had a con operating. Lark lured in unsuspecting men—gamblers, businessmen and the like—and then they made off with the unfortunate fellow's money and possessions. Seems a while back she stole more than her share from George and now she's on the run from him and the law."

Jesse turned to exchange a look with Sam. "Well, that sure explains her hangin' around here pretendin' she was hurt."

Sam looked stunned, but he nodded. "Who'd think to look here for her?"

"She wasn't in any hurry to go," Jesse thought out loud. "And she had money to pay her room and board."

"Stolen money," Milton Price added.

Jesse wasn't naive enough to believe everyone passing through on their way west was an upstanding citizen. That's why he wore his Colt at the ready and locked up the baggage at night. But learning someone who'd been under your roof, at your table—*in your room*—was a criminal was hard to swallow.

"Come on up to the house. You can have a meal and we'll compare what we know to help you catch her."

Mrs. Barnes had already served the other passengers, and they were just leaving to stretch their legs. Amy was carrying a ham from the pantry.

"Amy, this is Milton Price, a detective from Philadelphia."

After the introductions, Price described the con that Eden—Lark Doyle—and George Gray had been operating. He described George as fair-haired and having a distinctive scar above his eyebrow. None of them had seen a man like that.

Lark was without a doubt Eden, right down to Price's description of the pout and the wrinkling of her nose when she spoke.

Jesse told Price which stage she had been on when she departed and who the driver had been. Sam described her trunk and other baggage.

"Do you remember any other passengers who were here at the same time?" Price asked.

"William Hunter," Amy replied. "He was on the same train. Also a man by the name of Barnett."

"And that Castlewhite fellow," Jesse recalled.

"The Castlewhite who owns the Denver hotel?" Milton asked.

"That's the one."

"I'd better make sure she didn't go endear herself to him."

Price paid for his meal and Jesse saw him to the stage, then returned to the kitchen.

Wearing a weary expression, Sam remained where he'd been seated. He rubbed his jaw. "I don't know the first thing about people. About human nature."

Amy covered her father's hand with her own. "You just expect people to be what they say they are. Nothing wrong with that."

"I felt like an old fool before knowin' this," Sam said, shaking his head. He stood and went for his hat. "But I'm a bigger dunderhead than I thought."

"Daddy, she's a beautiful woman. She showed an interest in you. You're not the fool. She is. For not recognizing that it's wrong to deceive decent folks."

Sam waved away her comment and lumbered out.

Amy turned her gaze on Jesse. "*Now* I'm really mad. I was mad before, but this—*oh!*" She hit the table with a fist and a stack of clean plates rattled.

"Because she hurt your father?"

"Yes, because she hurt my father. And I'm angry that she tried to cause trouble for us." She flattened both hands on the tabletop and studied him. "At least we weren't stupid enough to let her trickery come between us."

"You were the wise one there."

She got up from her seat. "I hope Mr. Price finds that woman before she hurts anyone else."

As criminals went, a conniving female wasn't the worst. But obviously in Amy's book, anyone who hurt someone she loved deserved justice.

Jesse stood and moved to take her in his arms. Without resisting, she lay her head against his chest and leaned into him. "I love you, Amy."

She didn't respond, but neither did she pull away. It was enough for now. He didn't have his wife back the way she'd once been, but they'd come a long way.

A sound alerted them to someone in the room, and they drew apart.

Rachel offered a knowing smile and set a basket of apples on the table. "Don't mind me."

Jesse squeezed Amy's hand, gathered his hat and coat and returned to his work.

That Sunday Sam didn't attend church with them. Afterward Cay and Amy sat on either side of Jesse on the ride home. Jesse let Cay take the reins.

"The near-side rein lies on your index finger—" He showed him. "The off-side rein goes between your middle and ring fingers, like this. Keep equal tension on both. To turn the horse, ease him careful-like by movin' your wrist one way or the other. With some horses you need to use both hands."

Amy had taken to watching how Cay modeled his actions after his uncle, and right now he sat up straight, his hat lowered over his eyes in the same fashion. She guessed Cay had never had a man around to show him things before. He was as attentive to Jesse's everyday lessons as he was to their nightly spelling and ciphering.

When they arrived home Sam had a noon meal prepared, delighting Amy. The hands joined them and they ate together. Mrs. Barnes was off most Sundays, her day to visit her son, and Rachel had prepared a meal for Jack at the soddy, so Jesse stayed to help Amy clean up.

"Why don't you come out and watch Cay?" he suggested as they finished. "We're going to work a horse this afternoon."

Amy pulled on a scarf and jacket and accompanied Jesse to the stables. Cay joined them and, from a stall, Jesse brought a handsome Appaloosa with a leopard-patterned face and forelegs and black on white hips.

"We'll work on bridling today. Come over here on his left."

"Amy," Jesse asked, his voice always calm around the animals, "what must you protect when bridling?"

Jesse had been her teacher, too. "His teeth and ears need special care, but I'm thinking you mean your own head."

He grinned at her. "Right. You want to stand in close, Cay, so he can't butt you with his head. Saw stars a few times myself, before I got the hang of it."

He continued the lesson, warning Cay not to bang the

animal's teeth, which would make him head-shy and hard to bridle. He showed Cay how to get the horse to open his mouth, and how to make sure the bit wasn't giving the animal pain.

Jesse placed his hand on the Appaloosa's face to keep its nose down while he removed the bridle and handed it to Cay. "Now you do it."

"By myself?"

"Yep." Jesse backed away to stand near Amy, where she'd seated herself on a wooden keg.

Cay and the horse eyeballed each other for a full minute. Jesse and Amy exchanged an amused glance. Finally, Cay spoke to the horse and moved in close. He had trouble reaching, so Jesse found him a crate.

Following all the instructions Jesse had given, and with little hesitation, Cay competently bridled the horse. He kept glancing at Jesse, as though gauging his reaction.

"I swear that horse opened his mouth wider than he does for me. 'Bout time you got here to help out."

Cay's proud sheepish grin touched a place within Amy that she'd unknowingly left unguarded. His need for approval was so obvious that even she couldn't hide from it.

Jesse ruffled Cay's hair, and Amy's throat closed with bottled-up emotion. Their son should have been the one Jesse lavished praise upon. Their son should be learning from his father, getting spoiled by the hands and doted on by his grandfather.

Her boy.

No, she wasn't going to do this. She had moved on, and regret served no purpose. She stood, and her knees felt shaky.

"I think I'll go do some sewing."

She didn't miss the puzzled look Jesse cast her or the way Cay's smile dimmed.

Determinedly, she hurried to the house, where she got out the two dresses she'd been working on for the past couple of months and settled in front of the fireplace for an uninterrupted afternoon.

She made progress on the garments and finished the bodice and sleeves for both, then decided to try them on in case she'd made an error. She had used one of her older dresses as a pattern, but she didn't want to finish and not have her work fit properly.

Upstairs, she removed her shirtwaist and tried on the upper portions of the dresses, being careful of the basting in the darts. Turned out it was a good thing she'd been cautious, because somewhere during the process she'd made a mistake and she had to move the darts and the seams nearly an inch.

She had been eating better, she realized, turning to look at her reflection with new eyes. Her skin had more color, and her face was less drawn. Until today in the stables, she'd been feeling more like her old self than she had for a long time.

She vowed not to lose any ground she'd gained and allow her mixed feelings about Cay to erode her progress. The boy needed a home and a family. He was bright and respectful and so eager to please and to belong that it hurt to watch his face when he believed he was unobserved.

Since it was Sunday evening, Jesse set up the checker board, and he and Cay played while Amy rocked and finished one of the dresses. Occasionally Jesse stood and paced the room, each time returning to the game. Sam stopped by long enough for applesauce cake and coffee, and after he left, Cay said good-night and climbed the stairs.

"You want to take on the champ?" Jesse asked. He'd been pacing the room for a few minutes.

She put away her sewing and sat across from him at the table he'd made to hold the board. While they played, Jesse kept touching Amy's hand and sliding his leg against hers.

"Is this meant to distract me?" she asked with a smile.

"Only fair. You're distractin' me."

"I wasn't doing anything except sitting here."

"That's all it takes."

She couldn't help laughing.

"I need the distraction, you know."

"I know. I'm proud of you, Jesse."

Shrugging off her comment, he moved a checker. He had grown more serious. "I think Sam's takin' this thing with Eden—or Lark—whoever she is pretty hard."

Amy nodded. "He's being too severe with himself."

"Amy, I think he was poking her."

She shot him a look of surprise. "Jesse!"

He gestured with both hands in the air. "I do. He as much as told me so. He didn't say it like that, but now that I think it over, that's what he meant."

His words reminded her of her father's talk with her. "He said something about her…having an appetite for men." Amy's eyes widened and she brought her hand to her cheek. "*That's* what he was telling me!"

Jesse leaned in to say in a hushed tone, "Those Sunday afternoons they went for rides…. He was sure in a good mood on Mondays."

"No wonder he's so hurt. For a man like him that's a *promise*."

Jesse's gaze took in her expression. "I think the promises should come first. 'Cleave unto each other' and all that."

"He was lonely and she baited him. I hope she gets what's coming to her," she said. She stood abruptly and waved a hand in the air as though there was a bad smell. "Enough. I can't think about her with my father."

Jesse raised a brow and winked. "She went back for more—he must be a real stud."

"Jesse Shelby!" She picked up a fistful of checkers and threw them at him just as he stood up.

He laughed and caught her around the waist.

She spun from him and he chased her into the kitchen.

"I'll bet she put that smile on his face by—"

Amy turned back and clapped her hand over his mouth. "Not one more word, do you hear me? Not one!"

He drew her up against him and ran his hands down her back to cup her bottom.

She tried to keep her expression fierce, but her body turned to liquid heat at the suggestions in his eloquent eyes and hands. Through layers of fabric, he caressed her backside. Slowly Amy took her hand from his mouth. "If I move my hand, will you stop talking?"

"Only if I can start kissin'."

She laughed and met his lips with hers.

A week later, a tall slender man with slicked-down black hair arrived with trunks and cases and asked permission to set up a tent to the north, across the road from where the stages arrived and left.

"What's your business, Mr. Quenton?" Jesse asked, looking over the assortment of luggage.

"I'm a photographer, Mr. Shelby. I'm chronicling the Western advancement. There's much about this country that those back East still don't understand. The untamed magnificence." He gestured to the vast prairie. "The vision and struggles of men such as yourself. I want to bring it back to them."

"Sounds ambitious."

"As ambitious as embarking on a new life? As ambitious as paving the way for thousands of others? All of us have something to share. And something to leave for the future. My mark on the future will be photographs."

Jesse appreciated the man's passion. "I don't have a problem with you stayin' a while. You'll be expected to pay for your stay and your food, so you might as well enjoy a bed in the boardin' house."

"Thank you, Mr. Shelby, but I must keep a close eye on my equipment. I'll sleep in my tent and gladly pay for lodging."

"Suit yourself."

In the days that followed, Mr. Quenton joined them for meals and shared tales of his trips across the country.

A light snow was falling when Rachel entered the kitchen one afternoon the following week. She brushed flakes from the shoulders of her coat and hung it on a hook. "Do you think Mr. Quenton will show us his photographs soon?"

"I'd imagine so. He does seem to be everywhere, doesn't he?"

Rachel agreed with a smile. Over the past month, she had blossomed. Even the loose shirts and flowing skirts she wore couldn't disguise her burgeoning belly. Between Amy and Leda Bently, they had seen that Rachel had proper clothing, not only for daily chores but for church. In fact Amy had put aside her own new dresses until a few of Rachel's were altered.

Weeks ago, Amy had brought a plump cushion to the

kitchen and insisted that Rachel perform only chores she could do sitting down. Her baby would be born in a few short weeks.

Now Amy's throat tightened as she watched the cheerful young woman seat herself and reach for the bag of potatoes.

Rachel paused in her peeling to place a hand on her belly and frown.

"You all right?" Amy asked.

"I'm fine. This baby never stops moving. Even at night he's rolling around in there."

Amy almost told her it would only get worse, but she kept silent.

"Sometimes I can't believe our good fortune. Jack getting a job here, and you and Mr. Shelby giving us the soddy to use."

Her joyful optimism worked to dredge up feelings in Amy, but she fought them back. She was pleased for the young couple to have a good start for their marriage and their family. Jealousy was wrong and sorrow was a waste of time.

"Jack says after the baby comes he's going to teach me to ride."

"It's a good thing to know. I've noticed Jack is a good rider, and Jesse mentioned he's accomplished with the animals."

"He was a groomsman back in England." Rachel glanced around. "Where's Mrs. Barnes?"

Amy carried a cutting board to the table and placed

a stack of carrots beside it. "Stacking preserves in the root cellar."

Rachel peeled a potato and let the skin fall onto the sack protecting her white apron. "Jack heard from one of the hands that you'd had a child, Amy."

Amy's hand froze on the knife she held. The subject was completely unexpected. Completely unwelcome. And everyone knew that. Except Rachel. She picked up a carrot and scraped the sides. "I never talk about that."

"I'm sorry."

Silence stretched between them. They'd worked companionably for weeks. Rachel was a sweet young woman who wouldn't deliberately hurt anyone, and Amy felt the weight of guilt for creating a wedge between them. She'd already done it to everyone else. She looked up.

Rachel's gaze lifted and met hers. Amy saw only compassion in the other woman's eyes.

"No, I'm sorry, Rachel. It's a flaw of mine. You didn't know."

"It's okay. It's just that, well, sometimes I'd like another woman to talk to about things. I wasn't prying, really I wasn't."

"I know that."

They both resumed their peeling.

Amy had always had her mother to talk to and answer questions. Rachel was far from home with a new husband and a new life growing inside her. "Is something in particular troubling you?"

Rachel's cheeks flushed a becoming pink. She nodded. "It's not easy to talk about."

"You don't have to."

"But I want to ask."

Amy gave a little nod to encourage her. "Go ahead."

"Is it all right for Jack and me to, well…you know, be *close* so near to my time?"

Amy understood Rachel's concern and her embarrassment. She was a newly married young woman, in love with her husband, but her changing body seemed like a stranger's. She smiled. "You aren't the first woman who ever wondered that. You're afraid to hurt your baby, but you love your husband."

Eyes wide at Amy's understanding, Rachel nodded.

"I had to ask my mother, can you believe that?"

Rachel shook her head.

"She told me that she was sure Jesse was a very tender and considerate partner, and that as long as I was comfortable, there was no problem. There are many ways to make love, and being creative can be a good thing."

Rachel's eyes brightened. "Was she right?"

"She was very right."

Rachel smiled. "Thanks, Amy."

Amy nodded and sliced carrots.

"One more thing…"

Amy looked up again.

"It's embarrassing."

"More embarrassing than *that?*"

"Uh-huh. It's about gas."

Amy burst into laughter.

In the days that followed, Rachel seemed to glow even more, if that was possible. She took well to pregnancy, and from her shy smiles, Amy guessed she had shared Amy's advice with Jack.

Amy wiped her hands on a towel. "I thought I'd make cobbler for supper. What's your preference?"

"I love berries. Is that out of the question?"

"I have several jars of gooseberry. I could make an apple and a gooseberry." The root cellar was around back, so she put on her coat and took a bushel basket to carry supplies.

Returning to the kitchen, she stepped inside and froze.

A man she'd never seen before stood behind Rachel, holding a knife at her throat.

Chapter Ten

Amy dropped the basket, jars breaking at her feet. It took several seconds for her to comprehend what her eyes were seeing, and when she did, her heart lurched.

The stranger wore a dark coat and a hat that shaded his eyes. One of his hands covered Rachel's mouth, the other held the knife. Rachel stared back at Amy, her round eyes revealing fear.

"Who are you?" Amy took a halting step forward. "What are you doing?"

"Don't come any closer." He touched the blade to Rachel's neck, and behind his palm she let out an alarmed squeak. "Just stand right where you are."

Amy stopped, her heart thudding against her ribs. She couldn't grasp his intent. "What do you want? Let her go."

"I want a little information. Nobody's going anywhere until I get it."

"What do you want to know?"

"I want to know about a fetching woman with dark hair who was through a while back."

Eden again. "Wh-what about her?"

"She shared her pleasures with one of the men here."

Insult and anger stirred Amy's insides. She held her tongue and tried to assure Rachel with a steady comforting gaze. Rachel was gripping the man's forearms through the sleeves of his coat as though she could keep the knife from her neck.

"You know who that was?"

"I do."

"What's his name?"

"If you know about it, why don't you know his name?"

He tightened his hold on the already terrified young woman. Her eyes begged Amy for help.

"I asked his name."

Amy studied Rachel only a moment before improvising, "Sam Baker."

"You know where he lives?"

She nodded.

"Is he there right now?"

She shook her head.

"Listen carefully while I tell you what you're going to do. You're going to go out to the barn and get a wagon. If anyone asks, you tell 'em you're going for supplies. You bring that wagon right up to the house here. If you're not back with it in twenty minutes, she's going to bleed all over the floor."

"Let her go. She doesn't need to be involved. You can see she's expecting a baby."

"And let her alert the others? I'm not a fool."

"We'll leave her here and tie her up. I swear I'll get the wagon and go with you. Just leave her. Please."

For the first time Amy wondered what had become of Mrs. Barnes. She'd been emptying ashes the last time Amy saw her. And Cay's dog—any other time the animal was directly underfoot, but now, when he could have been useful in alerting them of danger, he was probably off chasing rabbits. She refused to think the worst. Even Mr. Quenton was nowhere to be seen. Dimly, she recalled his mentioning he'd be photographing horses in the pastures that day.

It could be noon before anyone came to the kitchen. Before anyone noticed something wrong…

"All right—" he said finally.

If he was thinking, he'd know two women would be harder to take with him than one.

"Get something to tie her with. Be quick."

Amy opened a cupboard and took out a stack of dish towels. "These. They won't hurt her. Let me do it."

Rachel gripped against his front, the man stepped forward and pushed her onto a chair. He took his hand from her mouth, but kept the edge of the blade at her throat. "Fast."

Amy's fingers had never felt so awkward as she tied Rachel's ankles together.

"Tighter!"

She obeyed and moved to secure Rachel's wrists behind her back.

Tears streamed from Rachel's eyes. "Amy—" She choked on a ragged breath.

With one hand, the man jerked a towel from Amy's hand and stuffed the corner into Rachel's mouth. "Now wrap her head so she can't spit that out."

Amy was careful not to pull Rachel's hair as she tied the knot securely. She turned her gaze to the stranger. There was nothing familiar about him, nothing that gave any hint of his motive or intent.

The point of the weapon pressed against Rachel's neck, he drew open his coat to reveal a pearl-handled revolver in a fancily tooled holster. "Twenty minutes, lady. If you let on, if you tell someone, if you make trouble, she'll die right here. Anyone besides you comes through that door, they eat a bullet. I won't get caught."

At the threats, she took a step back.

"Fast!"

With one last look at Rachel, Amy turned and fled out the kitchen door. Heart hammering, eyes streaming tears of fright, she ran toward the stables. Her head whirled with panicked thoughts. She could save herself and tell someone—Pitch or Hermie or anyone in the stable. Except for what might happen to Rachel. And her baby.

She entered the double doors and hollered. "Hello!"

A voice answered. "Right here."

Amy quickly dashed the tears from her face and hurried forward.

Pitch appeared from a stall. "What's on your mind, Miz Shelby?"

"I need a wagon right away. I have to make a trip to the mercantile. It won't take me long, but I have to hurry."

His shaggy brows rose. She occasionally took a wagon to the store, but never unplanned and never in a hurry.

"I, uh, have bread in the oven and I want to get back before it's done."

He shook his head as if women were unpredictable creatures and moved as quickly as his bowlegged stride would take him. Amy had perspiration under her arms and down her spine by the time he finished and she climbed onto the seat and took the reins. She still wore the coat she'd pulled on when she headed for the fruit cellar.

"You'd best wear a hat, ma'am," Pitch said. "Wind's a might chill today."

"I'll do that. Thank you."

"See you at noon."

She drove the wagon toward the house. If anyone saw her now, they'd think it odd that she was pulling the wagon so close, but she could be loading butter or eggs or something for trade, so her actions weren't entirely suspicious.

Desperate ideas raced through her mind. Once she had the man in the wagon with her, she could just drive him right up to the stable or the barn and jump down and run screaming. But he would likely start shooting—and who knew what else could happen, who else could be hurt? Was there a safer scheme than leaving with him? She didn't know what he would do to her or where he would take her.

She could get the horses running, then leap off the wagon, letting it carry him away. That sounded like the best plan. That way she'd be getting him away from the station and she could alert the men to go after him.

The scheme was definite in her mind when she stopped the team. She studied the door with trepidation.

Instead of seeing the back door opening as she had expected, she saw the man creep from the side of the house, dragging a coat-draped figure at his side. The skirt hem, bound ankles and shoes were plainly visible as his prisoner was hauled across the dirt. Horror crept up Amy's spine.

Fear rippled anew through Amy. She'd believed Rachel would be safe left behind, but he'd reneged on their agreement. Had she really thought she could trust him?

The man heaved the covered form over the tailgate and dropped the bundle on the wagon bed. Amy winced at the action and the muffled cry. He climbed in and covered himself and Rachel with the tarp.

Amy wanted to cry. Or scream. She'd wanted to keep Rachel safe. Now she couldn't let the team run away with the wagon, not while Rachel was tied helplessly in the back. She should have known he wouldn't give her an opportunity to thwart his plans.

"Go!" he ordered. "No tricks or your friend is dead."

Feeling as helplessly trapped as Rachel, Amy faced forward and clucked to the horses. They pulled the wagon with a *creak,* and she guided them toward the road.

As she passed the barns, she watched for someone to spot her, someone she could signal for help. But no one was watching and no one came out. In the far corral several men were working horses, but their labor and their own noise prevented them from hearing the wagon.

Jesse, she thought. *Where are you? Will I see you again?* She fought down rising panic in order to think rationally. A level head was imperative. What was the wisest and safest thing to do?

"Just keep going," the man called. "And don't look back. Head straight to Baker's place."

For reasons unknown to her, this man wanted to go to her father's. It had something to do with that wretched Eden. Did he plan to lie in wait for her father? For what purpose? Jealousy? Should she lead him elsewhere?

After playing out several scenarios in her head, she could only pray that taking him to Sam's was the best choice. Should her father come home, he would see the wagon and know something was wrong. And she prayed for someone to notice she and Rachel were missing.

The trip had never gone so quickly. Amy dreaded

pulling into the door yard at her father's place and learning what this man, whoever he was, had in mind.

She led the team to within thirty feet of the house and reined them to a halt. "We're here."

"Who else lives here?"

"No one."

"If you're lying, you're going to regret it."

"Why would I lie? I don't even know what you want."

The tarp moved and their captor threw it off and stood. He surveyed their surroundings, apparently assured they were alone. He drew out his gun, pointed it at Amy and then used the barrel to gesture. "Come get her and take her inside."

She tied the reins around the brake handle, climbed over the back of the seat and moved to where Rachel lay. The frightened girl stared at her wide-eyed.

"It's going to be all right." Amy helped her sit, and then moved to lower the gate so Rachel could awkwardly scoot herself to the edge. "I'm going to have to untie her ankles so she can walk."

He nodded.

She fumbled with the knots until they were loosened. Once Rachel had her balance, Amy helped her to the ground. Wrapping her arm around Rachel's waist, she led her toward the house.

Inside, the man pointed to the table and chairs. "Sit."

They obeyed. He yanked open drawers until he found towels and aprons, then tied the two women to the chairs. He wasn't gentle or careful, and he pulled the bonds tight, impairing circulation. Once he had them both secured, he turned his attention to opening drawers, overturning tables, rifling through everything he could find in a single-minded frenzy.

Amy met Rachel's brimming eyes. The young woman grimaced behind her gag and bent her head forward. A moan escaped through the cloth.

"Are you all right?"

Rachel shook her head.

"What is it?"

A tear rolled down Rachel's cheek.

A numb fear gripped Amy's chest. Rachel had been terrified, handled roughly. "The baby?" she asked softly.

Rachel nodded.

"Do you have a pain low in your belly—all the way through your insides?"

Again she nodded.

Oh Lord, not this. Not now. Amy prayed for help—divine or otherwise would be just fine by her. She'd done her usual best to ignore the fact that Rachel would be giving birth to a baby soon. She didn't know what she'd thought would happen. Leda would come to attend her—a midwife would be called. But Amy had never wanted to be a part of it.

From the one other room came crashing and banging sounds. What in the name of goodness he was looking for, she couldn't imagine.

The silence that followed was equally unnerving. She strained to listen.

Suddenly the intruder crouched in the doorway, startling her with his silent presence. He studied the floorboards, making a minute scrutiny of each board, perhaps checking for a loose one. He performed the same tedious investigation of the entire room in which they sat, even under the table and their chairs. Contact with the table leg knocked his hat off, but he didn't pick it up—just continued his search.

Rachel bent forward again, making a sound of discomfort.

Amy's head buzzed with the enormity of their situation. "Please untie her and let me help her. She needs to lie down."

"Shut up, lady."

"She needs help. Please."

He swore impatiently and sat on his haunches, studying his surroundings.

Amy had her first good look at him then. His hair was fair and neatly cut. He'd abandoned his coat somewhere, revealing a black suit and vest with a crisp white shirt. As he focused his attention on the rafters overhead, Amy noticed the scar that spliced one of his fair eyebrows in half.

A scar over his eye. The man the detective had described. Eden's partner. Amy tried to remember his name, but couldn't.

Eden. Once again that despicable woman had

brought suffering to Shelby Station. Amy should have snatched her hair out when she had the chance.

"If you tell me what you're looking for, maybe I can help. You can get it and go."

"I doubt that."

The detective had mentioned Eden taking more than her share from one of their scams and running from this man. "Did Eden take something of yours?"

He ignored her and poked around the back of the stove, checking the floor, the wall. If she had hidden something, she'd craftily chosen a place where it was unlikely it would be discovered. The rooms at the boardinghouse changed guests regularly and were cleaned daily. The shelves fell under his anger, and he tossed dishes and bins to the floor with resounding crashes. In obvious frustration, he kicked through the rubble.

The sight of a small velvet pouch brought a gleam of satisfaction, and he bent to pick it up. Making quick work of the drawstring, he dumped the contents into his palm.

From fifteen feet away Amy saw the gleam of gold and the sparkle of gemstones. Diamonds, emeralds, rubies. He held what looked like several elaborate sets of jewelry. Apparently worth chasing down, worth threatening their lives, worth whatever it took to get them back.

Anger replaced some of the trepidation coursing through Amy's veins. Eden had used her father, tricked him into thinking she had affection for him in order to hide these stolen goods.

She turned away from the man's gloating expression to the pain and fear obvious in Rachel's. "You've found what you want—now you can leave us here and head out. Untie me."

He seemed to be thinking over her words, when a shout came from outside. "Amy!"

Jesse's voice.

In the confusion, she hadn't heard anyone ride up. Or perhaps he'd ridden in silently. Lord, don't let him walk through that door and make himself a target for this greedy man. "Jesse, stay out!" she shouted.

Their captor shoved the jewelry back into the pouch and stuffed it inside his coat. In the same instant he had the gun in his hand and lunged for the window, where he used his elbow to shatter the glass and his sleeve to scatter it away from the frame. Standing to the side so he wouldn't be a target, he aimed through the opening and fired.

Immediately shots were returned, splintering the window casing and hitting the wall.

Rachel made a noise behind the fabric of her gag.

"If you want your women back alive, get on your horses and ride back out!"

"You're trapped in there," Jesse called. "Let them go."

"What kind of fool do you think I am? They're my ticket out."

Amy's heart felt as though it would hammer right through her rib cage. The man was desperate to escape now. He had what he'd come for and he wanted to get away with it. She and Rachel were still his best advantage. Jesse had to know that too.

Their captor lunged across the room and used the knife to cut the fabric and free Amy's legs. He hauled her up, her arms still bound behind her, and dragged her roughly to the window.

"Shoot now!" he shouted behind her ear.

From her position at the window, Amy focused her attention until she spotted the locations of at least four men, hidden in various spots. If she'd seen those, there were undoubtedly more concealed at the side and rear of the house.

"Let them go, you bastard!" The unmistakably English accent was Jack's.

"You've made a mess of things, Shelby." The man who held her was stiff with tension as he shouted a response. "You know I can't let them go and get myself out of here. I need another choice."

"Jesse!" Amy called. "Do as he says. Rachel is ready to have her baby and she needs help."

"I'm not leaving you, Amy!"

"Please, Jesse!"

The man shoved her back into the room.

"Let me help her." Amy turned her back, making her tied wrists available to him. "Untie me so I can get her into the bed and help her. So far you haven't hurt anybody, but you let her or her baby die and you'll hang for sure."

"God, I'm fed up with bossy women."

She waited, her head growing light.

Finally, she felt a tug and her bonds were cut away. She ran forward and untied Rachel. As she removed the gag, the young woman's cries broke her heart. Rachel could barely walk, and Amy had to support her weight and practically carry her into Sam's bedroom. Her skirts were wet and she was perspiring.

Once Rachel was in bed, Amy helped her remove her shoes, stockings and drawers, and urged her to let her see the baby's progress. The head wasn't crowning yet, but Amy guessed it wouldn't be long. She'd never delivered a baby alone before. She'd had her own mother and a doctor present when her child was born. And she'd been present for only one other birth. If something happened, she'd be responsible. *If the baby died...* Amy's chest felt as though the weight of the world rested on it. She couldn't be responsible for another child's death. She had to help her friend and make sure the baby was okay.

She looked into Rachel's eyes, trying to give her reassurance. "Try to rest. I know it hurts and you're scared, but try to relax your body and not fight this baby. I'm going to get water and towels and linens. You're going to be just fine." She smoothed the hair from Rachel's forehead. "Okay?"

"Okay," she whispered.

Marching out, she stirred the coals in the stove, then added kindling. In the litter on the floor, she found a bucket and carried it toward the door. "I'm going for water."

The man lurched toward her, but she opened the door before he could reach her. She would let that man kill her before she'd lose this baby. Leaving the door open, she walked across the yard to the well.

To her surprise and relief, her father was crouched behind the stones. He started to rise.

"Get down." She spoke low enough that her voice wouldn't carry. "He doesn't know you're here. I couldn't see you from the window."

Attaching the bucket to the hook on the rope, she turned the crank and lowered it.

"What's goin' on, Amy?"

"That's the man Eden was in cahoots with. The man with the scar."

"George Gray?" Sam asked.

"He found some jewelry in your place."

"What kind o' jewelry?"

"Something worth a fortune, I'm guessing."

"Eden hid it there."

"I'd suppose." She used the opportunity to glance about, locating Jesse, Jack and Pitch where they were concealed.

"This is my fault, then," her father said.

"If it's anyone's fault, it's that woman's," she whispered. The bucket was full and she cranked it back up.

"Rachel's baby isn't going to wait. Maybe a few of the men should leave, so he thinks you've all gone. Maybe he'll try to ride out then."

"You're goin' back in there?"

She unhooked the full pail. "I have to. Rachel needs me."

"Be careful, girl."

Carrying her load carefully, she walked back to her father's house, entered and closed herself in.

George Gray glared at her. She returned the look of contempt, walked past and poured water into a kettle on the stove.

She finally thought to remove her coat and noticed she was still wearing her apron.

"Leave that door open and stay where I can see you," George demanded as she headed back to Sam's bedroom.

Rachel's sounds of discomfort and distress had grown louder by the time she returned. Amy bathed the younger woman's face and hands with a cool rag and did her best to keep her calm.

The sound of riders drew her to the window beside the bed. She moved the curtain aside and spotted three men riding away. "They're leaving!"

She glanced to the other room to see that George watched the retreating men too.

"They're leaving us here?" Rachel's voice held dismay and her eyes were wide with fright.

"They're gone," Amy called. "You can leave us now."

"I'm not going anywhere until it's dark."

Amy's hopes sank. Rachel sobbed and she curled her hands into fists to keep from joining her. Amy had learned to hold in every emotion that threatened her composure, and she could hold back these as well. She would not panic. She would not give in to fear.

A movement beside the window caught her attention, startling her. She flattened her palm against her breast, then realized one of their men was hiding outside.

George was still at his station at the front. "You need a little air," she told Rachel, and eased open the window.

She made out Deezer's youthful face, etched with worry as he whispered, "Come quick, Miz Shelby. You and Miz Douglas slip out this winder whilst he's busy at the front."

Amy shook her head. "She can't ride."

And they both knew Amy wouldn't leave her.

She left the window open and pulled the curtains closed. It was only small reassurance to know he was right on the other side of the wall, but reassurance all the same.

"I didn't know it was going t' hurt this bad." Rachel bit her lip.

Amy sat beside her on the bed's edge. "Don't bite your lip, sweetie. You got a rough start, but we're going to do this together, you and I." Amy leaned to her ear and whispered, "Having a few men leave was just a distraction…to make him think they've all gone."

"Woman!" The shout came from George in the other room.

Amy got up and stood in the doorway.

"I'm hungry." He gestured toward the stove area. "Find me something to eat."

She looked back at Rachel, assuring herself the baby's arrival wouldn't be at that moment, and stepped her way around books and pans and broken dishes.

Fury rose like a fire in her neck and face before she ever reached the cooking area. He'd made a shambles of the kitchen and now he expected her to neatly whip together a meal. If she thought her father kept rat poison around, she'd gladly lace George Gray's food and watch him suffer.

The thought got her to thinking of something that might make him sick and not necessarily kill him. After adding wood, she found a tin of meat and another of beans and dumped them into a skillet over the hot stove.

She picked around in the debris, finding a metal plate and a fork. Her eye caught a familiar-looking medicine bottle that had apparently been inside a crock that now lay broken. With a quick check to see that George was looking out the window, she slipped it into her apron pocket.

"I'm going to check on her while that's heating." She entered the bedroom and sat beside Rachel, discreetly taking the bottle from her pocket to read the label.

"Is that for me?"

"No." She read the doctor's nearly indecipherable directions and remembered giving doses of the drug to her mother for pain during the last weeks of her life. "It's for him."

Rachel groaned and gripped the sheet with white-knuckled fingers.

"I'll be right back." Amy hurried out. With furtive movements, she uncapped the bottle and poured the entire contents into the cooking food, then recapped it and dropped it under the back stove lid, into the fire. With a wooden spoon, she stirred and scooped the meal onto the metal plate.

It steamed and smelled not half bad as she carried it toward George. She'd even poured him a cup of water so he'd think she was behaving herself. "Here. I'm going back in with her now. The baby's coming."

He eyeballed her and the plate and grabbed it with his left hand, studying the contents. For a horrible moment she thought he suspected, and she prepared for his anger. Her pulse battered her eardrums.

"That's what you said an hour ago."

She bit her tongue and forced herself to relax and walk unhurriedly while she got water and towels and returned to the bedroom.

Rachel was laboring in earnest now, trying to turn on her side and curl up to avoid the pain.

Amy washed her hands and took time to bath Rachel's face with cool water.

Time seemed to stretch endlessly. Birth was something a woman did all on her own, no matter how many people attended her, and Amy could only lend support and encouragement.

"Jack should be here."

"I know. He'll be here soon." She prayed that was true.

Another half hour passed and Amy crept to the bedroom doorway to peer out at George. He still attended his post at the window, but he was leaning heavily against the wall and he kept jerking the gun back up as though he was dozing.

Amy checked the baby's progress and placed Rachel's hands on the rungs of the metal headboard. "Hang on here. You have to push now."

"I don't think I can."

"You don't have any choice. I'll tell you when." She placed her hand on Rachel's belly and waited for the next pain to make the muscles taut. "Now."

Rachel gripped the metal rungs and pushed.

The baby's head barely moved.

"Do it just like that in another minute. Rest right now."

Eternity passed as they waited for another contraction. Rachel pushed again and made a little progress.

"Amy, is this normal?"

She assured her it was. "Rest in between."

A loud *thud* came from the other room.

"I'm going to go check on him." Amy tiptoed to the doorway and peered out.

George lay sprawled on the floor, the gun having skidded three feet from his open hand.

Chapter Eleven

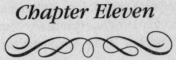

Bolstering her courage, she dashed across the littered floor to where he lay and grabbed the revolver. He didn't move. Had she killed him?

A shrill scream came from the bedroom.

Torn over what to do first, Amy ran to the front door and flung it open. She heaved the gun as far as she could throw and it hit the dirt, sending up a plume of dust. "Come get him! I think I've killed him!"

Jesse stood up from his hiding place behind the wagon. "Run out here now! Where's Rachel?"

"I have to go back to her." She turned and dashed back inside, leaving the door agape.

She heard Jesse at her heels. "Are you both all right?"

"We're fine. He's over there." She pointed to the body.

"I didn't hear a shot."

"I didn't shoot him. I drugged him." She slammed the

bedroom door closed behind her to afford Rachel privacy.

The young woman's face was contorted with pain. She made a sound between a scream and a growl that raised the hair on Amy's arms. Amy checked and found the baby's head crowning. Terror washed over her in a nearly paralyzing wave. More frightening than being kidnapped, more terrifying than nearly being murdered was the thought of letting something happen to Rachel's baby.

Amy wrestled with inadequacy and dread, then found courage somewhere deep inside her and coaxed Rachel to hold on just a little longer. The baby's head was nearly out now and Amy didn't have time to panic. Duty took over.

"You're doing great. Stop for a breath now."

The door opened and Jack rushed in and fell to the other side of the bed beside his wife. "What's happening? Is she hurt?"

"Far as I can tell, everything is the way it should be."

Rachel released her hold on the headboard to reach for her husband. Jack put his arm around her shoulder and she rested her head against him to cry.

"Prop her shoulders up and help her this time."

Jack did as instructed. After a few more pushes, the Douglases' baby struggled its way into the world.

After cutting the cord, Amy wrapped the squalling infant in a towel and washed her. "You have a girl." Placing her in a clean folded sheet, she handed the baby to Jack. "We have to finish up here."

Several minutes later, Rachel held her baby and Jack sat beside her. Until now Amy had handled each moment as it came, not allowing emotions to get in the way of her judgment or their safety. But studying the new family, emotion welled up inside Amy and threatened to spill out.

She efficiently tied soiled linens and towels in a bundle and carried them out, leaving the Douglases alone. She leaned back against the wall and caught her breath, fighting down the overwhelming feelings that threatened to overtake her.

Seeing the baby Rachel held and the way the couple sat with their heads together gazing down at her, widened the crack in the armor around Amy's heart. Now she felt like crying.

Underlying intense feelings of relief and fear was guilt-provoking envy, suffocating need and loss so severe she could barely breathe.

Jesse and Sam looked up with stricken faces. Jesse walked toward her.

"Is she okay? Are you?"

Amy took a moment to regain her composure. She glanced down at her bloodstained apron and added it to the pile of laundry. "She's fine. I'm—" She glanced from her husband to her father, recognizing the distress and worry etched on their faces. Another thought struck her with sick uncertainty. "Am I a murderer?"

Jesse lunged forward and pulled her against the warmth and strength of his chest. He felt so good, and she felt so safe in his arms. Tears stung her eyes and she buried her face, gripping the open sides of his wool jacket with both hands. His voice rumbled against her forehead.

"No, he's not dead. But he's out cold. What did you give him?"

Relieved, she retained her place of comfort in his embrace and raised her head to look at her father. "I found that bottle of medicine we used to give Mama. I poured the rest of it into his food."

Sam stepped toward them and Amy moved to give him a hug. "That was mighty quick thinkin', daughter."

Then she returned to Jesse's embrace, and he held her protectively against his side.

She gave Sam a weary smile and glanced around at the shambles of his home. "Sorry about your house, Daddy."

He nudged a tin funnel with the toe of his boot. "Place needed sprucin' up a bit anyhow." His gaze rose to hers. "If you'd have been hurt, it woulda been my fault. I brought that appallin' woman here."

"I won't tell you again, it's not your fault." She remembered George Gray's motive. "Did you see the jewelry?"

Jesse pulled the velvet pouch from his pocket. "Must be worth a fortune."

He opened the bag to show her the gems.

Amy picked up an earring and held it so the facets glittered in the late afternoon light. "Where would somebody wear a thing this fancy?"

Jesse held the other one up to her lobe. "On her ear."

She smiled at his teasing reply and put the one she held back in his palm. "What's going to happen now?"

"Deezer, Pitch and Hermie are seein' that Gray gets locked up in Liscom's root cellar behind the mercantile until the marshal arrives. They'll send a wire to that Price fellow while they're there. I'll lock these up 'til someone comes for them."

"How did you know to come out here to look for us?"

"Deezer saw the broken jars inside the door." Jesse dropped the gems back in the bag, drew it shut and tucked it inside his jacket. "Your coat was gone, but not Rachel's. Sam found Mrs. Barnes tied up behind the shed."

"Oh no! Is she hurt?"

"She has a lump on her noggin and a whopping headache," her father replied. "But she's fine. She'll be worried sick about the two of you by the time we get back, though."

"What about Biscuit?"

"He was with Cay as usual," Sam replied.

"Pitch told us you'd taken a wagon," Jesse continued. "And the tracks heading toward Sam's were the freshest."

"Rachel would like to see you," Jack said from behind them. "You men are welcome to come see the baby."

Jesse and Sam doffed their hats and followed Amy to stand at the foot of the bed. Rachel lay propped on the pillows, looking tired but happy. The baby lay sleeping in her arms. Amy deliberately didn't look at the child.

Tears glistened in Rachel's eyes before she spoke. "You're the bravest woman I know, Amy Shelby."

"You're very brave, too."

"You didn't fall apart or cry or lose your head. I'll never be able to repay you for staying and helping me." Rachel glanced at Jack, then at the other men. "There were several times she could have escaped alone, but she didn't—once, when Deezer was right outside this window, and she spoke to him. But she stayed for me."

Jack's eyes glistened, too. "Thank you, Miz Shelby."

"No more fussing about it—I did what needed to be done."

As she always does, Jesse thought. He observed his wife's obvious discomfort with their thanks. From the moment Deezer had run from the house to alert him of the broken jars and the missing women, Jesse had been distressed over what his wife was going through, worried that she was afraid or that she'd be harmed.

She had been a bulwark of strength and courage, however, quick-witted enough to talk with her father as he hid behind the well, clever enough to keep Rachel and herself safe, and bold enough to drug their captor, aiding their release.

Jesse felt inept and helpless in the face of all she'd done. He'd been frustrated and angry, hiding in the yard, unable to risk shooting or storming the house for fear of risking the women's safety. He was glad to be able to handle matters now.

"Can Rachel travel, or should she stay here?"

Amy looked at her young friend. "I think as long as she's carried and we make a bed for her in the wagon, she'll be fine. We'll send for Leda to come look over the two of them." She moved around to the side of the bed. "Rachel, let's get you home."

There wasn't much left of the day, but Jesse stuck close to Amy for the remaining hours. He drove the wagon with her seated at his side and the Douglases in the bed. He stood nearby as she greeted the hands and heard their mumbled words in response to their pleasure in seeing her safe.

Cay came forward hesitantly, stepping from the edge of the gathering of men who were returning one by one back to their chores. The boy wore an uncertain expression, his blue eyes filled with apprehension. Jesse hadn't allowed him to accompany them to Sam's. Cay hadn't challenged his decision, but he'd clearly been unhappy.

By the way his throat was working, Cay wanted to say something that refused to come out. Finally, he cleared his voice and spoke. "I had to stay here in case a stage came."

"That's a big responsibility," Amy told him. "Did a stage arrive?"

He nodded, and glanced at Jesse as he explained. "Driver was Pearly, so he helped me with the fresh team. He did grumble a might about no hot meal."

Amy smiled. "Now, that's a man for you. I'm toted off as a hostage and he's thinking about his belly."

Cay didn't share her amusement. He looked aside in embarrassment. "I'm, uh, I sure am glad you're back, Amy."

"Me, too, buddy."

The boy looked so forlorn and lost that Jesse nearly shoved him toward Amy, but the day's astounding events hadn't ended yet. Amy took a step forward, arms outstretched, and Cay moved right into her embrace to press his cheek against her breast.

Amy's hand trembled as she smoothed Cay's sandy hair and held him close. She pressed her cheek to the top of his head. Seeing the two of them like that brought a lump to Jesse's throat and he glanced away.

"Thanks for helping Jesse today," she said softly.

Cay pulled away and glanced around self-consciously, wiping his nose on his shirtsleeve.

Amy ruffled his hair. "Why don't you join us inside after we get Mrs. Douglas settled?"

In the soddy, Jesse started a fire in the fireplace. Jack carried in his wife and baby and placed them on the bed.

After making sure Rachel was comfortable, Amy said, "I'll be back to check on you later. Send Jack for me if you need anything."

At their place, Jesse watched Elthea Barnes grab Amy and hug her soundly, then step back to wipe tears from her eyes. "Why aren't you home resting?" Amy asked.

"They tried to get me to go, but I had to see you home safe first." Sam stayed in the kitchen as though he, too, didn't want to get far away. Cay joined them as well. It was obvious that everyone had been terrified for Amy's safety and was relieved to have her back in their midst.

"It's late." Amy looked to Mrs. Barnes. "Have the other men eaten?"

"You're not to worry about feeding us," Jesse said, going into the other room and returning with the rocker. "Sit and rest while Sam and I put somethin' together. After supper, I'll ready a bath for you."

Either she knew better than to object or she'd been more shaken than she let on, because Amy seated herself in the chair and eased back. "What happened to you this morning, Mrs. Barnes?"

The woman explained that she'd been struck over the head while dumping ashes behind the shed, and had come to gagged, with her feet and hands bound. The poor woman had lain there for hours until Sam discovered her.

"I hope you rested this afternoon," Amy told her.

"Much as I could, what with knowing you and Rachel and that precious baby were in danger."

Sam asked his daughter several questions about what had happened. Jesse worked and simply listened to her replies. Sometime later, when he looked over, Amy's eyes were closed.

"Here, darlin'." Holding a plate, Jesse knelt before her.

Her eyes fluttered open. "I'm not very hungry."

"You need to eat anyway. Try a little something."

The roast Amy had started that morning had cooked down to scraps. He had fried potatoes to go with it, and Sam had opened jars of green beans. Amy ate more than he had hoped she would, and drank a glass of milk besides.

"Did you save the drippings?" she asked.

He nodded.

"Good. I'll make gravy for flapjacks in the morning."

"Or you can stay in bed and be pampered for a day or so."

"Jesse, I'm not sick."

"And I don't want you to be." The thought of what might have happened today was like a dull knife in his chest. George Gray was a man with no conscience, as he'd proven by trying to use two innocent women for his own gain. Jesse had no doubt the man wouldn't have stopped short of injuring or killing both of them if he'd thought the deed would earn his freedom.

Thank God Amy possessed a level head, had used her wit and kept them alive.

The other men who'd been at Sam's all day came to eat, then one by one headed back to their chores, Cay joining them.

"Deezer, put a couple o' kettles of water on the stove in the bathhouse, will ya, please?"

The young man settled his hat with a nod. "Sure thing, boss."

Sam insisted Mrs. Barnes take a seat while he took care of the dishes. Sam seemed extremely attentive to the woman, finally offering to take her home so she could rest.

Jesse gathered clothing for Amy and walked her to the bathhouse, where he lit a lantern and filled the tub. Amy unbuttoned her shirtwaist and removed it, as well as her skirts and petticoats. She glanced at him shyly, then pulled her chemise over her head and skimmed off her drawers.

Her skin glowed golden in the lamplight, her alluring curves a delight to behold. Amy's tummy was rounded and her breasts plump. The impact of what that meant hit him with full force. *Amy was pregnant.*

She hadn't said a word to him.

He wanted to cry.

He wanted to laugh.

He wanted to go find Gray and kill him with his bare hands for endangering his wife and unborn child.

Amy must have noticed the swift rush of realization and anger that swept over him, because she settled herself in the water and gave him a puzzled look. "Jesse?"

He busied himself finding her fancy-smelling soap and a soft cloth. "Here you are."

She accepted the items. "Is something wrong?"

He knelt beside the tub, studied her lovely oval face and tenderly cupped her cheek. "Everything's fine now. You're home and you're safe."

She gave him one of those sweet smiles that made

him feel all soft inside. He loved her with every fiber of his being. Slowly, things between them were working out. There was a lot left unspoken yet, and Tim was still a barrier. But she no longer shut Jesse completely out. She had accepted Cay. And they were going to have another child.

Why hadn't she told him as soon as she suspected?

Jesse leaned over the edge of the tub to kiss her.

Maybe she wanted him to notice.

He ended the kiss and found a chair so he could sit nearby while she bathed. He didn't want to let her out of his sight. She slid down in the water and closed her eyes.

Jesse glanced around the room. The fire in the stove kept the bathing person warm, but the heat made it uncomfortable for those who were clothed. The laundry area was in the back of the building, and both sides used the same stove.

"I have a new appreciation for Adele, working in here most of the day."

Amy stood and lathered her body. "What about me? I used to do most of the laundry and heat the water for baths."

He hoped she was enjoying her bath as much as he. "I've *always* had an appreciation for you, Mrs. Shelby." He used a pail to rinse off the suds. "A *deep* appreciation."

He held her hand and she stepped from the tub to the absorbent padding he'd spread on the floor. Using soft toweling, he dried her shoulders and back, then knelt and rubbed the fabric up the length of her legs and over her bottom.

He couldn't resist kissing the places he dried, tasting her warm moist skin and inhaling her feminine scent. Amy locked her fingers in his hair, and he pressed his face to her belly and kneaded her hips, ran his palms down her silky thighs and up.

She gasped when he touched her intimately, her body jerking as he explored and teased with his tongue. In minutes her knees buckled and she lowered herself to the floor, lying back and inviting his caresses.

"Are the doors locked?"

"Yes, ma'am, both of 'em."

He leaned over to kiss her lips, and she framed his face with both hands, urgently meeting his rising desire with her own. She shifted her attention to his shirt and went to work on the buttons, then unfastened his trousers. Jesse shoved all his clothing off in a heap.

"The floor's too hard," he said. "I don't want to hurt you."

"You won't hurt me."

But he didn't listen to her denial, and lay at her side instead. The life inside her was too precious to risk harming for his momentary pleasure.

Impatiently, she pushed against his shoulder until he lay back, and then she rose to straddle his hips. She lowered herself onto him, her eyes closing and her lips parting.

Jesse treasured making love this way, free to caress her hips and breasts and to watch her artless reactions. Her skin flushed and the pulse at her throat throbbed. When she looked down at him, her dark eyes were dreamy and filled with passion.

She could make the lovin' so good that it took all his effort and control to make it last. But he didn't want it to end and he desired to please her, so he let her set the pace and take her pleasure, which she did with a tightening of her body and a sharp intake of breath. She trembled all over, but closed her eyes and smiled.

Jesse's body took over and he clutched her thighs and groaned as he came. She caressed his belly, dragging her nails in lazy circles. Jesse sat up, keeping her on his lap and hugging her. He pressed kisses against her temple and cheek.

"I love you, Amy."

She wrapped her arms around him and pressed her face to his neck. "Jesse," she whispered beneath his ear.

They held each other for a few minutes longer. Eventually he helped her to her feet and wrapped a towel around her while he added another kettle of hot water to the tub. They each took a quick turn washing, then pulled on their clothing and walked hand in hand to the house.

Cay was seated at the trestle table with a book open in front of him. He stood quickly. "I made you tea."

Jesse released her hand, and Amy took a seat on the bench beside where Cay'd been and waited while he brought her a steaming mug.

"Sugar?" he asked.

"Please."

Cay's attentiveness amused Jesse, though he realized he'd been fawnin' over her all evening, as well. He poured himself a lukewarm cup of coffee and found a few cookies, which he shared.

Cay sat back down beside Amy. She glanced at the cover of his book. "Did you start a new book on your own?"

"Yes'm. It's a good'un, too. Pirates and treasure." He told her what had happened in the story so far. They discussed the characters for a few minutes, but then the boy stood. "I can light my own lamp tonight. I'll be goin' t'bed now."

Amy nodded. "Good night then."

"G'night, ma'am." He glanced over. "Jesse."

"Cay," Amy said softly. "I know you're nearly a grown man and all, but maybe when no one's looking, like now, you could wish me good night with a hug. Only if you'd like to, of course."

Cay's cheeks seemed to darken in the glow of the lanterns, but he immediately leaned down to give Amy a clumsy, boyish hug.

When he'd gone upstairs, Jesse took Amy's mug and placed it with his own beside the dishpan. "I have to go check the stables and barns."

She stood. "I'm going to go out to the soddy and make sure Rachel is doing okay."

He watched her walk to the sod house and enter, then he performed his nightly check of the buildings and the storage locks and made sure all the lanterns were extinguished.

Hermie was making a check of the animals, and Jesse stopped to speak to him.

"The missus okay?" Hermie asked.

Jesse nodded. "You saw Gray put up soundly?"

"Watched Liscom padlock the door to that root cellar and checked it myself. I went to check on him tonight and Liscom said he woke up madder than a wet hen and pukin' his guts out. Gray's not goin' anywhere, boss."

Assured, Jesse thanked him for standing by them that day and wished him a good-night.

He met Amy on her way back to the house. He'd never felt the need to check all the windows and doors, but he did so tonight, making certain they were securely closed and locked.

Amy gave him a curious look, but said nothing. Upstairs she brushed out her hair while he shucked off his clothing and climbed beneath the covers. He stacked his hands behind his head and watched her.

"Cay was sure glad to have you home safe."

She removed the clothing she'd only recently donned, carefully hanging each piece on a wall hook. "We had to get used to each other is all." She opened a drawer and pulled out her nightgown.

"Forget that and come lie with me."

She held the gown against her breasts and looked at him.

"Come on," he urged.

"What if there's a fire?"

"A nightgown will protect you from a fire?"

"No, silly, but I'd have to run outside and I wouldn't want to be…"

"Naked?"

"Yes."

If he lived to be a hundred, he'd never understand the workings of a woman's mind. "We've never had a fire yet. We probably won't. So for fifty years, you're going to lay here every night in your nightgown, just in case?"

She shrugged. "I guess it does sound foolish when you put it like that."

He threw back the sheet and patted the mattress. Amy tossed the nightgown aside and climbed into bed with him. He wrapped the covers around them and held her close. She felt so good in his arms. So right.

She reached up to touch his jaw and skim her fingertips across his lips.

He kissed her fingers. "I hated thinkin' of you being scared today."

She seemed to be mulling over his words. "I *was* afraid. My head was filled with all manner of imaginings about what could happen. I wanted to come up with a brilliant plan to alert you. At first he was going to leave Rachel behind, but then, after I'd gone for the wagon, he brought her anyway. I was actually more afraid for Rachel than for myself."

Jesse gave her a gentle squeeze. "That comes as no surprise to me."

"Was my father in a state?"

"I'd never seen him that agitated. He feels responsible, you know."

"I know."

Jesse wrapped her tightly in his embrace and enjoyed the silken feel of her skin against his. It would take him a while to get over the fright he'd experienced this day.

"I wouldn't have been able to bear it if anything had happened to you." His voice came out thick and hoarse.

She kissed his chest.

"We've come so far these past months, Amy. I missed you so much before, and I want to make up for lost time and rebuild what we have." Several moments of silence passed before he spoke again. "If he'd hurt you…" He drew his hand down and splayed it over her belly. "If something had happened to the baby, Amy…"

Her body tensed almost immediately.

"We have a new beginning here," he whispered.

She withdrew, disentangling her legs from his, moving back several inches. "What are you talking about?"

"The baby. I'm talkin' about the baby."

"Rachel's baby?"

"No, of course not. Our baby."

She grew very still. "We don't have a baby."

Confused at her reaction, Jesse leaned on one elbow and reached again to place his hand over her stomach. "We do."

She sat up and scooted to the edge of the bed. "Why are you doing this?"

Fear, much like that he'd felt most of this awful day, weighed on his chest. "Why am I doin' what?"

"Bringing this up. You have to leave the past where it is and move forward, Jesse. All this talking you want to do is not helpful."

"I'm not talkin' about the past, I'm talkin' about now. About the future. About the child right there in your belly." He gestured.

Amy jumped out of bed and found her nightgown, then yanked it over her head. "I won't listen to this."

"Amy," he insisted.

"No! We are not having a baby! What's wrong with you?"

What was wrong with *him?* He got out on his side and moved around the end of the bed. "Amy."

She shook her head and backed away. "Leave it alone, Jesse."

Chill realization swept over him. She hadn't known. She hadn't told him because she hadn't realized. Or she hadn't been willing to admit the fact to herself. Why not? Why was carrying a baby so terrible that she couldn't let herself admit it? Of course—all this stemmed back to Tim and her invariable denial. She'd been unable to even look at a child for the past year.

But she was going to have to look at one soon—theirs. And no amount of avoiding would make a baby go away.

He was torn. Did he force the issue now, or would that make things worse? Should he wait until she was ready? When in God's name would that ever be?

She was trembling now, this woman of strength and courage, this woman who didn't fear for herself, but whose mind protected her in its own defensive way. He would never deliberately hurt her or force her to face something too painful to deal with. She'd already taken huge strides in making changes within herself. He would have to trust and pray that the rest would follow.

"It's okay," he said in his most reassuring tone. "Never mind, it's not important right now." He moved to take her in his arms and she folded herself against him.

He guided her back to the bed. There they lay together in silence, her breath gradually returning to normal. The trembling stopped. It still felt right to hold her. But his heart dealt with a sharp new pain. The fact that she was denying the child they had made.

Long into the night, long after Amy slept, Jesse lay awake.

And ached.

Chapter Twelve

Sam spent the next morning with a shovel and buckets, hauling the broken debris from his home and dumping it down the outhouse pit. He was going to dig a new one next spring anyway. Cay had come with him, and he enjoyed the boy's quiet companionship.

As many times as Amy told him not to blame himself, he felt responsible for what had happened. Eden had been taking a diversion while she found somewhere to stash the jewels she had hoped to keep for herself.

"Did you go to school when you was a boy, Sam?"

Sam righted a chair and leaned against the back. "Never did, lad. Learned numbers and letters from my ma."

"What about Amy—did she go to school?"

"She did. When we lived in Ohio, it was just a short walk to the schoolhouse. Then when we moved to Nebraska, there was a schoolmarm who took turns living with the families nearby."

"There ain't no schoolmarm around here, though, huh?"

"I reckon with more families movin' in, we should find us one. We do have a church, after all. We should probably have a school."

"I had a man teacher back home."

"You thinkin' you might wanna be a schoolteacher?"

"Nah. I like workin' with the horses. Don't think I'd wanna be in with a bunch of kids all day when I could be outside."

"You learn from your uncle Jesse and you'll be a fine horseman one day."

"How'd you and Jesse come upon a plan to run the station, anyhow?"

Sam explained how they'd been in the army together and how they'd recognized the need for stations along the routes that so many were taking as the West expanded.

"Livin' in the city, I never saw so many people ever day as we see coming through Shelby Station," Cay told him.

"And every one of 'em paying for food and a good portion of 'em wantin' a bed and a bath." Sam winked. "A dollar for each."

"You must have a lot of money by now."

Sam looked at him. "I guess I do."

"Whaddya gonna do with all of it?"

He glanced around. "Maybe I need a new house."

Cay followed his gaze. "A really nice one. With a porch."

Sam nodded, but his thoughts turned to a bigger house with only himself to occupy it. "Might be kind of a waste. Just me livin' in it would be foolish."

"Maybe so." Cay picked up the broom and started sweeping inward from a corner. "You could get married. I knew a lady back in Indiana went clear to Colorado to marry a man what sent for her."

Sam paused in picking up a pile of books to glance at the boy. "That's a common practice, but I don't think I'd want to take a chance like that."

"You could get a real stinker, huh?"

Sam laughed. "I think I'm a might old for sending for a woman, lad."

Cay used a dented dustpan to pick up his pile of dirt and china chips. "Yeah. Prob'ly somebody more like Mrs. Barnes who cooks good and wouldn't make you cut your hair all the time and stuff."

The boy's words caught Sam by surprise. Mrs. Barnes? He tried to remember her first name. Ethel? Evelyn? He'd seen her nearly every day for the past six years and didn't know her name.

She was a widow. Well, so was he.

She had a grown son. And he had a grown daughter.

She was pleasant enough and not hard to look at. But a *wife?* He must be plumb loco for havin' these thoughts. He wasn't young and looking to start a family. He had a simple, settled, more-than-adequate life.

But something is missing, an internal voice taunted. What happened with Eden had shown him that he had been missing a relationship. He'd made a mistake with that one, but that's what he deserved for taking up with a woman he didn't even know.

A respectable woman who simply wanted companionship as he did—now that was another thing entirely. He'd have to look Mrs. Barnes over with a new eye. And…he'd have to pay attention to see if she ever looked at him in any certain way.

"I am an old fool," he said to himself. And laughed aloud.

The diversity of people who passed through Shelby Station never ceased to amaze Amy. Hopefully they'd seen the worst of the lot with Lark Doyle and George Gray. Once news came the following week that the marshal had arrived, and Jesse and Amy told him their stories, the lawman took custody of Gray and hauled him away for trial.

The jewelry had been returned to its rightful owner. That chapter was behind them, but not entirely forgotten. Jack confided in Jesse that Rachel had nightmares almost every night. Amy's sleep was disturbed by dreams, as well, but she rationalized by day that the danger was over, and moved forward.

Mr. Quenton had proved to be an interesting fellow, joining them for meals and often sitting with the men of an evening. One morning, soon after the news that Gray had been taken away to stand trial, Quenton extended an invitation to come to his tent to see his photographs. That night a few hands at a time took him up on his offer, followed by the Shelbys.

Snow fell as Jesse, Amy and Cay ran across the rutted road and entered the spacious tent. The man sat writing in a journal by lamplight. He removed a pair of wire-framed spectacles and welcomed the visitors.

"You've come to look at my work." He opened a case and carefully took out a stack of large photographs.

"Have to admit we've been curious," Jesse said.

Mr. Quentin gestured for them to take seats on nearby trunks. With heads bent over the pictures, the three of them viewed image after image. Some pictures of men working on the railroad, cowboys herding cattle, and families standing outside tents and soddys. Others depicted children and animals and farmland.

"Mr. Quenton, these are incredible," Amy told him. "You've caught *life* on these papers." There was a candid quality about his work, a stark reality that somehow captured the lives and the determination of the people that the viewer couldn't help recognizing and appreciating. "It's like—like you've lassoed a tornado and brought it to a stop, with all its power visible."

"Mighty impressive," Jesse agreed.

Mr. Quenton smiled at their praise and moved to a folding table. "I've just developed these."

Amy took the smaller stack from him and looked at the first one. A likeness of Pitch made her smile. He was leaning on a corral rail, his hat cocked back, squinting into the sun. His gold front tooth gleamed.

Another was Jesse, his shirt molded to his chest in the wind, one hand flattened on a dark gelding's neck as he adjusted a harness. Amy's fingers hovered above the picture. "He looks so real. I feel like I could touch him." She glanced up. "Not like the daguerreotypes where the person is posed and sober. This is…well, it's the real *Jesse*."

"I consider that a supreme compliment." Mr. Quenton gave a little bow.

Among the collection, were photographs of Sam and Cay, and one of Amy standing on the porch, one hand shading her eyes. She stared at an Amy so different from the person she saw in the mirror each morning and night that she barely recognized herself. This woman seemed in harmony with her surroundings, at peace with her life. She moved on to the next picture—an image of the windmill. Another showed the soddy, smoke curling from the chimney.

Amy paused over the last picture, and beside her Jesse lowered his head for a better view. Three wooden crosses poked through a dusting of snow, the names painted on them legible. Amy's breath caught. It was a picture of the slope where their mothers and their son were buried.

Jesse felt as though the air had been sucked from the tent. Amy seemed to stare at the likeness as though she'd never seen the sight before, as though it was one of the previous pictures from Kansas or Wyoming and not a spot a few hundred feet from where they now sat. Wind buffeted the canvas overhead.

And Jesse realized then that she hadn't ever seen it. Not like this. Not like he had when he'd planted roses and tended the weeds. In all the time since Tim's death she'd only been there the day they'd buried his mother, and she had carefully avoided looking at Tim's grave.

Unaware of the tension, Cay pointed. "I helped make that one."

Quickly, Amy handed the stack back to Mr. Quenton. "Thank you for showing us your work."

She stood and ducked out the tent flap.

Jesse watched her exit and turned to Quenton, who wore a puzzled expression. "She liked them. So did I. See you in the morning."

Then he and Cay followed Amy to the house. She had gone directly to wrap several loaves of bread she'd baked after dinner, and stood arranging them. Jesse took his nephew into the parlor to work on his numbers.

Amy had become predictable in her dogmatic refusal to talk or even think about anything where their son was concerned. Now there was another child to consider, and that concerned him even more. Her denial wasn't healthy, and his patience had worn thin. He was going to handle things differently this time. He wouldn't end up frustrated and tempted to lose himself again.

"Uncle Jesse?" Cay looked confused. "What happened to your little boy?"

Jesse gazed at the fire. When he spoke it was to say

words he had never said before. "He drowned in the creek." A simple explanation for an event that had changed his life. "He was just three."

"And his name was Timothy." Cay had read that on the marker.

Jesse nodded. "We called him Tim." Just saying his son's name aloud was liberating.

Cay's attention shifted to a spot behind Jesse. Jesse turned to see Amy standing inside the room, her hair still damp from the snow. She wore an expression of betrayal, as though telling Cay the truth somehow made him unfaithful to her…or to their son.

Without a word, she gathered her hem and climbed the stairs. Jesse and Cay exchanged a look and returned to the lesson.

Jesse didn't think Amy slept that night. She was too still, too quiet. Each time he woke, he could feel the emotion emanating from her. This was the way it had been before he started drinking. In shutting out her feelings, she was shutting out him. But he wasn't going to let it go this time. He wasn't going to feel like he was doing something wrong.

"Amy," he said softly into the darkness. "Maybe if we could just talk…"

"Let it go, Jesse."

"You keep acting like if I let it go, everything will be all right. Well, it won't. You think you've let Tim go, but you haven't. You haven't even grieved, and I don't understand how you can *not*. You haven't allowed me to grieve. Why can't we share this?"

When Amy threw back the covers and stood, Jesse got up and padded across the floor to strike a match and light a lamp. Amy wore her gauzy nightdress that revealed the slight swell of her belly. Her braid draped over her shoulder and across her breast, and her eyes were like dark bruises in the soft light. She stared at him as though he were deliberately trying to hurt her.

"Don't keep lookin' at me like you can't figure out what's goin' on." He thrust a hand into his hair and gripped until his scalp hurt. "Denying we had a son or that he's gone won't fix this. Denying that you're carrying a child now won't make our loss go away."

Amy covered her face with both hands and released a sharp cry. "I don't want another child! I don't deserve another child!"

He'd never seen her this anguished, and her distress almost made him feel guilty, but he caught his thoughts before he regressed. Jesse approached her slowly. "Amy, this baby didn't have anything to do with the past. He deserves to be loved and wanted."

"I know," she said from behind her fingers.

He peeled her hands away from her face, but she didn't look at him. "We can't pretend this child isn't comin', and we can't deprive him of our love just because we feel guilty."

"I know," she said again with a nod.

Encouraged, he gently cupped her jaw and turned her

face up to his. Her eyes were dark and liquid, but no tears marred her cheeks. He drew her into his arms, aching for all she held inside, needing her to face the truth.

"We're going to be parents."

She clung to him, her fingers biting into his flesh. "I'll do better, I promise."

"Don't promise me anything, except that you'll always love me and that you'll love our baby." He led her to the bed and lay down with her in his arms. He stroked her back and shoulders until she relaxed against him, and eventually slept.

She had taken a huge step in recognizing her pregnancy, and for that he was grateful. Perhaps this baby would be the key to helping her let go of Tim. Jesse prayed it was so.

The following morning, Jesse tapped on Cay's door on his way past, calling, "Mornin'!"

Amy joined him in the kitchen and he kindled the fire in the stove for her before going out to start chores before breakfast. An early stage arrived, and he changed horses while the driver and passengers made their way to the kitchen for coffee. When the stage had moved on, Jesse returned to the house.

The warm interior smelled like bacon. "Did you have time to feed 'em?"

"They got bacon and toast. I haven't been out for eggs yet."

"Cay still hasn't come down? He could've gathered the eggs for you."

Jesse ran up the stairs and knocked on the door. No response.

Letting himself in, he found the room unoccupied. The bed was unmade and a drawer stood open. Jesse moved forward. The drawer was empty, so were all the others.

He glanced around in bewilderment, a sick feeling in his stomach. He thundered down the stairs. "Did you see Cay this morning?"

Amy and Mrs. Barnes shook their heads. Pitch entered and gave the same answer.

Jesse ran across the yard to the stable. Hermie was just propping a pitch fork against a stall. "Seen Cay?"

"No, boss."

"Are all the horses here?"

Together they checked the stalls and found three empty. "Who's ridden out already?" Deezer's horse was gone. And the one Jack rode. They had been assigned to check fences and probably got an early start. He stood before another empty stall. "The dun mare," Jesse said.

He glanced at the rack of saddles. "How would we even know if there was tack missing? Or a saddle, for that matter?"

"There was a saddle on this divider last night," Hermie replied. "I remember because I was gonna oil it if'n I had a spare minute."

"Why would he take a horse and head out on his own?"

Hermie shook his head.

Amy was heading toward him when Jesse started back toward the house. "Did you find him?"

"Appears he's taken a horse and saddle."

She stared, wide-eyed. "What? Where would he have gone?"

"I don't know."

Biscuit ran up to them then, tail wagging, and they exchanged a worried glance.

Having just ridden in, Sam dismounted and joined them. "Somethin' troublin' you?"

"Cay took a horse and rode out," Jesse told him. "Probably sometime during the night."

Sam looked from one to the other with a puzzled frown. "Why would he do that?"

Jesse shook his head.

"He heard me," said Amy.

"What?" Jesse asked.

"Last night," she continued. "He must have heard us talking. I was upset. I said I didn't want any more children."

Jesse studied the horizon, his jaw set in a grim line.

"It's my fault," she said.

"Oh, for cryin' out loud," Jesse said in disgust. "I'm fed up to here with the two of you takin' the weight of the world on your shoulders. How full of yourselves are you? People do things—bad and good—without your permission. Without you givin' 'em the idea or the reason."

Amy stared at him, but Sam inclined his head in acceptance of the criticism. "Point taken. What do you want to do?"

"Ride after him. Snow last night should assure tracks."

"I'll go with you," Amy said.

"I wasn't plannin' on takin' a buggy."

"I'll ride. I'm going with you, Jesse."

She'd ridden during her first pregnancy, though it had been a while since she'd been on horseback. "We'll take a buggy," Jesse said.

"No, that will slow us down. I'm perfectly capable of riding. I'm going to pack a bag. I'll get your things, too. And I'll have Mrs. Barnes put up food." She turned and headed back to the house.

Jesse looked at Sam. "She's carryin' a child."

Sam's throat worked and he thrust out a hand. "That's good news, son."

Jesse shook his hand. "Maybe it's a blessing in more ways than one. Tell the men I'll figure wages when I return. Tomorrow's payday, and I don't know how long we'll be."

"Nobody's goin' anywhere but you. They'll wait."

Dressed in her winter coat and warm boots, Amy returned before he had the horses ready. She stood aside as he finished saddling and tied on their supplies.

"How would he know which way to head, Jesse? The

prairie all looks the same out there. He'd get lost within an hour."

"He's smart enough to follow the stage trail."

"He heard us quarreling, didn't he. That's why he left."

Jesse gestured for Amy to mount and helped her into the saddle. He shortened the stirrups. "I can't say, but it's likely."

"He's hours ahead of us already if he left then."

"Don't talk more worry into it than's already there." He shrugged into his coat, pulled on gloves and put a foot in the stirrup to swing onto his horse.

Sam stood outside the stable, the dog nestled under one arm to keep it from following them. "Looks like he headed west. Don't worry 'bout the station. We'll handle everything."

Amy reached down and Sam took her hand, closing his fingers over hers. When he released her, she straightened and pulled on her wool mittens, and they rode out. Jesse double-checked the tracks Sam had pointed out and agreed Cay had ridden in that direction. They nudged their horses into a trot.

By mid-morning, Jesse was confident that Cay was following the stage trail. His tracks were obliterated by the morning stage in some places, but plain in others. "He won't get lost," he assured Amy.

At noon Amy dug biscuits and bacon from her saddle bag and offered Jesse a portion. They slowed the horses so they could eat as they rode. They had just

shared a drink from his canteen when Jesse's attention
shifted from the rutted trail to a horse running toward
them. The animal was saddled, with the stirrups hooked
over the saddle horn. To prevent fright and injury, Jesse
had taught Cay to never leave them dangling when the
horse was saddled.

Jesse jumped to the ground and raised one arm.
"Whoa. Whoa, easy, girl." The animal recognized Jesse,
whinnied and trotted right up to him. Jesse took the
reins and looked over the animal.

"That your horse?" Amy studied the landscape in
concern.

"It is."

"The one Cay was riding?"

Jesse nodded. He handed Amy the reins in order to
check hooves. "He's fine. Nothin' wrong."

He mounted, leading the bay behind, and they rode
on. If Cay had been thrown or fallen, he would be along
this trail and they would find him.

Half an hour later, the tracks of hundreds of stage
wheels veered south toward a scrawny patch of trees that
grew alongside a meandering stream. For a quarter of a
mile the trickling stream flowed here to the lowest point,
then disappeared to the south again, but it was obvious
that drivers used the area as a stopping point to rest the
animals and allow passengers to stretch their legs.

This time of year, there was even water flowing in
the bed. Jesse had seen the spot before, knew drivers
carried buckets of water to the horses before moving on.

He dismounted and helped Amy down, then led the three horses to the water, where they lowered their heads and drank. Amy made a trip behind some bushes while he checked the ground for signs of Cay. Farther up around the turn and behind an outgrowth of weeds, he found a flattened area. A close look revealed Cay's boot prints and hoofprints where the dun had been hobbled.

"He hid back there," he told Amy, returning.

She stayed back as he looked at the ground around the trail. He walked forward along the path the stage had taken and found no further evidence, then returned and stood with his hand resting on his holster.

"Looks like he left here on the stage."

Amy blinked. "The driver would have recognized him."

He nodded.

"It was Ben North this morning," Amy recalled. "He'd have asked Cay what he was doing out here. Not that he could have done anything except take him on and turn him over to the law when he reached Fort Crowley."

"Unless he never saw him."

"What do you mean?"

"Cay freed the bay deliberately. He could have slipped up to the stage while Ben and the passengers were down here for water, and stowed away."

"Wouldn't they have seen him? Where's to hide?"

"On top, amid the luggage. It snowed yesterday. That

load was tarped. Clever boy—small, nimble. He could've sprinted right up top and hid himself."

Thinking of Cay's determination to run away hurt Amy. "Didn't he know we wanted him? Was he unhappy with us?"

Without answering Jesse went to bring the horses back up the bank.

"We'll find him, won't we, Jesse?" she asked.

"We'll find him."

Amy's entire body ached by the time it grew dark and they stopped for the night. Jesse found a spot overlooking a river, built a fire and tended to the horses. She made them biscuits and opened a tin of beans while he found branches and set up a small lean-to to keep them dry and the fire out of the wind.

"Do you think the stage has arrived in Fort Crowley yet?" she asked.

"It's a full day's ride with a strong team and a good driver. It's possible Ben got them there by now."

"I guess we could have pushed on."

"It's too dark to risk the horses," he replied. "We'll be there in the morning."

They ate in silence, then cleaned up and bedded down. Jesse tucked Amy alongside him beneath the bedroll, combining their body heat to stay warm.

"I'm not slowing you down, am I?" she asked.

"No. We made good time today."

"Maybe by tomorrow night we'll be home with Cay and in our own bed."

He didn't respond.

Amy closed her eyes and concentrated on Jesse's warmth. She remembered the words she'd spoken the night before, her denial, her blind refusal to accept the changes in her body. She'd been too afraid to admit what Jesse had wanted her to see. Too afraid to acknowledge a new life being entrusted to her.

When she'd had to adjust her new dresses, she'd attributed her growth to simply regaining weight she'd lost. It was easy to lose track of menses and forget she'd missed several. Jesse, on the other hand, wasn't easy to ignore, wouldn't be pushed out of her mind, and she clung to the hope that knowledge gave her.

In his infinite love and concern, he wanted only what was best for her. He had shown her how to be courageous, how to make a change by his own example. Could she be nearly as brave? Could she look into her heart and face her fears and inadequacies as he had?

Amy peeked into the ugly truth that hid in the dark recesses of her mind and shivered.

Jesse hugged her close.

She didn't know if she was strong enough to face it all, to take out the buried memories and expose them to the light of day. If she did, she would know once and for all that she didn't deserve another child.

And so would Jesse.

Chapter Thirteen

Amy had never been to Fort Crowley, but Jesse knew his way around. Inside the log walls of the fort was a lively community. Men and women traveled the boardwalks, calling greetings to one another, and the shops bustled with activity.

The Shelbys started their search by checking at the livery station where the stage had stopped. The attendant didn't remember a boy, and the stage had already moved on, having left only one passenger behind.

Jesse located the man, a printer by trade, and inquired about Cay.

"No lad on the stage," the man told him.

"Did you notice a boy after you reached Fort Crowley?"

The man shook his head.

Jesse returned to Amy, where she waited with the horses, and told her he'd learned nothing. She glanced around, overwhelmed by the impossibility of finding Cay.

"How will we find him, Jesse?"

"He's a city boy. He'll find his way around. He'd need food first off." He left her again to search.

The restaurant owners hadn't seen Cay, but the man who ran the trading post recalled a lad who bought jerky and inquired of a job.

"What did you tell him?"

"Told him I didn't need no one, but that Bartholomew over at the saloon always needs help sweeping and emptying spittoons."

"Thank you, sir." Hopeful, Jesse crossed the street and found the saloon. He turned back to where Amy waited near a water trough, anxiously watching, before he pushed through the bat-wing doors.

The stale smells of smoke and whiskey assailed him. His attention was drawn to rows of bottles filled with amber liquid lining the rear counter, and his stomach lurched. He moved to the scarred wooden bar. A tremor ran through his hand as he touched the surface, and he pulled back.

A beefy man with an apron laid down a pearl-handled .45 he'd been oiling, and lumbered over. "Want a shot, mister?"

Jesse could almost feel the burn of whiskey sliding down his throat; he relived the warmth in his chest as alcohol numbed his senses. He looked directly at the man and shoved aside the insidious thought.

"No thanks. I understand you might have hired a lad to sweep just this morning."

"The kid belong to you?"

"He's my nephew."

The man cocked his head. "Mr. Bart hired a kid. He's probably still out back emptying ashes from the stove." He gestured with a thumb. "That hallway leads to the rear."

"Thanks." Encouraged, Jesse followed the directions, boots clomping across the worn floorboards.

He discovered a storage room stacked with crates of liquor and bins of empty bottles. Another door marked "Private" was locked, so he moved on to the exit. As he pushed open the grimy paint-peeling door, the rusted hinges squeaked. He stepped out.

The sound of a pail dropping alerted him, and he discovered Cay running in the opposite direction down the alley. Relieved to see his nephew, Jesse took a second to recognize that Cay didn't want to be found and to get his feet moving. He shot after the boy, who dodged barrels and trash bins, and darted around a corner.

The narrow passageway between two buildings opened out onto the main thoroughfare. Ahead of him, Cay dashed into the street, narrowly avoiding a horse and buggy, and startling another horse and rider. Jesse was at his heels, ignoring the curses shouted after him.

From her position, Amy spotted Cay. She quickly tied the horses to a hitching rail and raced after him, too, as he entered another alley. Jesse caught up with her and they ran until they reached the backs of the buildings.

The boy was nowhere in sight.

Beyond was the log wall of the fort. To the right, a fence too high for him to jump. The only path he could have taken was to the left, and they immediately set out that way.

A cat yowled and startled Amy. She froze for a moment, then pushed onward. They had stumbled into the residential section of town, and ahead lay tiny yards with outhouses, wood piles, and clotheslines hung with flapping laundry.

Winded, she paused. "Why is he running? He could be anywhere. There are a hundred places to hide. Why won't he talk to us?"

Jesse caught his breath. "I'm prepared to check a hundred places. Are you?"

She nodded.

They split up to investigate yards and privies and wood bins. Jesse called Cay's name a few times, and once a back door slammed shut as he passed. Irritation kicked aside some of the worry he'd been fighting down. Confound the boy, he had to know they cared for him! What kind of fool stunt was he pulling?

After half an hour, Jesse rose from peering beneath a porch and came nose-to-gun-barrel with a lawman. The deputy wore a sheepskin coat with a tin star on the front.

"What are you lookin' for, mister?"

Jesse raised both hands to show he wasn't holding a gun. "My nephew, Cay Shelby. He ran away from home yesterday and we tracked him here. I came upon him out back o' the saloon, but he got away."

"You beat him?"

Jesse stiffened and lowered his hands. "Of course not."

"Shelby, you say?"

Amy came up beside Jesse.

"Name's Jesse Shelby. This here's my wife, Amy. We run a—"

"Shelby Station," the deputy interrupted. "I know who you are." He holstered the gun. "You riled a few womenfolk, sneakin' through their yards, Mr. Shelby. Maybe you'd best let the law look for your boy."

"We've looked everywhere." Amy's voice and her expression showed her heartfelt concern.

Jesse noticed that her nose was red from the cold and her eyes held a haunted look. "My wife's tired. I'm gonna find us a room."

"Carolyn Bridges runs a clean place and the eats are decent. You'll find it if you head out on the street and take a left."

"Thanks. You'll look for Cay?"

"I will. If I find anything, I'll look for you at Carolyn's."

"Thanks."

Jesse took Amy's hand and led her back to the street, where they found the boardinghouse. He paid the rotund woman who greeted them. "I'd like a bath for my wife and something to eat, please."

"Surely." She handed him a brass key.

Jesse led Amy up the stairs and opened the door. The room was plain, but clean, with a bed, a lopsided chest of drawers and a washstand. "I'll go put up the horses at the livery. You rest."

By mid-afternoon, Amy had bathed and napped and they'd both eaten. Jesse went to find the sheriff's office, but none of the officers had turned up anything. He spent the rest of the day asking business owners and citizens if they'd seen Cay.

By evening, discouragement weighed on him as he stood in their room staring down at the street.

"Jesse." Amy lay on the bed. She rolled to her back, "I'm sorry."

He met her gaze. "It's okay, Amy."

"You were right all along. When Cay first arrived, I resented him being with us. I don't know why. I told you I was afraid he'd run away. And now he has. But not because he was a troublemaker. Because I ran him off."

"You didn't run him off. You did the best you could. He just misunderstood somethin' he heard, that's all."

"But if he'd known how I truly felt about him, he wouldn't have misunderstood. I should have told him I love him."

Jesse turned to look back down at the street lit by gas lamps. How long had he stifled the longing to hear those words himself? "You haven't even told me you loved *me* for a long time."

He shouldn't have said that. Amy didn't respond

well to pushing, but he wasn't much for holdin' back what he was thinkin'.

Her clothing rustled as she sat up. A board creaked and her reflection came into view in the pane of glass. If he'd made her angry, at least she was still willing to talk to him. He studied her wavy likeness without turning around.

"I love you, Jesse. I do."

Her admission touched that place of need in his heart. His throat tightened. He composed his emotions, let the curtain fall into place and turned.

She'd never had to worry about being vulnerable to him. Never. He returned her love, relished it, gloried in it. Why had it taken her so long?

Amy looked into Jesse's blue eyes and saw her love returned. She'd been afraid of being vulnerable to *herself.* Of opening up a flood of well-sealed emotions and letting herself feel *anything.* Even love for him.

But love him she did. Amy confessed the truth as much for herself as for him. And the admission made her feel lighter than she had for a long time—for months, for more than a year. Loving too much hurt sometimes, and she'd pulled into herself for protection. But not letting herself love hurt just as much. Maybe more.

"I shut you out," she told him, her voice unsteady. "I thought if I didn't love, I wouldn't hurt. I did the same thing with Cay."

He took her in his arms and held her against his

chest. Jesse was warmth and safety and comfort, but she'd never let him be those things to her before. Feeling safe and warm made her again think of Cay.

"Where do you think he is tonight? Where will he sleep?"

"I don't know."

She leaned away and grasped his forearms as a horrible thought struck her. "He wouldn't take another stage and leave Fort Crowley because he knows we're looking for him, would he?"

"I don't know. I didn't think he'd run away at all."

"Maybe you'd better go to the freight station and the livery and ask them to watch for him in case he tries to leave."

"That's a good idea." He grabbed his coat and hat. "I'll check the saloon again, too, in case he went back for his pay."

After Jesse left, Amy turned the key in the lock and stepped to the window, where she watched the street below as Jesse crossed and headed down the boardwalk.

An hour later he was back with a pail of warm water and a cup of coffee, which they shared.

Jesse removed his boots and socks and hung his holster on the metal bed frame. He wearily removed his shirt and washed at the basin.

Hours later, he and Amy lay side by side on the bed, the unfamiliar noise from the street below as much of a detriment to sleep as the worry they shared. Amy turned on her side and rested her head on Jesse's chest.

A knock sounded on the door.

They sat bolt upright in the darkness, and Jesse grabbed his Colt from its holster and stepped to the door. "Who is it?"

"I got somethin' to tell ya," returned a small voice.

Jesse turned the key and the knob and opened the door enough to see who stood in the hall. He immediately dropped the gun to his side and took a step back. "Who are you?"

A small boy with shaggy brown hair and a tattered jacket stood in the opening. "How much're you willin' to pay to know where your kid is?"

"You know where Cay is?" Amy climbed from the bed and pulled on her coat to cover her nightdress.

"He's clean and has hair and eyes like you," he said to Jesse. "Wears a nice coat and boots."

"Where is he?" Amy asked.

"I figure you're rich enough to pay b'fore I tell."

"Pay him, Jesse."

Jesse moved to the belongings he'd placed inside the top drawer of the chest. He took six dollars in coins and held them out to the urchin.

The child's hazel eyes lit with appreciation when he saw the money. "I'll take you to 'im. But first you gotta give me the money."

Jesse dropped the coins into his grimy palm. "I'll give you half now, and half when I see Cay."

The young boy scowled, but he tucked his three dollars safely away.

After pulling on his boots and shirt, Jesse strapped on his holster. Amy handed him his hat and coat, but her eyes were on the child with the dirty hair and clothing. The toes of his shoes were worn clear through the leather. What kind of parent let a child dress so poorly and roam the streets at this hour of the night?

She watched them leave and then ran to the window, but didn't see them down on the street.

Jesse followed the boy through the alley behind the hotel. He'd traveled enough alleys that day and sure didn't want one of the deputies to spot him back here again.

"Where are we goin'?"

"Ssh." The ragamuffin held a finger to his lips.

"Sorry," Jesse whispered. "Where are we goin'?"

"I'll show you."

"What's your name?"

"They call me Scrap."

"How do you know where Cay is?"

"Found 'im and showed 'im where to sleep."

"Where's that?"

"I'll show you if you quit yappin'."

Jesse stopped trying to talk and followed. The boy called Scrap led him behind a brick building and across a vacant lot to where a few tents sat. Beyond those was a grassy area that held broken wagons and cannon carts. Scrap pointed at a spot beneath a lopsided wagon, where layers of newspaper covered what appeared to be a sleeping form.

Jesse looked at Scrap, who met his eyes in the darkness and nodded. He held out his hand.

As yet unconvinced, Jesse crawled under the wagon until he could see hair and an ear. Scrap followed. Stealthily, Jesse raised a layer of newspaper and made out the side of the boy's face, finding it familiar. Relief and anger assailed him.

Scrap tugged on his coat sleeve and Jesse reached in his pocket and handed over the last of the coins. Closing his fingers over them, Scrap scrambled backward from beneath the wagon.

To assure Cay didn't escape again, Jesse clamped onto the boy's shoulder and pulled him out from under the wagon. Cay awoke startled, and struggled to get away from his captor. Newspapers flew in all directions. Jesse got a steady grip on him by holding him against his body and locking his forearm over Cay's chest.

"Stop," he told him. "It's me. Uncle Jesse."

The skirmish ceased. "Uncle Jesse?"

Jesse turned the boy to face him. "I warrant you are in a serious fix about now, so you'd best stop struggling and come along."

Cay obediently stopped struggling and stood as though prepared for whatever might befall him. "Why'd you make such a fuss over comin' after me, anyhow?"

Jesse took his arm and glanced around. The other boy was nowhere to be seen. "Why d'ya think?"

"I dunno. I'm a bother, so you should be glad I left."

"We've got some talking to do." Jesse made his way to the street and along the fronts of the buildings. He led Cay into the boardinghouse and up the stairs.

After a quick rap, he said, "It's Jesse."

The key was turned from inside and Amy opened the door. Her expectant gaze lit on Cay, and she reached for him, pulling him inside and hugging him soundly. She buried her face in his hair.

After a few minutes, she released him and moved to sit on the edge of the bed. "Do you know how worried we've been?" She patted the edge, indicating he should join her, and he did.

He shook his head. "No."

"We followed you and we've been looking all over. Why did you run from Jesse today?"

He shrugged.

Amy drew a breath as though gathering her composure. "I know why you ran off."

"You do?"

She nodded. "You heard Jesse and me, night before last. I was upset and I said some things I didn't really mean. Can you understand that? Have you ever said things you didn't mean?"

Her question was met with another shrug.

"You heard me say I didn't want more children, didn't you?"

Gaze on the floor, Cay nodded.

"And you thought that meant you."

"It ain't like you wanted a kid," he said. "You din't

ask for me. You just got stuck with me, like my gran did."

"Your grandma loved you very much. That's why she wanted to make sure you were safe with us. Most times we don't choose the family we get. Just like havin' your own baby, you can't pick the one you want."

"But leastwise a baby's yours," he replied logically.

"And how do you get a baby?" she asked.

Cay's cheeks pinkened, and Jesse wondered where she was going with that question.

"From God, that's where. He gives you a baby when he thinks you're ready. Like he gave you to us."

"My ma din't want no baby," he said defiantly.

Amy's expression showed her compassion. "But she loved you enough to give you to someone who would take care of you and love you like you needed."

He raised his gaze then, skeptical but interested. "How would you know that?"

"If your mother hadn't loved you, she could have let you die. Or left you at a foundling home. But she didn't. She took you to your grandma because she knew that would be best for you. Just like your grandma brought you to us."

Cay studied Amy's face as though he'd never before considered the possibility that his mother had loved him. Jesse himself had always doubted it, having known his sister's impulsive, selfish nature, but Amy's explanation made it believable. She'd just given Cay something extraordinary, something no one had ever given him before: belief that his mother had cared.

"Cay, Jesse and I love you. We already had problems between us before you ever came to us—you didn't cause them. In fact, you've helped us." She touched his hair and tilted his chin up on her palm. "I love you. Promise you won't ever scare us like that and run away again."

"I promise." Cay threw himself into Amy's arms and laid his head against her breast.

She smoothed his hair and rocked him as though he were an infant.

Swallowing back tears, Jesse hung his coat and hat. "Are you hungry, Cay?"

Cay shook his head. "Scrap got us food tonight."

"How did he pay for it?"

"I dunno, but I paid him for my share."

"You used your earnings?"

He nodded.

Jesse tilted his head as though to say, well, it was Cay's money. "What do you know about Scrap?"

"Nothin'. Just that he lives back there where you found me, and that he knows how to get food and stuff."

She glanced at Jesse. "Where did you find him?"

"Sleepin' under a wagon."

"And Scrap *lives* there?" Amy asked.

Cay nodded. "I asked him about his family, and he said his pa had left 'em a long time ago and his ma died."

Amy looked from Cay to Jesse in shock. "And he's allowed to live without a home or anyone to care for him?"

Jesse shrugged. "I'll inquire about him at the sheriff's in the morning."

"That won't be long now." She glanced toward the window. "We'd better get some sleep."

Jesse locked the door. "Cay, you take the bed with Amy, and I'll stretch out on the floor." He opened both bedrolls, which had been stacked in the corner, and made himself comfortable.

Cay shucked down to his union suit and lay on the bed. "Think Sam's worried, too?"

"He is," Jesse replied. "I'll send a telegram to Liscom's first thing, so he'll know we found you."

Cay pulled the blanket up to his chin. "Okay."

"Where did you sleep last night?" Amy asked.

"Same as tonight—under the wagon," he replied. "Scrap found me last night and showed me the place to hide out."

"Weren't you afraid?"

Cay didn't say anything.

"Men don't admit to being afraid," Jesse told her in the darkness.

"Pardon me. Did you miss us? Would that be okay to admit?"

"I missed home somethin' awful." A few minutes passed. "I'm glad you found me."

"Me too," Amy answered.

Reassured now that Cay was with them, and pretty

certain that the boy understood he was wanted at Shelby Station, Jesse closed his eyes.

Cay had called it *home*.

While Jesse visited the sheriff the next morning, Amy led Cay into a dry goods store and he helped her shop for fabric and ready-made shirts for Jesse and her father. She purchased two shirts as well as two new pairs of dungarees for Cay.

The store carried rows of footwear, and she insisted Cay try on boots until he found a pair that fit him well. "It'll be getting colder and you'll need warm socks," she told him.

Cay looked down at the new pair of boots thoughtfully. "There will be lots of snow soon, huh?"

She nodded as she looked over spools of thread.

"Scrap don't have very warm clothes," he said.

Amy stopped in reaching for a package of needles and looked at Cay. She'd been unable to get the other boy out of her mind. Surely someone would take care of him before winter set in hard.

Jesse found them, and he and Cay carried the packages to the boardinghouse, then returned and met Amy in front of an eatery with red-and-white checked curtains in the windows.

Inside, they seated themselves, and a tall young woman with braids wound around her head brought them cups and a slate with the day's menu. They ordered and she hurried away.

Amy folded her hands on the table. "What did the sheriff say?"

"He knows about the boy, of course. Seems he's been taken by the authorities before, but always manages to run away. Apparently that Bartholomew fellow at the saloon said he'd be responsible for him, and lets him sleep in a back room when the weather is bad."

"That's unacceptable," Amy responded. "What about the families in town, the church women? Why doesn't someone take him in and provide for him?"

"Seems his mother wasn't respectable enough for them," Jesse replied. "They look the other way."

Amy's compassion and sense of injustice had been riled. "If I lived here, they'd have a piece of my mind."

"I'm certain they would."

Steaming plates of roast beef and mashed potatoes were delivered. Jesse and Cay picked up their forks.

"Well, we'll just have to take him home with us, then."

Their forks paused midway to their mouths and similar blue gazes turned to her. Jesse laid his fork on his plate, the bite uneaten.

"Are you sure?"

"Can we let a child spend the winter under a wagon or sleep in the back of a saloon?"

He raised a brow and couldn't disagree. "I reckon not."

Amy looked over at Cay. "What do you think? Do you object to inviting Scrap to come live with us?"

Cay seemed to consider for only a few seconds. "I think everybody should have a family."

Amy's smile made her appear less weary. "Then we'll go to the sheriff and tell him what we're thinking. Then we'll find the boy and ask him. If he wants to come with us, the sheriff will have to take whatever steps he must to make it legal. We should probably consult an attorney while we're here."

Jesse had no objections. Amy made it sound like the only thing they could do.

Cay set down his cup and grinned with a milk mustache. "Boy, will Sam be surprised."

Chapter Fourteen

Jesse bought a springboard from a man selling his possessions to move back East. He made the best of the day, buying supplies and a few extras, and treating Amy and Cay to meals in the restaurant.

In the afternoon, the sheriff sent for them, and the Shelbys entered the lawman's office. Jesse walked forward.

"You wanted to see us?"

"I rounded up the kid for you. I wired Denver and heard back that the foundling home there will send papers to make you taking him legal."

Amy glanced around. "Where is he?"

"In the rear."

She took note of the solid door behind him. A terrible suspicion filled her mind. "Are you holding the child in a cell?"

"Ma'am, he fought tooth and nail just getting him here—what was I to do with him?"

"Let him out right now!"

"He'll just run."

Amy looked to Jesse for help.

"Once he's turned over to us, that will be our problem, won't it?" Jesse asked.

"It sure will."

"Let's go talk to him." Jesse gestured for Cay to take a seat and wait for them.

The sheriff opened the door and led them along a narrow corridor with half a dozen small, caged cells.

"There he is. Name's Richards by the way. Toby Richards."

The boy who'd come to their room the previous night sat on the end of a narrow cot. He glared at them, anger and resentment in his hazel eyes. Amy experienced a slice of pain in her chest. The urchin looked so alone and so young, and the inhumanity of locking up an innocent child chafed. She hoped he'd be open to their invitation.

She moved to the bars. "Unlock the door and let us in, please."

Apparently seeing no harm, the sheriff used a brass key to turn the lock, then ushered them in. Amy entered first and Jesse followed. The sheriff closed the cell door behind them.

Amy turned and pointedly stared at the sheriff, and the man returned to the outer office.

She took a step toward the young boy, deliberately

keeping her distance so as not to frighten him. Beneath the belligerent scowl he wore, she recognized his apprehension. "You know who we are?"

"Know I helped you catch your kid and then you done this to me."

She didn't argue with him. Instead she asked, "How old are you, Toby?"

"Old enough to know I don't want to live in no orphan asylum."

"We don't want that for you, either. How about living with us? Think you could tolerate that?"

The boy narrowed his gaze and scratched at his dirty neck. The action made Amy cringe inside. "What're you fixin' to pull?"

"Nothing. You helped us, now we'd like to help you."

"What for?"

Jesse spoke up. "We can always use hands. We operate a stage station. Cay helps us, too. Did he tell you anything about it?"

Toby nodded. "An' I told him he shoulda stayed long wise he had a bed and food and stuff."

"We had a misunderstanding, the three of us," Jesse explained. "But it's all settled now. He's comin' home. We just thought—since you helped us and all—and since we could use the extra hands—that you might want to come along too."

Amy appreciated Jesse's man-to-man approach and the way he spared the child's pride.

The boy had a difficult time covering his surprise, but

it was obvious he wasn't convinced the offer was plain and simple. "You'd pay me?"

Jesse nodded. "Cay earns wages. You would, too."

"Cay also works on his lessons each night," Amy added, hoping that wouldn't scare him but needing him to understand what they would expect. "We would want you to learn to read and write so you could help Jesse with the lists and the ledgers and so forth. Have you been to school?"

"No, ma'am. But before my ma died, she was teachin' me to figure."

His polite address touched her. "Well, that's a good start."

Jesse stood with one hand on the iron bars. "You understand, Toby, that we'd be wantin' to make this legal? You would become part of our family. It's more of a family position we're lookin' to fill than a job."

The boy glanced from one of them to the other. "Couldn't nobody take me away after that? Make me go back to the orphan asylum?"

"No one could do that," Jesse assured him.

"What if you decide you don't like me? What if your boy don't like me?"

Jesse shrugged. "What if you don't like us?"

After scratching his head, Toby stood up. "Guess we'll all be takin' a chance, eh?"

"We will need your word that you won't run away," Amy told him. "It's too fearful hard on parents when they don't know where their young'uns are."

"Can I talk to Cay first? B'fore I give my word and say yes?"

"Surely. A man's word shouldn't be given lightly."

Toby's proud posture conveyed that Jesse had spared his dignity.

Jesse stepped to the front of the cell and called for Cay. The sheriff let him in.

"Toby would like to talk to you," Jesse said.

Jesse and Amy followed the sheriff out, leaving the two boys alone. A few minutes later, Cay called, "It's okay. You can let us out."

The sheriff opened the cell and Toby walked out beside Cay, obviously with no intention of bolting. He was thinner and shorter than Jesse's nephew, but Amy would almost have guessed him to be older. Perhaps it was just the life he'd been living and the lack of decent food that had added years.

"I'm set to go with the Shelbys," Toby Richards told the sheriff.

"All right, then, son. An agent will visit you before the papers are finished. You tell the agent then if you want to stay for good."

If the boy felt awkward leaving with them, he didn't show it. He strolled along the boardwalk beside the Shelbys, big as you please, grinning at anyone who gave them a second look or stopped to gawk.

"Let them look," Amy said. "If a one of them had a shred of decency, they'd have taken you home with them."

Amy paused, and her three companions turned quizzical eyes on her. She looked Toby over, then surveyed the street. Her attention lit on a painted sign on the other side.

Jesse, Cay and Toby turned to see what had her so interested. Then Jesse placed both hands on his hips and looked down at the boy. "Come with me, lad. We have a stop to make."

Amy smiled encouragingly. "Cay and I will pick up a clean set of clothes and Cay will run them over to you."

Toby accompanied Jesse into a narrow building boasting hot baths.

Amy and Cay exchanged a glance, then hurried to run their errand.

It was nearly an hour later that Jesse and his young companion located them in the dry goods store. Amy widened her eyes and flattened her palm over her breast. "Well, if you don't beat all! There was a handsome lad under all that dirt and hair."

Jesse had even seen to getting Toby's hair cut. It was wet and dark and parted on the side. The boy had a handsome forehead and dark brows. His hazel eyes sparkled. Amy gave him an impulsive hug. He didn't return her embrace, but he allowed it.

She proceeded to select shirts and dungarees, boots and union suits for him. "And a coat," she told the proprietor. "He'll need a warm coat and a pair of gloves."

That evening, they sat in the restaurant with the red-

and-white checkered curtains and tablecloths. If the grin on his face was any indication, Toby relished sharing a place at the table more than the meal. Amy stared back at a couple who were unnaturally interested in the Shelbys, and they looked away.

After one more night at the boardinghouse, this time with Cay and Toby on the floor, they rose before daylight, packed the wagon, and set out with the three horses tied to the rear.

The light snow that fell didn't hinder the boys who sat in the back pretending to shoot Indians.

Amy smiled at Jesse on the seat beside her, and he took her mittened hand.

"Our family is really growing now, Amy."

She leaned into him. "Is my father ever going to be surprised."

The closer they drew to home and the more Amy thought over everything that had happened, the more she worried about what had made Cay run away. She considered what she'd said that had hurt him so. She loved Cay. She hadn't meant to feed his insecurities. She'd just been so afraid. Afraid of the new baby. Afraid of hurting Jesse more. Afraid she didn't deserve to have children.

Saying what she had so that he could hear it was quite likely proof that she couldn't be trusted with kids. All she'd ever wanted was a husband to love, a home and children. Lots of children. Amy drew her coat tightly around her and felt the chill air seep into her bones. She'd nearly ruined things with Cay. Now she'd taken on Toby. She might make more mistakes. Might make mistakes with the new baby. That thought terrified her. Could she do this? Could she really do this?

Mr. Quenton's photographs had been unavoidably realistic. She'd seen herself, her father, Jesse, the hands all looking so natural and so genuine. Pictures pointed out details. They were memories a body could see.

And some of those memories haunted her. Those she'd wanted hidden. Those she couldn't face.

Still couldn't face.

But they were there, nonetheless. And each feeling she admitted drew her closer to those she couldn't allow. Dark memories just under the surface. Huge responsibilities. And the worry of a new baby.

A baby.

Amy let herself really think about it, finally. Just like Rachel, she would have a tiny life to nourish and cherish. She was being entrusted with a life much more helpless and needy than Cay or Toby.

That grave in the photograph proved how well she'd done the last time.

The station came into view, and the boys scrambled to stand behind her and hold onto the back of her seat for balance. Jesse smiled ear to ear, and Cay shouted, "There's Sam!"

Inside, Amy was a jumble of doubts and regrets, but she plastered a smile to her lips. All along she had thought she'd let things go, but just as Jesse accused time and again, all the turmoil had been right there inside her, waiting for her to open herself up and let it churn.

She felt so different from others. Like the shell of a person she pretended to be on the outside, while underneath hid the real person, the Amy no one would love or accept if they knew her true identity. She felt alone in her guilt.

Now that all these emotions had been stirred up, it took a lot more effort to tamp them down. Determinedly, she chose to lay all that aside and share the joy of this reunion, as well as the introductions.

Sam met them in front of the stables, a grin on his face. He opened the double doors and stood to the side. Biscuit gave an excited yelp and appeared from the interior, tail wagging.

"We've been waitin' for you," Sam called.

Jesse led the team inside.

Sam helped Amy down and hugged her soundly. "How'd you do, girl?"

"Just fine, Daddy."

Cay bounded down from the wagon and ran to where they stood. Biscuit sniffed at his ankles and trotted alongside. He paused to pet the animal's fur and received a lick on the chin. "I'm back, Sam!" he called, standing up and taking a step forward.

Sam released Amy and hooked the boy around the neck, bringing him up against his coat in a gruff hug.

Cay's hat fell off and Sam ruffled his hair. When Sam released him, Cay picked up Biscuit.

Sam's attention centered on the other young person who still stood in the bed of the wagon. His curious gaze shot to Amy.

"Come on down, Toby," she called, and gestured for him to join them. "This is my father, Sam Burnham."

Toby approached the older man hesitantly. Biscuit barked at the new arrival and Toby glanced at the dog in Cay's arms, but spoke to Sam. "How do, sir."

"Toby helped us find Cay," Amy told him. "We asked him to come home with us."

"I see," Sam replied, but it was obvious he didn't.

She would tell him all about it later.

Jesse closed the stable doors and unloaded the crates.

Cay set down Biscuit and picked up a stack of brown-paper-wrapped packages containing their new clothing. "Where's Toby gonna stay?"

Amy turned toward Jesse, who paused in his work and removed his coat. They studied each other thoughtfully. They hadn't discussed sleeping arrangements. She didn't want Cay to feel they were crowding in on him, but neither did she want Toby to think he wasn't part of the family. And the only empty bedroom would be needed for the baby. Of course, the baby could always sleep in their room for some time….

"Can he bunk with me?" Cay asked. "I'd like havin' the company."

Relieved, Amy smiled. "I think that would be perfect."

When Amy pushed open the kitchen door, Rachel and Mrs. Barnes were drying and stacking dishes from the noon meal. Her arms were filled with packages.

"Amy!" Rachel ran forward. "Sam told us you'd be back today."

Amy dropped her packages and spontaneously hugged the young woman, then found herself giving Mrs. Barnes a hug as well. Mrs. Barnes looked surprised, but she didn't let Amy's greeting fluster her.

"Something agreed with you. You seem different."

"I am. And it's so good to be home. I ate out at a restaurant every day we were in Fort Crowley. But by this morning I was ready to be in my own kitchen. She took off her coat and hung it. "Where's that little girl?"

Catherine, as Jack and Rachel had named her, was sleeping soundly in a cradle beside the fireplace, a soft knitted blanket tucked around her. She lay with her head to the side, her fists at her ears and her dark lashes against her cheeks. Amy's heart tugged at the sight. She reached out and her finger grazed her tiny knuckles. "She grew while I was away."

"She's such a good baby," Rachel told her proudly.

Amy turned back to pick up the wrapped bundles and place them on the table. "I have gifts."

Rachel came forward with a hand pressed to her breast. "For *us?*"

Without wasting a moment, Amy untied and unwrapped, revealing her purchases. "These are for you," she said, presenting Mrs. Barnes with a pair of white gloves and a belt with a filigree buckle.

The woman carefully dried her hands before accepting the accessories with obvious pleasure. "I have just the dress to wear these with—thank you, Amy."

"And this is for you." She handed a stack of fabric with spools of matching thread atop to Rachel. "I'll help you, and we can make dresses for you and for Catherine."

"This is too generous," Rachel said with tears in her eyes. She'd gotten by with very little until she and Jack had started earning wages at Shelby Station. New dresses must seem like a luxury to her.

"I couldn't get along without either one of you," Amy said truthfully. "And I don't just mean the work you do." She knew she'd never been quite so forthright with her feelings, and Mrs. Barnes wore an expression of appreciation and pleasure.

"I have a few things for Adele and Maggie, as well," she said. She wrapped the last items and set them aside. There was something else she needed to say. Gathering her courage, she faced the two women. "I'm going to have a baby."

"Oh! A baby!" Rachel squealed and hugged her again.

Mrs. Barnes gave Amy an assessing look of concern. "Is it going to be all right?"

The woman had been around Amy long enough to know this was a change of heart. "It's going to be all right," she assured her.

After wiping the corner of her eye on her apron, Mrs. Barnes said with all sincerity, "I'm so happy for you and Jesse."

Amy read relief on the woman's face.

The commotion of feet hitting the porch floor and the dog excitedly barking arrested their attention.

Amy drew a fortifying breath. "There's someone else I need to tell you about."

Both women eyed her curiously.

Just then the back door opened and Cay burst through the opening, Toby on his heels. "Is there any dinner left?" Cay asked.

The two women looked at the pair of boys in surprise. Then both smiled and hurried to bring the youngsters a meal.

Toby ate like there was no tomorrow, and for much of his life he hadn't been certain there would be. Amy had excused his manners until now, but she knew she wouldn't be doing him any favors by not teaching him correctly. In order not to single him out, she would incorporate mealtime etiquette into their lessons. True, they would be sharing a table with the hands most of the time, but many city travelers came through. Besides, Cay and Toby would be young men someday, and they should know how to present themselves.

That evening, she set the table for the four of them—Jesse, Cay, Toby and herself. She poured drinks, placed a napkin at each setting and served apple strudel. With patient tutoring, she taught the lads to use their napkins, eat slowly and swallow each bite instead of washing it down. Apparently amused by her calm lesson, Jesse listened with half a smile and joined them in each step.

"When you're finished, thank the cook and ask to be excused."

"What for?"

Toby's puzzled frown almost made her laugh. "Simply say, 'Thank you for the fine meal. May I please be excused?'"

Toby leaned toward Jesse and said man to man, "I din't pass no gas."

To his credit, Jesse kept a straight face. "A lad asks permission to leave the table, son."

"Oh." Toby sat back and looked at Amy. "Fine strudel, ma'am. Best I ever et. Can I be 'scused? Er, please?"

"Thank you, Toby, and yes you may. You boys wash up now and get ready for bed."

"I already washed this mornin', din't I, Cay?"

"We wash before bed, as well. When the weather's warm, you can wash at the basins on the back porch. When it's cold, you take a pitcher to your room and use the bowl. Water's on the well on the back of the stove. And clean your teeth."

"Again?"

She nodded.

"I ain't never knowed people what washed and cleaned so much. I don't know how you got any skin left."

"As you can see, our skin is all still intact, so it won't hurt you a whit," Jesse replied.

Cay filled a pitcher with water and Toby followed him out of the room. Their feet sounded on the stairs.

"This is all new to him," Jesse said.

"He's doing well." She picked up their dishes.

"I'll be checkin' the buildings and the animals now."

In his absence, Amy washed up their dishes and worked on the finishing touches of her dresses. She probably wouldn't be able to wear them for long. A funny feeling made her stomach dip. She would have to open the chest of clothing she'd packed away and bring out the clothes with drawstring waists and over-shirts to accommodate her growth. With the last hem in place, she heated the iron and pressed both dresses.

She'd carried them upstairs and hung them in her wardrobe, Jesse's voice drifted after her. Peering into the hall, she discovered him standing at the opening to Cay's—to the boys'—room. She joined him and they stepped inside.

Cay and Toby were seated on the bed in their union suits. Amy went to the chest at the foot of the bed and took out another blanket. "You might be needing this." Both of them scrambled under the covers, and Jesse helped her settle the blanket over the boys.

For a few seconds an awkwardness hung over them, but she refused to revisit the same mistakes she'd already made. She had never come in and wished Cay a good-night. She'd been uncomfortable with that—he wasn't a small child, after all, and she hadn't wanted to embarrass him. But he needed to know he was cared for and wanted. Everyone needed to know those things. She was starting over right now with both of these youngsters, and she could only pray they would accept her affection.

Because she stood nearest to Toby, she bent to tuck the covers around him. "I'm glad you came home with us. We'll all have to get used to each other, and some things we'll just have to work out. But this is a new start for all of us."

His eyes were dark in the glow of the lantern. He simply returned her gaze.

"Good night, Toby."

"Ain't nobody called me that since my ma," he said.

"Well, it's your name, and it's a fine name." She bent and kissed his forehead.

Jesse stepped back as she moved around the end of the bed to Cay's side, where she fussed with the blankets. "Remember, you made a promise to us."

"I remember. I won't never run away again."

"Because we're a family," she confirmed.

He nodded.

"And we want you here with us." She bent to kiss his forehead, and he brought an arm out of the covers to wrap it around her neck and kiss her cheek.

Emotion welling inside her, she turned down the wick, plunging the room into darkness.

"'Night, fellas." Jesse took her arm and led her from

the room, closing the door and following her to their room.

She changed into her nightdress and sat at her dressing table, where she removed the pins from her hair. Dressed in only his trousers, Jesse padded to stand behind her. He took the brush from her hand and brushed the ends of her hair first, working out any tangles, then stroked from her scalp to the tips. When they were first married, he used to brush her hair like this often. She closed her eyes and enjoyed the tingling pleasure and the relaxing sensation that washed over her.

Laying down the brush, he drew her hair to one side, exposing her neck. He leaned to kiss her skin and nuzzle her ear, then traced a finger along her collarbone and inside the neck of her gown, creating delicious shivers.

"Cold?" he asked. "Maybe we'd better get under the covers."

She accepted the hand he extended. He led her to the bed, then extinguished the lamp, divested himself of his drawers and climbed in beside her.

Gently, almost reverently, he caressed her shoulder, then her breast. His touch moved across the swell of her belly, his hand warm through the fabric of her gown.

Wanting to be closer, Amy worked the hem upward, and he helped her cast the nightdress aside. She took his hand and placed it on her abdomen again.

Jesse drew the covers down so he could press his lips to the place where their child grew. Amy stroked his hair and freed her heart to accept. Accept this new life they'd created. Accept her responsibility.

As though a spiritual connection bound all three of them, a tiny flutter, like delicate wings, quickened in her womb. Their baby made its presence known for the first time. Her heart skipped a beat at the same time Jesse raised his head.

"Amy, I felt that."

A myriad of feelings pushed their way past Amy's defenses. The first tear she'd cried in forever leaked from the corner of her eye and trickled down her temple, followed by another, and another. Her chest quaked and a sob was retched from her being. She clamped her hand over her mouth.

Immediately Jesse pulled her hand away. He bracketed her face between his palms and kissed her eyes, her cheeks, her temples, speaking to her heart without words. She heard devotion in the beat of his heart, *experienced* calming peace in the touch of his lips and the earnestness of his concern.

"Jesse," she whispered.

He covered her mouth with his, breathed her name, sated her every need and longing as only he could. She clung to him and wept with newfound joy and worth.

"Yes," he said against her cheek. "Yes, Amy."

Eventually her tears subsided. Jesse took her in his arms and she lay with her head on his shoulder. Night closed in around them, and when they slept, it was with his hand on her stomach and her face turned to his.

* * *

In the days that followed, Amy told herself everything was resolved. She had come to terms with a new child. And she had, but there was more. More newly resurrected emotions vied for prominence, ate at her peace, eroded her small victory.

The dream of the crying baby returned, and she woke nearly every night with a start and the sound of that pathetic wail ringing in her ears.

Jesse's understanding and devotion only added to her conflict and self-recrimination. Remembering all the times he'd tried to comfort her, looking for solace and peace and partnership in his wife, she blamed herself for shutting him out. For turning him to the cold comfort of a whiskey bottle. Her fault. All her fault. Because Tim's death had been her fault.

Mr. Quenton had packed and left the week before, gifting them with a few photographs, among them the one of the graves. Amy had been tempted to tear it up and throw it away, but instead she'd buried the photograph in the bottom drawer of their bureau. As if guilt wasn't enough punishment, she'd taken it out and looked at it more than once.

One brisk morning, she woke before Jesse, the dream echoing through her head. She moved to the bureau and silently took out the photograph. In the semidarkness, she could barely see it, but she remembered well enough.

Moving to the window, she parted the curtain and

looked out toward the slope. She would let herself feel. She would let herself love again. The walls guarding her heart had been breached. And now she remembered Tim....

She pictured him as he'd been—an active, smiling, beautiful child, the apple of his father's eye. And she remembered the worst day of her life—that horrible afternoon—and Jesse's reactions. Then she pictured her son the way she'd seen him last. Still. Pale. Gone.

Amy put on her stockings and a shawl and made her silent way downstairs. At the back door, she pulled on her boots and coat and trekked outside. The frost crunched beneath each step that carried her away from the house, toward the slope and the crosses that marked the graves. She didn't notice the cold or the dog that sniffed at her ankles and then chased a small creature into the brush.

The place she avoided had always been this close to where she worked and slept, but she'd never before had the courage to climb the hill.

To see Tim's grave.

The marker was there, between the two others. Rosebushes, now dusted with snow, had been planted at the head of Tim's. Jesse, of course, had planted and cared for them. Just as he'd built the coffin as an expression of his love and grief, he'd kept this place tended.

But not Amy. Amy hadn't felt a thing, hadn't cried, hadn't grieved and hadn't allowed anything or anyone to remind her. She couldn't live with the fact that she'd been responsible for their loss, for the grief Jesse endured. All along she'd accused Jesse of not moving forward, while she'd been blind to the fact *she* was the one who hadn't dealt with Tim's death.

How could he forgive her? She didn't know, but she had to ask him.

How could she forgive herself?

Denying herself forgiveness brought only agony.

"Forgive me, Tim," she said aloud. Saying his name for the first time unleashed a flood of grief. She dropped to her knees on the frozen ground. Sobs racked her body in a long-denied expression of pain. She cried so hard her throat hurt, her chest ached, and the cold seeped into her knees. The pain was excruciating…but it was a testament to life. She was alive and she could no longer refuse to live.

She sensed his presence and turned to see Jesse standing silently several feet away. Tears streaked his cheeks. As always, he was there for her, giving her space, allowing her time.

"Jesse," she said, her throat dry and constricted. "It was my fault."

Looking confused, he took a few steps closer.

"I was in the kitchen, using the quiet time to bake. I didn't check on him. I never thought to make sure the front door was locked in case he woke."

She staggered to her feet, but Jesse didn't move toward her. He simply listened.

"By the time I went up to check on him and saw he

was gone, it was too late." Her voice was rising and her face contorting as she remembered. "It was my fault. *My fault*. How can you ever forgive me?"

She didn't wait for him to respond. She let her feelings spill out. "I shut you out. But what could I have done? I couldn't crawl into this grave with Tim." She looked at the ground, then squeezed her eyes shut and dropped her head back. "I couldn't go back to that day and change it. I couldn't even scream loud enough."

She curled her hands into fists. "So I shut off. Insulated myself from everything and everyone to keep this one tiny shred of sanity inside from slipping away. Something snapped inside me." Beseeching him with her eyes once again, she brought both hands over her heart. "I looked at you and saw you feeling and taking action. I stopped feeling and there was nothing I could do. But by blocking out Tim's memory I kept myself from healing. And I kept you from healing, too."

Silence stretched between them. Wind caught the hem of her coat and flapped it against her legs.

At last Jesse took a few steps to stand before her. "Tim's death was not your fault. There's no one to blame. It just happened and we'll never understand why. If there was anything to forgive, I would."

"But there is! I told you, I didn't check. I didn't lock the door."

"We've never locked the front except at night. But okay, I forgive you. I do. You'll have to forgive me, too, then, because I didn't think ahead and lock the door when I was at the house at noon. And I never warned him not to go to the creek alone."

She shook her head and reached to brush the tears from his cold cheek. "No, Jesse, no."

"You see, we could blame ourselves forever, but it wouldn't bring him back. Forgive yourself, Amy. That's what you have to do first."

"I shut you out. It's my fault you started drinking."

"I'm responsible for myself. I made my own mistakes. Don't take on the weight of the world."

"I shut out Cay."

"We've been through all that. It's done."

"I'm afraid I won't be a good mother to this baby," she admitted finally. "What if I let something happen?"

He grasped her by the shoulders. "Amy, we can't do anything about the past, and the only one who knows the future is God. If we let ourselves worry about what might happen, we'd never go out of the house in the mornin'."

"After all this you still love me?"

"Always, Amy. Always."

She collapsed against his solid form, and he wrapped strong arms around her. After several reassuring minutes, she turned to observe the graves in the first streaks of dawn. "It's just like you said. Tim's with his grandmas."

"We don't have to forget him, Amy. If we talk about him and share what we're feeling, we'll keep his memory alive. Remembering can be a comfort."

"I want to do something," she told him. Taking his hand, she led him back to the house. She tugged him through the dark kitchen and into the parlor, where she found a match beside the hearth and lit a lamp. Jesse shrugged out of his coat and took hers as well, laying them on the back of a chair.

Amy walked to the mantel and opened the round glass door on the clock she'd taken in trade. With a simple touch of one finger, she set the pendulum in motion. Closing the door, she stood back.

The ticking sound filled the room.

"From this moment on, we move forward," she promised.

Jesse took her in his arms and kissed her, the new life they embraced a tangible presence between them.

"Thank you," he whispered.

"For what?"

"For givin' me hope again."

Overhead, the sounds of feet hitting the floor caught their attention. Minutes later, the steps creaked and two tousle-headed boys peered at them from the foot of the stairs.

"What's goin' on?" Cay asked. "I don't smell no breakfast cookin'."

Jesse released Amy but kept her hand in his. "We have somethin' to tell you boys."

"What is it?"

"It's about another new person in our family."

As the rising sun ushered in a new day, beams of light filtered through the curtains and spotlighted the Shelby family.

Two miles down the road, Sam pulled a buggy up to Matthew Barnes's home and walked to the door.

Elthea greeted him with a surprised smile. "What are you doing here so early?"

"Just stopped by to see if you'd like to ride in with me this mornin'."

His place was the opposite direction, and she knew it. She called inside to her son. "Sam Burnham's come by for me. I'll be going now."

She gathered her mittens and coat, and Sam held the garment while she slipped it on.

"This is a pleasant surprise, Sam. Thank you."

"You're welcome, Elthea." He led her to the wagon and assisted her up to the seat.

Matthew Barnes and his wife stepped out on their porch and watched as the buggy pulled away. They waved as the sun broke over the horizon.

Epilogue

❧

Shelby Station, Nebraska, 1874

Amy's daughter flounced into the kitchen carrying the carved wooden revolver her big brothers had fashioned for her. "I don't wanna wear this dress, Mama. I wanna wear a holster and ride one of Papa's horses."

"But this is a special day, little miss," Amy said to her four-year-old daughter. She tied Miranda's shiny gold locks into place with a yellow ribbon and adjusted the ruffles of the dress she'd spent hours making. "It's your birthday, and our friends and the hands are waiting to eat cake. Catherine will love your dress." The shaded side yard had been turned into a picnic area with makeshift tables, and their guests were waiting for the birthday girl. Amy had been trying to get Miranda into this dress for the better part of an hour. "You want to look pretty at your party, don't you?"

Miranda shook her head, and her shiny ringlets bounced. "Nuh-uh. I wanna ride a horse. I can wear dungarees and eat cake."

Any threw up her hands in surrender. "All right." She unbuttoned the row of buttons down the back of the dress. "Run back to your room and change. Quick, now."

Without releasing her favorite toy, the child threw her arms around Amy's neck, hugging her soundly, then placed a damp kiss on her cheek. "Oh, thank you, Mama!"

Amy watched her run through the house toward the addition Jesse and their boys had added that held three more bedrooms.

The sound of a spoon hitting the floor warned her that one-year-old Thomas had run out of patience waiting in the high chair. She washed his hands and face and lifted him out, holding him on her hip and kissing his cheek. "I can't get that sister of yours into a dress, Tom. What am I to do?"

The baby grinned and patted her cheek.

The kitchen door creaked and Elthea entered with an empty platter. She set it on the table and smiled brightly at the child Amy held. "Your grandpa was looking for you, Tom."

Amy handed over her son, and the older woman kissed his cheek adoringly. Elthea and Sam had married two years ago and were living happily in Sam's small house at the homestead. She rode in with him nearly every morning to help Amy with the meals and the children.

"She's not going to wear the dress." Amy uncovered a cake and carried it toward the door.

Elthea followed. "She'll grow into being a young lady eventually, Amy. You'll see."

Jesse was standing with a group of men when Amy approached, and he strode toward her with a wide smile. "Is she ready?"

Amy set down the cake and slipped her arm around his waist. "Wait and see."

Two young men approached them, and Amy's heart softened as it always did when she looked at her two boys. At sixteen Cay was the tallest, with blue eyes and a disarming smile like Jesse's. He had plans to go to the university in another two years.

Beside him Toby was downright handsome, broader, though not as tall. A lock of obstinate dark hair fell over his forehead and his hazel eyes were full of mischief. At eighteen, he was Jesse's right hand.

"Where's our girl?" he asked. His deep voice never ceased to amaze Amy. She remembered the scrawny distrusting boy they'd brought home and adopted.

"You'll see," Amy promised.

Leda Bently's family joined them and the doting hands gathered around, as well. Miranda had been the darling of Shelby Station since her arrival.

Finally the back door opened and Miranda darted across the porch, down the steps and out into the yard. The golden ringlets Amy had so carefully arranged were stuffed beneath her favorite wide-brimmed hat, the yellow bow nowhere to be seen.

She wore a pair of dungarees that had seen better days on one of her older brothers. The shirt was new. Amy had seen to it that the boys' shirts were given away and that Miranda had shirtwaists in more feminine colors. Her hand-me-down boots were scuffed, and the holster with the wooden gun covered her from hip to knee.

She smiled from ear to ear and surveyed the crowd of family and friends who'd come to celebrate her day.

Jack and Rachel's Catherine, not even a year older than Miranda and dressed in a frilly blue pinafore, was the first to break the silence. She stepped forward and linked her arms through her friend's. "Happy biwthday, Miwanda."

Sam followed Catherine's lead, an indulgent smile on his face. He picked up his granddaughter, and she hugged him around the neck.

Jesse turned his amused gaze on his wife. She read pride and love in his blue eyes.

Cay and Toby exchanged a look that said they didn't much care what their kid sister wore. She was the apple of their eyes no matter what she did.

Conversation broke out then and food was shared. After the cakes had been cut and everyone had eaten their fill, Miranda opened her gifts.

Sitting on the lawn in a mountain of paper, a doll on

its back staring at the sky, and a new red handkerchief around her neck, Miranda looked up with a puzzled frown.

Jesse stood nearby with Thomas on his shoulder. "What's the matter, pumpkin?"

"There's no present from Grandpa."

Elthea and Sam gave each other a knowing grin and Sam removed his hat to scratch his head. "I knew I was forgettin' somethin'. Where did we put that present?"

"I do believe you hid it in the barn," his wife replied.

"That's right. Fetch it for me, will you, Cay?"

Cay lit off toward the barn.

Toby knelt and spoke to Miranda, distracting her for several minutes.

Voices murmured and heads turned. Miranda stood up and craned to see around the milling guests and the brother who blocked her view.

Guests parted and Toby moved aside. Cay led a dun colt forward on a rope lead.

Miranda ran toward the horse. "Whose baby horse is this?"

"He's yours," Sam told her. "He's your present."

Wide blue eyes examined the animal, then surveyed each member of her family with awe. "But I'm only four. Am I big enough?"

"You need help learning to ride and taking care of him," Jesse told her. "You always have to have one of us with you until you're bigger."

"Okay, I promise," she agreed solemnly.

Promises were serious business at Shelby Station.

Cay had promised never to run away again and he'd held his promise to this day, though Amy had never seen any indication that he had any call to leave.

Jesse had promised to love her all their days, and she rested in that confidence. She, too, had made a promise. She'd vowed that past mistakes would never again overshadow the present or the future. She and Jesse had grieved for their first son, missed him every day. He still held a place in their hearts and memories. But Tim was no longer a stumbling block to their marriage or their love.

That night after company was gone and their children were all in bed, Jesse and Amy held hands and walked to the hillside where the graves of their mothers and their son were still carefully tended.

Moonlight illuminated the small crosses.

"Are you disappointed?" Jesse asked. "About Miranda not wantin' to wear the dress and all? I know you put a lot of work into it."

"I think it was one of those fanciful hopes," she said with a wry smile. "I had visions of her in ruffles and ribbons, but I pretty much knew all along that she'd hate it. She wants to be wherever you and the boys are. And that's okay."

Jesse nodded. "Did you see Cay and Toby around Leda's girl today?"

"I did. She's a pretty young thing. Sweet, too, and she can cook."

"Don't be marryin' 'em off already," he teased.

"No, I'm keeping them here as long as I can," Amy replied. "I don't even want to think about Cay going away to university."

"It's his dream."

"And we know about dreams, don't we? Shelby Station was one of yours."

"That…and you," he said, wrapping an arm around her waist. "I dreamed of you from the first day I met you."

"I remember that day," she said. "And the manure caked to your boots. You really made an impression."

He laughed. "Must not have scared you off. Nothing has, it seems."

"I guess you're stuck with me." Amy raised her face to kiss him. "Love me?"

"Always, Amy. Always.

* * * * *

If you enjoyed what you just read,
then we've got an offer you can't resist!

Take 2 bestselling love stories FREE!

Plus get a FREE surprise gift!

Harlequin Historicals®
Historical Romantic Adventure!

FROM KNIGHTS IN SHINING ARMOR TO DRAWING-ROOM DRAMA HARLEQUIN HISTORICALS OFFERS THE BEST IN HISTORICAL ROMANCE

ON SALE MARCH 2005

FALCON'S HONOR
by Denise Lynn

Desperate to restore his lost honor, Sir Gareth accepts a mission from the king to escort an heiress to her betrothed. Never did he figure on the lady being so beautiful—and so eager to escape her nuptials! Can the fiery Lady Rhian of Gervaise entrance an honor-bound knight to her cause—and her heart?

THE UNRULY CHAPERON
by Elizabeth Rolls

Wealthy widow Lady Tilda Winter accompanies her cousin to a house party as chaperon and finds herself face-to-face with old love Crispin, the Duke of St. Ormond. Meant to court her young cousin, how can St. Ormond forget the grand passion he once felt for Lady Tilda? Will the chaperon soon need a chaperon of her own?